HER
FROZEN
CRY

BOOKS BY CAROLYN ARNOLD

HER FROZEN CRY

CAROLYN ARNOLD

bookouture

Published by Bookouture in 2022

An imprint of Storyfire Ltd.
Carmelite House
50 Victoria Embankment
London EC4Y 0DZ

www.bookouture.com

ISBN: 978-1-80314-211-1
eBook ISBN: 978-1-80314-210-4

PROLOGUE

She stoked the fire, hoping its warmth would coax the cold from her bones. She couldn't shake the feeling that someone was watching her. But there was no one around. Surely, she was being paranoid, her mind fed by too many horror movies set in secluded cabins. Much like the one she was in right now. Alone. Isolated. Surrounded by nothing but wildlife and trees, with miles separating her from the nearest neighbor.

Earlier, rain had battered the roof and fat drops pinged against the windows. Instead of soothing her, nature's lullaby had her on edge. She jumped at every creak of the old cabin and had to repeatedly assure herself the structure was sound. It was likely fortified by many secrets made and kept within the walls, some of which were ones she'd deposited herself since arriving yesterday. But she had needed to get away, slip out of her life, re-evaluate. Step back.

The flames in the fireplace grew and danced wildly. She watched, entranced, and felt herself let go, just a little. But the chill was still in her, as if someone's eyes were crawling over her skin.

She got up and dared to look outside. Nothing but blackness. She'd draw the curtains, but there were none in the living room. Why had she ever left her beautiful home and family for this place, even for a couple nights? She must be crazy.

But her secrets were at risk of exposure if she didn't handle things just so, and that meant facing her demons in stillness and silence. Their voices grew loud, and she could feel her day of judgment drawing near. So many regrets and fears ricocheted in her mind. There would be no escaping them any longer.

She left the fire and grabbed the blanket from the couch. Wrapping it around her shoulders, she slipped into the bedroom. She'd get ready for bed and pour another glass of wine until her mind quieted and gave way to indifference, and possibly courage. Only then would she be able to slip into a deep, peaceful slumber.

She checked everything off the list and settled back on the couch beneath the throw, sipping her wine, and looked at a photograph she'd brought with her. The people in the picture were what was most important to her above all else—they made her want to be a better person, to *do* better—but her vision blurred. She blinked deliberately a few times, but it didn't offer much improvement. And now her head was spinning.

What the...? She hadn't drunk that much.

She tried to return her wineglass to the table, but it shattered to the floor.

She was dizzy, and she couldn't catch a full breath. It was like her heart was slowing down.

She gripped her chest, and the photo slipped from her lap.

She suddenly felt so weak, so very cold, so very tired.

Tears fell, hot against her cool cheeks.

This was it. The end—how and when she died. But this wasn't right—the timing so unfair. There was so much more she wanted to do with her life, so many things she wanted to make right.

As the darkness claimed her, a figure outside in the night moved to leave. Their mission was now complete.

ONE

The place was set back in the woods, remote. No one would have heard her screams, if there had been any. That felt like such a macabre thing to think, but it ran through Detective Amanda Steele's mind all the same.

Wednesday afternoon, and she was standing in a rustic cabin in Gainesville, a rural part of Prince William County. Her partner on the job, Trent Stenson, was next to her. The medical examiner, Hans Rideout, and his assistant, Liam Bakker, were tending to the deceased while two crime scene investigators bustled around collecting potential evidence.

The decedent was a thirtysomething woman and someone that Amanda recognized on sight. Alicia Gordon. She was one of the most successful entrepreneurs in the county—and possibly in the state of Virginia—for founding New Belle, a successful and lucrative cosmetic company.

The victim was in a seated position on the couch, an ancient number with its plaid cushions and bare pine frame. A wool blanket only partially across her lap. The rest of it had draped to the floor.

Her eyes were closed, her lips slightly parted like she'd just fallen asleep, but the scene revealed more. A wineglass was shattered on the floor, and red wine had pooled on the pine boards and crept into the cracks.

Across the room was a wood-burning stove, the fire long run out. The cabin held a slight chill and smelled of death and something sweet. A perfume, perhaps?

Amanda noticed a folder on the side table with some papers sticking out of it haphazardly. She confirmed it had been photographed by the CSIs and picked up the folder with gloved hands.

New Belle financial reports. At a swift glance, all appeared in good order. The company fiscally profitable.

Also a few colored printouts—ads for a perfume called Abandon. Apparently, New Belle was expanding their product line.

She handed the folder and paperwork to CSI Isabelle Donnelly to bag as evidence. "Thanks," Amanda told her. She turned to Rideout and asked, "Cause of death?"

"This one's a bit of a mystery, I'm afraid."

"Surely, someone her age doesn't just drop dead," Trent inserted. "Suicide?"

"It's far too soon to say. I won't even comment on COD until I have her back at the morgue." Rideout pressed his lips. "Sorry, I can't give you more."

Amanda understood that in cases of suspicious death it was necessary for Homicide to be present on scene. Everything needed to be treated as if a murder had taken place. Once the scene was released, there'd be no turning back the clock to collect evidence. "Time of death?"

"Rigor is telling me anytime between nine last night and midnight. As always, I'll conduct more tests at the morgue to determine that with more accuracy."

The time would explain the pajamas, the blanket, and the burned-out fire. While the daytime weather in the area was warmer than some states in March, nightly temperatures still dipped to about freezing.

Amanda signaled for Trent to follow her, leaving Rideout and Liam to their work. She went first into the bedroom.

"Something you're looking for?" Trent asked.

"I'd like to know if Alicia had company." She paced around the small room.

A single-size bed, a small dresser, and a simple nightstand with no drawers. On top was a deer antler lamp and a bottle of liquid sleeping aid.

"Just one suitcase," Trent said and had her turning. He'd opened the closet door.

Amanda pulled out one of the dresser drawers. Alicia had laid out her clothing in neat, folded piles. Nothing indicated a romantic getaway or liaison. They'd get more information from the woman who had found Alicia though—the owner of the cabin. A Pamela Zimmerman. She'd be able to tell them how long Alicia had booked the place and possibly her purpose for coming there.

"Detectives." CSI Donnelly stood in the doorway, holding a frame in her hands. "You might want to take a look at this." She handed it to Amanda, and Trent came up next to her.

A family portrait. A young man about twenty and a boy about ten years old. Alicia was positioned next to a man relatively close to her age, possibly older—likely her husband or significant other.

Amanda's gaze froze on his face. This couldn't be. She blinked, scrutinized the image closer, and confirmed her initial suspicion. He had aged and now had a full head of silver hair, but she knew him. Tony Bishop. Her legs became a little weak. This investigation just got personal.

Trent was staring at her profile, his head angled. He seemed to have developed this ability to sense her shifts in mood and read her mind. She wasn't quite sure she was comfortable with it.

She subtly shook her head, not about to get into it right now. "Where, ah, did you find this?" She could barely get herself to speak and nudged her head to the photo.

"It was under the blanket, found when Rideout removed it."

Amanda shifted her gaze back to the photo. How the lives of these people were about to take one hellish turn. She should have known it was too much to wish that this week go by without needing to notify next of kin that a loved one had died. And this time, it had to be someone she knew...

"I'll take that back if you want," Donnelly said, offering Amanda a gentle smile as she reached for the frame.

"Thanks." Amanda handed it over, and Donnelly put it into an evidence bag and proceeded to write the particulars on it— where it had been found, etcetera. "You didn't happen to find her phone, did you?"

"We did. Under the edge of the couch."

"Did you try accessing it?"

"CSI Blair told me to just bag it for processing at the lab."

Emma Blair was the senior CSI and held the transgressions of Amanda's father against her. He'd had an affair with Blair twenty-some years ago that resulted in a child. Amanda had a half-brother who was a firefighter for the Dumfries-Triangle Volunteer Fire Department. But all this was just exposed about four months ago, and Amanda was still reeling from the bombshell.

"All right. Keep us posted on that." Some battles weren't worth waging. The three of them left the bedroom. Amanda poked her head into the living room. "Anything else we should know before we head out? Any signs she may have died by suicide?" She opened that question to everyone in the room.

"No note or letter to loved ones," CSI Donnelly said.

"She have a laptop or tablet with her?" Trent asked.

Donnelly shook her head.

The absence of a letter meant nothing—not everyone left a note for loved ones. But didn't a woman like Alicia Gordon have everything to live for? Though outward appearances could be deceiving. "Keep us posted on the time for the autopsy," she told Rideout.

"Will do."

"Thanks." She stepped outside with Trent and took a deep inhale of the cool afternoon air. Was it too much to ask that it clear her mind? That photograph. His face. Chills wormed through her coat and seeped into her bones.

"So what was Ms. Gordon doing up here in a cabin—all alone? Looking at a photograph of her family?" Trent screwed up his forehead. "Reminiscing? Trouble in her marriage? Maybe we *are* looking at suicide. And what was up with your reaction to the picture? It was like you saw a ghost."

I kind of did...

"Amanda," he pressed.

"It was nothing. Just not looking forward to the notification. That's all." Only it wasn't *just* that, which Trent would find out soon enough.

"Never fun when there are kids left behind."

The portrait had been found at Alicia's feet, so it would seem she'd been looking at it before she died. Maybe it was as Trent had suggested and Alicia was depressed, possibly missing better days.

"We'll need to ask the husband about the marriage." Trent pulled out his notepad, flipped its pages. "Guy's name is Tony—"

"Bishop," she punched out, cursing her impulsiveness.

"Do you know him?"

Her answer was carried on a sigh. "You could say that."

TWO

After seeing his face *and* saying his name, Amanda's world tilted upside down. Tony Bishop, a person from her past. Way, way back. One stolen moment. One kiss that never should have happened. One secret she'd been carrying around since high school. She'd been a junior, him a senior—and five years older than her because he'd been held back a grade in elementary school. They'd first met fighting over the last cheese-and-bacon bagel in the school cafeteria and had an instant connection that lasted for years even after he left for college.

Trent narrowed his eyes, a smirk toying with the edges of his mouth, as if he were awaiting some juicy tidbit of gossip. "Just how well do you know this guy?"

She nodded. Not an answer, but all he was getting.

"I see you're talkative on the matter."

"Let's just focus on what's in front of us, go from there." There was no sense getting carried away about the case being a conflict of interest. They didn't even know for sure if Alicia Gordon had been murdered. There might not even be a case for her and Trent to investigate. But until then, she wanted the chance to explore the circumstances surrounding Alicia's death.

She at least owed that to Tony, didn't she? The question curdled in her stomach with an instant reply. She didn't owe him anything.

There was a span of silence, then Trent said, "All right, then. Keep your secret, but it might complicate things."

She raised her eyebrows. "You think?" *He had no idea.* And maybe her response was a little snarky, but she was doing her best to insert some space between herself and Trent these days. Sarcasm seemed to work rather well at pushing him away. When that didn't work, she diverted to business. After all, nothing good could come from getting involved with a colleague. Not that she had time for a romantic indulgence anyhow. She had recently adopted a six-year-old girl, Zoe Parker, and the child came first.

Amanda nudged her head toward a police cruiser in the lane. Its exhaust was coming out in plumes of white smoke in the cool air.

A shiver tore through her.

Officer Wyatt was in the front with a woman, presumably the person who had found Alicia. Wyatt would be taking her initial statement in the shelter and warmth of the vehicle, but Amanda and Trent would need to follow up with their own questions.

Amanda led the way over, and Officer Wyatt got out.

"Detectives," he said. "It's pretty straightforward. Pamela Zimmerman owns the cabin, and she found the deceased at one thirty when she arrived to clean the place for the next renter. They're due in on Saturday."

"Okay." Amanda glanced at the property owner. She was dabbing her nose with a tissue. "You pull a background on Zimmerman?"

"Sure did, and nothing flags."

"Did Ms. Gordon ever rent from her before?" Trent asked, impressing Amanda. Establishing that might factor into the investigation. If Alicia had made a habit of staying there, it could make it easier for a killer to target her here—assuming this was murder.

Wyatt shrugged. "I didn't think to ask that."

"All right, well, we'll take it from here," Amanda told him.

"Ah, where do you want to question her? You want me to take her to Central?"

Central Station was where the PWCPD Homicide Unit was stationed, but it was located in Woodbridge about a half-hour drive away. She flicked a finger toward the cruiser. "Seems she's comfortable in your car. Could we just pick things up in there?"

"Yeah, I guess." Wyatt glanced around, his eyes holding desperation and the look of someone who was lost. He obviously wasn't looking forward to standing outside.

"Here." Trent handed him the keys to their department car. "Make yourself at home."

"Mighty appreciate it." Wyatt held up the keys and dipped his head.

Amanda sat behind the wheel, and Trent got into the rear seat without any complaint about the hard plastic on his backside.

"Ms. Zimmerman, I'm Detective Steele, and this is Detective Stenson." Amanda angled her body toward the console and gestured to Trent.

Pamela craned her neck to look at him.

Amanda continued. "We know you just gave your statement to Officer Wyatt, but we need to run through everything with you quickly. Procedure." She tagged on that last bit in the hopes of quelling any grumblings Pamela might have about repeating herself. The disclosure only worked a third of the time. This instance was one of them as Pamela didn't raise any objections. "What time did you get to the cabin?"

"It was right around one thirty. I ate lunch and came over after."

"And where do you live?" Amanda asked.

"Just fifteen minutes down the road."

"Do you know if Alicia had company?" Amanda wasn't holding out hope, given the distance between the woman's home and the cabin.

"I wouldn't know. I can just tell you that she booked as a solo."

That didn't rule out visitors, but Pamela wasn't going to be a help in that regard. "When you got here, did you have to unlock the door to let yourself in?"

"Uh-huh. Well, I knocked first." Pamela dabbed her nose with a tissue. "I could see that her vehicle was still in the drive-way. She should have been gone already."

Amanda had noted the Mercedes when she first arrived on scene. She'd circle back to how long Alicia had rented the cabin for, but first she wanted to narrow in on something else. "So the door was locked?"

"It was, and that's why I hesitated to go inside. But some-thing inside me was pushing me to do so." Pamela laid a hand over her stomach. "Guess it was a good thing I did."

Locked door. All alone. Perhaps Alicia Gordon *had* died by suicide? Then again... "How does the lock on the cabin door work? Does it require a key to lock it from the outside?" Some locks could be engaged with a simple twist and pulling the door shut. The answer could go a long way to determining if someone else had been in the cabin with Alicia.

"It's a single deadbolt and requires a key."

Which meant either Alicia had locked it from inside or someone had taken the key. "I assume she was given just one copy?"

"Yes."

They'd need to verify it was still in the cabin.

"Did Ms. Gordon ever rent from you before?" Trent practically had his face pressed against the bullet-resistant plexiglass that separated the front and back seats.

"This was the first time."

"And how did she find out about the cabin? Do you know?" Amanda asked.

"Harold Armstrong. He works for Alicia, and he recommended the place. He actually called on her behalf, told me she'd be calling. I did her a favor..." She stopped talking there, her eyes taking on intensity. "Some favor."

"How did you do her a favor?" Amanda asked.

"I usually only rent the place out on a weekly basis."

"You made an exception for Ms. Gordon?" Trent said, beating Amanda to the question.

"Yes." She glanced at Trent, and somehow it emphasized how strange a sight it was seeing a cop in the back of a squad car. "She was booked for just a couple of nights. She checked in on Monday, and she was supposed to leave today."

Today was Wednesday, and Alicia had died last night. "Do you know why she planned such a brief stay?" Another question in Amanda's mind was why Alicia had even come here. Assuming Alicia lived in Woodbridge that was so close. Was she seeking solitude for some reason? Or had there been marriage problems, as Trent had suggested? Had she come out here to rendezvous with a lover—one who didn't leave a trace? One who killed her and made it appear as if she'd just fallen asleep? Had she come to end her own life, out of sight from her family?

"I don't know all the details. Just that she wanted a quick getaway. Ah, she did mention something about clearing her head."

Someone in Alicia's position would probably have a lot weighing heavily on her. There'd be a lot of responsibilities—not only on the professional front but personally. The younger boy in that picture would likely live at home with her. Amanda was relearning what it was like to have a young child to care for. It was almost seven years ago that she'd lost her husband, Kevin, and daughter, Lindsey, in a car crash to a drunk driver. Adopting Zoe Parker had reminded Amanda that balancing work and family was tough to pull off. It seemed one or the other always suffered.

"Did she mention why she might need to clear her head?" Trent asked.

Pamela shook her head. "No, she wasn't telling me that. I was a stranger to her."

Amanda was thinking the two people they should start with were Tony Bishop and Harold Armstrong.

Trent was scribbling in his notepad but paused long enough to ask, "Did you happen to be here when she arrived?"

"I was actually. Normally it doesn't work out that way."

"How did she strike you?" Amanda interjected before Trent could speak again. Often when people sought a getaway, there was something pushing them to do so whether that was stress, depression, or just the need to relax.

Pamela eventually said, "Distracted. Confused possibly." She flicked a hand in the air. "Probably explains her needing to clear her mind."

Amanda nodded, but she needed more to explain it away. In fact, depression could be a factor, as well as the feeling of being overwhelmed. Amanda gave her card to the woman. "My partner and I may be in touch with you again, but feel free to call me if you think of anything else that might help our investigation."

"Will do, but before you leave, I have a question for you. Was Alicia murdered?"

Amanda stiffened. "Her death is being treated as suspicious. We would appreciate that you keep what happened here to yourself to respect her family's right to be the first to know."

Not that Amanda saw Pamela as the type to run off and blather to the media, but the latter had a way of slinking out of hidey-holes when talk of a death hit emergency response radios.

"No problem there. It's not exactly something I'd want to advertise." Her eyes blanked over and settled on the cabin. "If she was, uh, killed here, I might end up selling the place. But it's going to break my heart to do it. That cabin's been in my family for three generations."

"Well, there's no need to rush into any decision." Amanda smiled gently at her.

"Yeah, suppose you're right."

Amanda and Trent thanked Pamela for her cooperation and got out of the squad car. He was hobbling a bit and seemed to be struggling to stand straight.

"You all right there?"

"I will be."

"Uh-huh. But how's your ass?" The words slipped out, and her cheeks burned. "You know, because those seats in the back are molded plastic..." She was desperately trying to backpedal.

Trent smirked. "It's a bit tender, if you must know."

There was yet another victim on this property. Her. Cause of death: embarrassment.

THREE

Before Amanda and Trent left the cabin, they confirmed the key was inside. With no sign of forced entry, by all indications Alicia had died alone in a locked building.

She and Trent were now parked in the driveway of Alicia's family home, but Amanda couldn't convince herself to move. It wasn't the dread of serving the notification itself, but the recipient causing her hesitation. Tony Bishop.

"You okay?" Trent looked over at her from the driver's seat.

"I will be. Thanks." She hurried out of the vehicle now—just to discourage any further conversation on the topic of Tony. As much as her feelings toward him were conflicted, no one deserved to hear their spouse was dead. Even if Tony hadn't been there for her much after her husband, Kevin, had died, she could be the bigger person and show him genuine sympathy and kindness. She understood some people weren't comfortable being around widows, even convincing themselves they were doing the one left behind a favor. But the decision to withdraw wasn't about those mourning; it had to do with a person's own level of discomfort.

She navigated the walkway to the front of the house. Such a

stately structure, impressive even, and she was rarely impressed by such things. Beige brick with white trim and black shutters, it boasted a large architectural footprint with a side porch and double front doors.

The surroundings were also luxurious. The yard was primly manicured, and stone statues adorned the property, which butted against woods at the back. In the summer, the trees would have been aglow in all shades of iridescent greens, and the colored leaves of fall would have the landscape appear on fire.

She stepped up to the landing, sheltered beneath an over-hang with two columns on each side.

Trent said, "Wow. This place is incredible."

She rang the doorbell, and a mini symphony chimed inside the home. Alicia's money had probably paid for the place. Amanda had never known Tony to be wealthy. He worked as an accountant for a medium-sized firm last she knew, earning a decent wage—but nothing anywhere close to being able to afford this place. Then again, the last she knew, he'd also been married to a woman named Claudia.

She had her finger over the bell to push it again when she felt subtle vibrations beneath her feet. Someone was coming.

One of the doors was opened by a young man of about twenty. He must have seen them pull into the driveway; he wasn't dressed for going out. Next to him was a boy about ten, swooping a model airplane through the air. No question that they were the children in Alicia's photograph. At least the eldest must be Alicia's, probably the youngest too. As far as Amanda knew, Tony had one daughter, Bethany, with his previous wife, Claudia. And, wow, Beth would be in her early twenties by now.

"Yeah?" he said and raised his eyebrows.

"Hi there. We're looking for Tony Bishop. Would he happen to be home?" Normally she'd be quick to identify herself and Trent as police, but she felt the urge to shelter these boys from her purpose here for as long as possible.

The young man shook his head. "Not at the moment. What's this about?"

"It's best that we speak with him directly," Amanda said pleasantly. "Do you know when he'll be home?"

"Should be soon. You friends of his?"

Simple question with a complicated answer. Even Trent was staring at her awaiting her response.

"I knew Tony a long time ago." She answered honestly, steering clear of confirming any sort of relationship.

"If you want, you can come in and wait. He should be here soon."

Amanda considered the offer. It might be best to wait outside, but given the expectant way both boys were looking at them, she agreed to enter the home.

The younger boy asked, "What are your names?"

"This is Trent, and I'm Amanda. What's your name?"

"Leo."

Amanda moved her gaze from the kid to the older son.

"Brad Slater," he said without further prompting.

The background Trent had pulled on Alicia listed her as thirty-eight. She must have had Brad when she was around twenty, just out of high school or while in college.

"My last name is Rossi," Leo put out with a grin.

"Nice name." It also confirmed Leo was Alicia's son too.

"Thanks."

"Just come with me." Brad locked the front door and led them to a sitting area. It was part of a large, open-concept area. The ceilings were two stories high, and a walkway on the second level, with a bar railing, traversed down the center of the house. The color scheme was neutral in grays, creams, and light beiges. Wainscotting turned an otherwise boring wall into a work of art and provided character. The furniture arrangement consisted of two chairs, two sofas, and four cubes that were pushed together to make for an eye-catching coffee table. They could also double as additional seating. Every touch elevated the home on par with a fancy hotel. Such a far cry from the modest two-story home Tony had shared with Claudia.

"Champ, why don't you go upstairs and play?" Brad put the question to Leo as if all sorts of adventures awaited him.

"Okay." Leo sounded far from enthused but ran off.

She and Trent sat on the dark-gray couch, while Brad dropped into one of the chairs.

He took out his phone. "I'll just text Tony to let him know you're here."

"Thanks."

"Yep." Brad sent the text. "So are you two police?"

"We are. Prince William County PD." She'd leave out mention of their ranks and department. He was a young man more than child, but the news of his mother's death was going to profoundly affect him.

"What do you want with Ton—" Brad's phone chimed, and he looked at it. "He just pulled into the garage."

A few seconds later, there was the sound of a door opening and shutting. "Brad?" a man called out.

"In here."

Tony rounded a wall, balancing a pizza box on one forearm and carrying a few cloth grocery bags. He stopped when he saw her. "Amanda?"

She felt Trent watching her profile but refused to acknowledge it.

"Ah, Brad, come get all this, will you? And put it away?" Tony said.

Brad got up but didn't rush into action by any means. He took the items from Tony into the kitchen, which was straight across from the sitting room, and placed them on the counter.

Tony locked his gaze with Amanda's as he walked toward

her. He stopped a foot away and took her in like she was a unicorn. "It's been a long time since I've seen you."

"The better part of seven years." Her heart was thumping. Even her stomach was fluttering. Tony had hurt her deeply when he'd pulled away after Kevin's and Lindsey's deaths. Still, her heart was breaking with what she had to tell him.

"You're looking good." Tony offered a genial smile.

"Thanks." He was too, truth be told. He'd stayed slender and had a thick head of hair, which had turned silver early but gave him a distinguished look. She should just get to the point of the visit, but her mouth was so very dry.

"And this is...?" Tony nudged his head toward Trent.

"Detective Stenson," Trent said. "I'm Detective Steele's partner."

"Oh?" He dragged his eyes from Trent to her. "I thought Amanda the Great didn't take partners on the job? Or is he—"

"On the job," she emphasized. "And he kind of got thrust on me." She smirked at Trent, taking advantage of the lighthearted detour. But she couldn't put off the bad news forever. "There's something we need to tell you." She paused there, gathered her strength to see this through. "You might want to sit down."

"Ah, sure." Tony's eyes darted from her to Brad in the kitchen, who had slowed his movements. Tony dropped on the other couch in the room.

"There's no easy way to say this," Amanda began, taking her time—more as a favor to him or herself? "I'm sorry to inform you that Alicia was found dead this afternoon in a cabin up in Gainesville. It's believed she passed last night."

"Excuse me?" He panted, his eyebrows shooting down in harsh arrows. "That can't be.... That's not possible."

Brad left the kitchen and sat next to Tony. His face was knotted in anguish. "Mom's... she's... What...?"

Tony put a hand on Brad's knee and jutted out his chin. "Tell us what happened," he said to Amanda.

She recognized the tough front, the armor of steel erected in an effort to protect the heart. But the damage had been done. "We're unsure as of yet." The most honest answer she had to provide at the moment.

"What do you mean unsure? How can you not know?"

"How was your wife's health, Mr. Bishop?" Trent asked.

"Great. She was healthy as an ox." He shook his head. "She'd kill me if she heard me calling her an ox. But this just makes no sense, but you know that. That's why you're here. You work in Homicide. Assume you still do?"

Brad's eyes widened, and he rubbed his arms. "Mom was murdered?"

Amanda held up a hand. "No one is saying that yet, but her death is being investigated as suspicious."

"And you're on this, Amanda? Tell me you are."

She blinked, trying to suppress the tears that threatened. "I am." She gestured toward Trent. "*We* are."

"Wow. I just can't believe this." Tony took his hand back from Brad's knee and raked it through his hair.

"Did you know she'd rented a cabin for a couple nights?" Trent asked.

"Yes, of course."

"And why was she there?" Amanda volleyed back.

"She just wanted to clear her head about a few things," Tony said.

That's rather vague... "What specifically?"

"She was strongly considering selling New Belle."

Surprising factoring in her success, but that could explain the financial reports she had with her. It didn't explain something else, though. "Was she to be working up there?"

"Yes and no."

"We didn't find a laptop or tablet. Would she have had either or both with her?" Had someone been in the cabin with her, after all, and taken them?

"No, I think she left both here. She took her phone, though."

"Did you hear from her since she left?" If she had called or texted Tony last night, it might help narrow down time of death.

"No. And I didn't expect to. She needed time to herself. I respected that."

"Why did she want to sell the business?" Trent asked.

"It just had her on the go all the time," Tony replied. "She wanted to spend more time with Leo. Oh God, Leo, where is he?" Tony looked at Brad, who jabbed a finger toward the ceiling in response. Tony let out a deep breath. "I don't even know how I'm supposed to tell him about his mom."

"It won't be an easy conversation," Amanda empathized. She didn't envy Tony that job—at all. It was awkward enough sitting across from her former friend and delivering this news. "When did you and Alicia get married?"

"Six months ago next week." His face pinched in grief as the realization must have sunk in that he wouldn't be celebrating that milestone with Alicia. "We just hit it off right away. My divorce from Claudia was working its way through. Alicia had broken up with her boyfriend six months before we met. Neither of us were looking for anything serious, but you can see how that turned out. We completely fell for each other."

Amanda was curious what had happened with his marriage to Claudia. She felt awkward prying into Tony's personal business, but this could be a murder case, and there were always injured parties in a separation. Until they knew exactly what had happened to Alicia, all possible motives needed to be considered, which opened the suspect pool to include exes. Given that the two boys had different last names, Alicia had at least two former partners. "I'm guessing things with Claudia and Alicia's partners ended amicably?" She'd give all parties the benefit of the doubt.

"Relationships have a way of running their course," Tony

began. "Seth Rossi—that's Leo's dad—he and Alicia share custody. She lived with him for over ten years. He's who she broke up with just before we met. Brad's father was a..." He stopped there, seeming to hesitate about finishing.

"You can say it," Brad stepped in. "I'm not a kid. My mom hooked up with him in college. I'm the result of a one-night stand. But he's part of my life," he added quickly. "Seth too."

"That's great to hear." Amanda gave him a gentle smile.

Trent pointed his pen at Tony. "And your ex-wife? How did things end there?"

"Claudia was over us before I was. She saw fit to take up with her Pilates instructor."

"Sorry to hear that," Amanda said.

"Don't be. If my marriage to Claudia hadn't fallen apart, I never would have found Alicia." His shoulders hunched forward, and it was like his entire body went slack like a puppet whose strings were cut.

"Where did you and Alicia meet?" Trent asked, voicing the question in a gentle manner.

"One year ago in Washington. I was there for a conference on accounting tax law, and Alicia was meeting with a client in the area. We found ourselves at a hotel bar one night. We both ordered a double shot of Jameson on the rocks—at the same time. Our eyes met, and the rest was history. We were married six months later." His eyes filled with fresh tears, and the corners of his mouth turned downward.

Brad shifted on the couch. Discomfort, grief? Both? "This must have felt like a whirlwind to you," she said, directing this to Brad.

"It was... at first. But Tony made Mom happy. That's all that really mattered."

He seemed rather nonchalant about his mother's fast run down the aisle with Tony. And she had to wonder if it was a tough front he was putting on. She hadn't heard Brad call Tony

"Dad" once, but she said, "You two seem to have hit it off as well." She drew a finger from Brad to Tony.

Tony patted Brad's knee. "He's a good kid."

Brad gave him a tight smile, emotionally reserved. "You're all right."

"Jeez, thanks." Tony's voice was light, but it was overshadowed by grief.

"You live at home, Brad?" Amanda asked, longing for a better feel of the family's dynamics.

"No, I rent a place in Washington with some friends."

"He goes to Georgetown." Tony peacocked with pride.

"Oh, impressive. And you're home now because... Oh, it's spring break?" Sometimes her college days felt like a lifetime ago.

"Yep, until the twenty-seventh."

And yet Alicia saw fit to get away now? Tony had just told them one of the reasons Alicia was looking to sell her business was to spend more time with Leo. By extension and factoring in the photograph, one would take that to mean the family as a whole. "This may be tough to answer, but do you know if Alicia was feeling depressed?" This particular question she was directing at Tony.

"No way. She was on top of the world. Why do you ask?" Tony's face shadowed.

Trying to rule out suicide... "Just part of the investigation."

"Part of the invest—" Tony's body collapsed into itself with a giant sob. He wiped away the tears that now fell and held up a hand. "Sorry, I-I just can't believe this is happening, *has* happened."

"There's no way Mom would have hurt herself. Someone did this to her. Had to have..." Brad sniffled and wiped at his eyes, falling apart next to Tony.

Shock had acted as a buffer and absorbed the initial blow, but it had subsided, visibly leaving both men with raw grief.

"No need to apologize. At all." Sadly, she could relate to what Tony was going through. There were days in the last seven years she didn't think she'd survive the pain of losing her husband and daughter. And her previous friendship with Tony somehow had her taking on his sorrow. But she had to deny those feelings, or they'd capsize her. She had to focus on the cold facts.

Alicia had been a prominent businesswoman and likely worth a lot of money, if business statements were any indicator. Someone in the wings may be impatient to inherit. She glanced at Brad. The poor kid was disintegrating in front of them. She cleared her throat, reminding herself to remain professional and objective. It was also possible that despite lavish appearances Alicia was in major debt, even near to foreclosure on her house. It couldn't be ignored either that given her social presence and profile, Alicia would have attracted enemies. "Do you know of anyone who might have had an issue with your mother?"

"Now you're, ah, talking murder?" Brad swallowed roughly, and Tony wrapped an arm around him.

"I realize it must be hard to think it's possible, but—"

"No." Brad cut Amanda off. "Why would anyone?" He passed a cutting gaze to Tony, and he withdrew his arm.

There could be many reasons, but Amanda would let that avenue go unexplored fully—for now. "What happens to Alicia's money and the business now that she's gone?"

Tony blew out a large puff of air. "Most of it falls to me, including the business."

Amanda didn't like the sound of that. They'd married quick, and the inheritance could be seen as motive.

Brad pulled back. "You don't want it? Is that why you're puffing over there?"

"I never once said that I didn't."

"Sure sounds like it."

Tony's jaw clenched for the briefest of seconds, then he

faced Brad. "New Belle was your mother's dream, and I supported her with that. I will do whatever she would have wanted."

"Sell it? You're going to sell it?" Brad's voice was rising incrementally with every word.

"Please," Tony beseeched him. "I don't know yet. It's far too soon for me to even..." He massaged his forehead. "I can't even make sense of all this right now."

"It's understandable you'd need time," Trent said.

Tony and Brad remained quiet.

Trent went on. "While Alicia was at the cabin last night, where were you?"

"Here with the boys."

Here with the boys... Alicia had left home to think about the future of her business, something she wanted to sell to spend more time with her family. Yet she'd chosen this time—when her eldest was home—to slip away for a couple of days? Possible, but a little hard to reconcile. The fact Alicia had been reflecting on a family portrait would almost suggest she was struggling with the decision to go ahead with her plan to sell. Maybe family wasn't as important as her business after all. Or maybe she was trying to tell herself selling was the right decision—the faces of her family enough to bolster her courage. Amanda glanced at Brad, and he met her gaze. Maybe she was making too much out of Alicia's brief getaway. Brad was an adult child and wouldn't need as much attention as Leo. And just because Brad was in the area for spring break, that didn't mean he planned to spend every waking moment with his family. He probably had plans to hang around with his friends in town.

"Did you slip up to the cabin to visit her since she checked in on Monday?" Trent asked.

Amanda was grateful Trent had assumed the lead in trying to obtain an alibi—a necessary step, especially if Alicia had been murdered. That still didn't make it any easier to be witness to this conversation when it pertained to an old friend.

"I was here with the boys," Tony pushed out, his cheeks flushed with irritation.

"This is just procedure," she told him.

"He was here," Brad said. "We had Chinese food delivered. Tony's not a cook." He offered Tony the briefest glimmer of a smile.

"No need for that." Tony attempted to play along, but any joviality fell short.

Her gaze flicked to Brad. They should mention the photograph and explore the possibility of suicide more, but she didn't feel comfortable doing that in front of Brad. It might be best if he left the room at this point. "Brad, would you be able to give us time alone with Tony?"

"Ah, sure." Spoken as if he were questioning why he had to leave, but not pushing the issue. He got up and left.

After Amanda heard his footsteps go up the stairs and fade away, she asked her next question. "You told us Alicia needed to get away, that she had some business matters to think about. But Alicia had a family portrait with her at the cabin, and it seems she was looking at it just before she died. Do you know why that might have been? Were the two of you having problems?"

"She had a picture of us?" Tony's voice cracked.

"She did. We thought maybe she was reminiscing about better days," Trent inserted.

"No." Tony shook his head. "We weren't having any issues. I don't know why she would have had the photo."

Amanda considered another option that occurred to her earlier. Alicia was using the picture to remind herself why she was giving up her business. Surely it wouldn't have been an easy decision for her. "Alicia never took your last name. Why was that?" It didn't necessarily mean anything, but Amanda wanted to hear the answer and gauge for herself.

"You never took Kevin's either, but you two were happy."

You two were *happy...* Now there was a twisted blade to her heart. "We were."

"So why didn't you take on the surname James?" Tony's lashes were soaked with tears.

Tony knew the answer to that. She'd idolized her father growing up and wanted to follow in his footsteps to become police chief for the PWCPD. Keeping the last name of Steele could only help as she climbed the ranks. Now her father was retired—for about seven years—and Kevin was dead. If she could go back, she'd have taken her husband's name. "Due to professional reasons," she pushed out, making eye contact with him as she did.

He gestured with an open hand. "Same for Alicia. When I met her, which was only a year ago, may I remind you, she'd already built her cosmetics empire. Why would I expect her to take my last name?"

"Understandable," Amanda said. "I need to ask again. You are certain that Alicia wouldn't have taken her own life?"

He pierced her gaze with his. "There is no way."

There would likely be more questions they'd need to ask in the days ahead, and she might even need to press harder on the subject of suicide, but they'd covered enough for today. "There will be an autopsy conducted to determine what exactly caused her death."

"And when will that be?"

"Soon. I'll let you know more as soon as I do. Is there anyone you need me to call? We could get someone from the department to sit with you..." Victim Services, from the police department, would spend time with those who were affected by crime.

"No, we'll be..." Tony didn't finish.

If he was going to say *fine*, he wouldn't be for a long time to come. "I'm so very sorry for your loss." She stood and started for the door before anyone could see the tears in her eyes. Despite the distance between them in the last seven years, she felt Tony's pain as if it were her own.

"Ah, Mandy?"

The abbreviation of her name stopped her short. She spun and faced Tony. "Yeah?"

He stepped outside with them, shutting the door behind him. "I didn't want to make a huge deal of this in front of Brad, but you think someone killed Alicia, don't you? I mean, that's why you were asking about who hated her and where we were, right?" His focus was solely on Amanda, wanting to pull on their personal history so she'd level with him. "Is there more you're not telling me?" he added when she had yet to respond.

"If I knew more, I would tell you," she said.

He scanned her eyes. "You really don't know?"

She shook her head. "As I said, the autopsy should bring us more answers." She put a hand on his shoulder and squeezed. "Just hang in there, okay?" Such a stupid thing to say, and she could hit herself for it.

He pulled her in for a hug. It was long and uncomfortable, but he clung to her, desperate. She rubbed his back, not wanting to give in to the embrace.

He withdrew. "Sorry, I probably shouldn't have done that. It was just seeing you after all this time and"—he sniffled—"you know what I'm going through." He didn't voice an apology, but it seemed unspoken. "Please find out what happened to her."

"I will." She licked her lips, instantly regretting her words. They spoke of a promise, and there were to be none of those in this line of work. It made things easier, didn't set high expectations or give more cause for disappointment. She'd crossed a line. This was a prime example of why police business and a personal connection didn't mix—it messed with the mind *and* the heart.

FOUR

It had taken longer than anticipated to deliver the news to Alicia's family, and by the time Amanda and Trent were headed to Central, it was going on six o'clock. Amanda fired off a quick text to Libby Dewinter, Zoe's "aunt," to let her know she was running a little late tonight. Libby had been scheduled to stay until five thirty, but she understood that Amanda's job wasn't always set hours.

"We'll just update Sergeant Malone and call it a day," she said. "Start fresh tomorrow." A message had come in from Rideout advising the autopsy was tomorrow morning at nine.

"Works for me." Trent pulled into the lot for Central.

The station was one of three belonging to the Prince William County Police Department. The building itself was mostly a single-story redbrick structure with the exception of one second-story office tower, sided with formed aluminum panels. It was situated on a country lot surrounded by trees and would have been a serene setting if not for the nature of the investigations that went on within the station's walls. In addition to Homicide, there were bureaucratic offices, including the one that belonged to the police chief.

Trent parked but didn't turn the car off. He looked over at her. "Just how well do you know Tony Bishop?"

Given the way he was looking at her and the tense energy in the car, he wasn't going to take a brush-off. "He was a friend."

"A close friend?" he countered. "He calls you Mandy, and he hugged you."

Jealous? The idiotic thought passed by in a flash. "It's nothing. We've known each other since high school. He married Claudia, and I married Kevin. End of story." Not exactly, but she wasn't getting into the nitty-gritty.

"I see," he said slowly.

He probably didn't, but she wasn't going to challenge his claim. She pointed toward the building. "Shall we?"

His mouth opened, shut, then he said, "Sure," and got out.

They bypassed the warren of cubicles belonging to Homicide and continued on to Sergeant Malone's office. They found him at his desk, typing something into his computer. "There you are."

"Here we are," she parroted. Malone had sent a text about an hour ago requesting a briefing but hadn't followed up. Scott Malone and her father had been best friends and that made the sergeant a family friend. As such, Malone extended her more leash and patience than he did others working under his command.

She sat in one of the chairs across from him, and Trent got comfortable in the one beside her. They filled him in on the little they knew.

Malone leaned back in his chair and swiveled. "When is the autopsy scheduled?"

"Tomorrow morning at nine."

Malone barely nodded. "Could it have been suicide or an accident?"

"This case could go any way. Even natural. As for suicide,

we did ask the husband if he'd noticed if she was depressed. He didn't think so."

"Suicidal behavior involves far more than just visible signs of depression. You might want to do some research on the matter and revisit the husband."

Amanda wouldn't look forward to that conversation. "Will do." She got up and left, Trent on her heels.

He leaned in toward her. "You're not going to tell Malone about knowing the vic's husband?"

"Not unless it becomes absolutely necessary."

She met his gaze, and his eyes questioned her.

She put up her hands. "What?"

"Nothing."

But it was something. He was judging her, questioning why she hadn't just told Malone. And maybe the "family friends" connection with the sergeant could extend her favors, but she wasn't willing to test it right now. "I'll bring it up when and *if* it matters."

Trent nodded.

They stopped in the section of hall that split—one way toward the exit, one toward the Homicide Unit. "If you want to stay and look into signs of suicidal behavior, be my guest, but I need to go," she said.

"I understand."

And he probably did more than she wanted to admit. Trent seemed to *get* her, and it probably hadn't escaped his notice she was reeling from the events of the day. "I'll see you tomorrow. Here, eight twenty, and we'll head up for the autopsy together."

"All right. I'll bring us coffee."

She dipped her head. There were times it felt like he was too good to her, and too good to be true. Dangerous territory, and something she had fought so hard against at the beginning of their partnership. Somehow over time, though, the barriers had lowered and their relationship had grown comfortable and casual. "Night," she said and left.

Amanda got into her Honda Civic and headed home. She lived in Dumfries, a ten-minute drive from Woodbridge, but tonight, in some ways, she wished it was longer. She wanted to get home to Zoe and hated being late for her, but Amanda's mind was a mess. It kept serving up memories of all the times she and Kevin spent with Tony, and his wife, Claudia. How much fun they'd all had whether it was a night in or on the town. Tony must have been at a loss for what to say and do, and that's why he'd withdrawn. And while she let the friendship dissolve, Tony and Claudia should have been there for her. It was hard to forgive either of them for that.

And as if running into Tony wouldn't have been hard enough to handle on its own, his bride of six months was dead. Murdered? Death by suicide? Accident? Or natural causes? In one sense, the result was the same no matter what manner of death—a loved one was lost. Of all the options, though, murder could provide firm closure, if the killer was caught and held to justice. There would be an answer to *why*, even if it was bitter to swallow.

Amanda pulled into her driveway. The bungalow she'd bought with her husband seemed to be staring at her, as if it had eyes. The clock on her car's dash told her it was six thirty-three. She should be rushing to get inside, but she sat there, just for a few minutes to get her bearings, to soothe herself. She took several deep breaths. Then she went inside.

"Sorry I'm late," she called out, but no one came to greet her. Zoe was often on the couch in the living room that was to the left of the front door, watching TV with Libby.

Amanda hung her jacket on the full-sized coat tree in the entry, and her gaze caught on the small one there for Zoe. It had belonged to Lindsey. Amanda thought it would be hard to see it being used again, but somehow knowing that it was repurposed filled her with hope for a brighter future.

She slipped out of her shoes and started down the hall toward Zoe's room. Hearing peals of laughter, Amanda smiled. The girl had filled the home with light and love again, worming into Amanda's heart and healing her.

Amanda poked her head through the doorway and found Zoe and Libby playing *Frozen*. Zoe was in the Elsa costume Amanda had bought her for Christmas. It came with a gown, tiara, wand, braided-hair extension, and gloves. Zoe was decked out in every piece. Libby wasn't dressed up but was apparently playing a scared townsperson, with her arms flailing in the air.

"Hello, guys." Amanda inched her way into the room, and Libby laid a hand over her heart.

"I didn't hear you come in."

"I called out but—"

"Mandy!" Zoe ran to Amanda, and she lowered to receive the big hug that was coming her way.

Amanda pulled back after the embrace and stood to full height. She poked at a tip of the tiara. "How's my little princess?"

"Doing great. Aunt Libby's playing *Frozen* with me."

"I see that." Amanda smiled at Libby. "Sorry I was late."

"No problem at all. It happens sometimes."

Though overtime didn't happen for Libby. She taught third grade at Dumfries Elementary, where Zoe attended, and had predictable hours. "More than I'd like."

"Never a problem. You know I love spending time with our girl."

Amanda never corrected Libby when she referred to Zoe as *our girl*. Libby was chosen family to Zoe's parents before their murders, was even designated as Zoe's godmother, but changed life circumstances hadn't permitted Libby to take Zoe in. "You two look like you're having fun." Amanda was still smiling, the expression common when she was around Zoe. "You must get into this as much as Zoe."

"It's all about being young at heart, and I put my heart into everything I do," Libby said, and Amanda had no doubt. "Well, I should be going, kiddo."

Zoe giggled and then stood tall, her expression serious. "It's not *kiddo*. It's Princess Elsa, thank you very much."

"Oh, my apologies, *Princess*." Libby bowed to Zoe as if to royalty, then pecked a kiss on her forehead. The girl hugged her in response.

"Bye." Zoe straightened her tiara and waved at Libby.

Libby said goodbye to Amanda and left the room. A few moments later, Amanda heard the front door close.

"So, what would you like to do now?" As Amanda said the words, she noted the stark contrast in her life. Leaving work to come home to this girl was like walking out of a dark pit into the sunlight. If only she could exist here, in this bubble, all the time —but she would eventually grow restless. She was born to be a cop. It had her thinking about Alicia Gordon's plan to sell her business. Had that been Alicia's idea, or was she being influenced or coerced to do so? Surely, just like Amanda was a cop in her blood, Alicia must have felt that bond to her work, to the empire she'd created.

"Mandy?" Zoe tugged on Amanda's sleeve.

"Uh, yeah, sorry, sweetie. I drifted. What would you like to do?"

"Play more?" Her eyes were sparkling.

"Sounds good. I'm just going to grab something to eat, then I'll join you."

"Okay."

Amanda headed for the kitchen, and Zoe trailed her. "You ate, didn't you?" It had become a standing thing over the last several months that if Amanda wasn't home by five thirty or hadn't reached out to Libby, she'd make dinner for Zoe. There was the faint smell of food lingering in the air, but Amanda couldn't put a finger on what it was. She was hoping for leftovers, though. That would make dinner easy.

"Yeah." Spoken like it was a given. Her Aunt Libby would never let her starve.

"And what was that?"

"Fish sticks and french fries."

"Oh, sounds wonderful."

"It was really good. She made extra for you. It's in the fridge."

Eating leftovers lost its appeal. Room temperature would have been better. Cold, the breading would be soggy. Still, Amanda smiled. "Very nice." She could rewarm it in the oven, but that didn't sound overly appetizing either. Good thing tartar sauce could cover a multitude of sins. She grabbed it along with the container from the fridge and turned to sit at the kitchen peninsula. She found Zoe seated on one of the stools there. "You can play while I eat if you want."

"No. I'm good."

Amanda's heart warmed. The girl loved her company as much as Amanda loved hers. "Do you want anything to drink?"

"Nope. But I'll take one of your fries." Her hand was out of its glove, and her index finger was curled as she moved it toward Amanda's plate.

"Okay, just because you're you." She winked at Zoe and gestured for the girl to help herself.

Amanda dug in. She just hoped the food stayed down—not to insult Libby's culinary skills. Amanda was just feeling the weight of this case bearing down on her.

FIVE

Being without answers wasn't just frustrating, it was like being adrift in the ocean. A person was at the mercy of the waves, not able to act, just to *react*. Amanda preferred being proactive, and she hoped this morning Rideout would provide some direction.

She and Trent were heading through the morgue doors at eight fifty, caffeinated and ready to go.

Rideout was standing next to a steel gurney where Alicia Gordon's body was covered with a white sheet. He was already in his smock and gloved up, and they wished each other good morning.

She envied how Rideout never let the darkness of his job stain his energy or his mood. He was comfortable around the dead, a benefit for someone who spent so much time with them. She could compartmentalize and detach, though it was harder with children. Today, it was the wife of a man she knew well. She had to squeeze out thoughts of Tony and not take on his grief. She'd just focus on the job and bring him closure if possible. "So, what can you tell us?" She gestured toward the cadaver.

"I received her medical records. She only had one

prescription which was birth control. She'd really been in fine health until..." Rideout waved a hand over the sheet. "So what caused her to drop dead, as you put it, Detective Stenson? I have drawn blood to send to the lab for toxicology testing to see if it shows any poisons, drugs or toxins in her system. I'm also hoping to learn something when I open her up."

"Murder," Trent said in a low voice.

"Possible, but not necessarily," Rideout said. "She could have come into contact with something unknowingly... or knowingly, for that matter." He looked at Amanda.

"We don't have reason to believe death was by suicide. Not yet." She and Trent had talked about what he'd found out last night on the way here. Those with suicidal thoughts exhibited many signs, and these differed for each person. They had to explore that angle more, and that meant another conversation with Tony.

"I'll leave manner of death to you to figure out," Rideout said.

"You mentioned drugs. Do you have any specific ones in mind?" Amanda asked.

"Until I know cause of death, it would be premature to even guess."

"The woman who rented Alicia Gordon the cabin described her as being sort of dazed," Amanda put that out there, appreciating it might not steer Rideout toward one specific drug.

"As I said, I need to determine COD first. But she'll tell us, I'm sure." Rideout nudged his head toward the body. "Are you sticking around?"

"For a while, yeah." She wanted answers and hoped some would present themselves before she and Trent had to leave.

Rideout got to work and opened Alicia up. He paused on her lungs and examined them closer.

"You have something?" Amanda felt like she was breathing down his neck. Maybe because she was.

"The lungs show petechial hemorrhaging, and there is some frothy fluid in her bronchi." He looked at her, then Trent. "This tells me she had labored breathing."

"Does it tell you what might have caused it?" Amanda realized she was being stubbornly persistent, but the desire for answers was strong.

"No." Rideout smiled before going back into Alicia's body cavity with two hands. He came out with her liver. "You don't have to stay for all of this. It might be a while before I could give you anything definitive anyway."

They might be best to leave and see if they could pin down *manner* of death. "You'll keep us posted?"

"Don't I always?" Rideout's tone was far too light to jibe with him holding a person's organ in his hands.

Amanda and Trent loaded into the car and headed back to Woodbridge. Amanda updated Malone on the way.

"Continue treating it as a homicide," he told them.

"Thought you'd feel that way. Thinking we'll stop by New Belle next." She glanced at Trent in the driver's seat, and he nodded. She continued. "We'll take a look around, see if we can talk to Harold Armstrong who recommended the cabin." She'd included his name in the briefing they'd given Malone last night.

"Keep me posted." With that, Malone hung up.

"To New Belle." Trent headed in the direction of the cosmetics company. "Armstrong might be able to let us know his thoughts on Alicia too. Whether she showed signs of suicidal impulses or..." He stopped speaking, but the tension in the car had Amanda looking over at him.

"Just say it," she dared him.

"Maybe we should talk to Bishop again first and discuss the possibility of suicide more."

"We'll talk to him again, but he's grieving. Let's give him some space and get an outside perspective first."

"All right. Armstrong might be willing to share his thoughts on their marriage too, whether there were any issues."

"Tony had nothing to do with her death." Her conviction surprised her. She really owed Tony nothing after all these years, but the man she had known would never have killed anyone. Then again, she should know from life experience that anyone—even those you least expected—was capable of murder.

"I know Tony's your friend."

"He *was* my friend." And in some ways, that felt like so very long ago. "Regardless, every case deserves an open mind. We can't convict him for the same reason we can't release him from suspicion, but you're right, the marriage might not have been as solid as he sold it to us. One thing niggling at me is where she died. What was she really doing there? Maybe it was for the reason Tony mentioned—to sit with her decision to sell New Belle. But that doesn't exactly gel for me. She wants to sell her business to have more time for family, but her son is there on spring break and she leaves? And how does a woman who spent her entire adult life building a business just up and let it all go?"

"You think someone was squeezing her out?"

"Well, they might have got their way. She is out." The latter part of her response was short and clipped, and she felt horrible for that the second it left her mouth. She rushed to try and bury her snappy comeback. "If she was murdered, which we are going to assume from this point unless told otherwise, that doesn't happen to people without enemies. That means Alicia had skeletons in her closet. We need to find out what those were."

"Agreed. I am allowed to agree?"

"Why wouldn't you be?"

He raised his brows.

"Sorry for being a little short." She wasn't doing very well at the "pushing him away" thing. It came in spurts. The truth was the guy was just so damn nice to her—and loyal, a trait she highly respected and admired.

"As for being short, you can't help how tall you are." He put it out there drily, and it took her a few beats to stitch together his meaning. His smirk helped.

"Hey, I'll have you know I'm taller than the average height for a woman. Five foot nine."

"Uh-huh, short stuff."

She laughed but briefly. She hated how light she felt around Trent despite the fact they were constantly surrounded by death. Somehow he made it all a little easier to handle. He grounded her, and she found his presence comforting, but these days even more than that. She was starting to feel *something* for him. "Look, Trent, we need to stop this, whatever *this* is." She fanned her hand between them.

"Not sure what you're talking about."

"You really don't?" *What am I doing?*

"No, I don't."

She scanned his face. Either he was an amazing actor, or he really didn't feel the sparks between them. *That's not at all embarrassing...* "If you don't, then I'm not explaining it to you. Forget I said anything. Just take us to New Belle."

"Aye, aye, boss." He kept his eyes firmly on the road, and she stared for a few seconds at his profile.

Did he really not have a clue as to what she was talking about? And if not, then why the hell was he wearing cologne all the time lately?

SIX

Amanda had driven past the New Belle factory many times but never had reason to go in until now. It took up a decent chunk of real estate with a large parking lot. Spots near the front doors were marked for visitors and assorted staff. Alicia Gordon's spot was in the prime location with a space for Tony next to it. Both of their areas were empty. The one beside Tony's was assigned to Harold Armstrong, and a silver Dodge Ram occupied it.

The receptionist told Amanda and Trent that Harold Armstrong was on the premises but on a conference call. "He shouldn't be too much longer," the twentysomething added. "I'll let him know you're here."

"Thanks." Amanda took in the lobby. The area was outfitted to market New Belle products, taking advantage of anyone passing through. Posters were on the wall, and a six-foot-tall cardboard ad was freestanding near the counter and advertised Abandon perfume—the fragrance in the marketing materials Alicia had at the cabin. This time, Amanda paid more attention to the slogan. *Dare to live the life you deserve.* Cliché yet powerful. Modern. Edgy.

A woman with supermodel looks came through the front

door. She flashed a winning smile to anyone who glanced in her direction and walked to reception with an emphasized sway to her hips.

"I have an appointment with Tony Bishop," she said to the woman there.

Amanda studied the model. There was something familiar about her, but Amanda couldn't quite place why. And whatever business this woman had with Tony was none of Amanda's concern. Then again, his wife had just died. Was the relationship between Tony and this woman professional or personal? Did it have any bearing on the investigation?

"Detectives?" An overweight man, in his late sixties and with a balding head approached them. He carried himself tall, shoulders squared with confidence, but there was something in his eyes that undermined him.

She gave the introductions and said, "Harold Armstrong?"

"That would be me. How can I help?"

Does he not know Alicia is dead? "We need to speak with you about Alicia Gordon."

His face pinched. "I was afraid you might say that. This way."

She and Trent followed Harold to his office. The nameplate on the door announced him as distribution director. Huge space. Big enough to be a conference room, and it had a meeting table and eight chairs.

"Sit wherever you'd like. Would either of you like water, coffee, tea?"

She declined, and so did Trent. Harold helped himself to a glass of water from a pitcher on the credenza. Then he joined them at the table where they'd already seated themselves.

"I assume by now you've heard that Alicia Gordon was found dead yesterday afternoon," Amanda began.

Harold took a long drink of his water and set his glass on the table. He nodded and wiped his mouth with the back of his hand. "Do you know what happened to her yet?" Wrinkles lined his brow, and the corners of his mouth tugged downward. "Tony said you didn't know..."

"We don't. Yet. But we're working on getting answers," she said.

"I honestly can't believe it. She was healthy, you know. She worked out and ate right. This makes no sense."

"Everyone knows death is a fact of life, but it rarely makes sense, Mr. Armstrong," Amanda pointed out.

"Suppose you're right, but this time it really doesn't. So young." Harold rubbed the top of his head, buffing it to a shine.

"We understand that you recommended the cabin in Gainesville to her," Trent said. "Is that correct?"

"That's right." His voice had become tight, his eyes narrowed, and his posture stiffened. "She said she needed to get away for a few days, and she didn't want to go too far from home."

"Do you know why she was looking to get away?" It never hurt to verify stories. Amanda held her breath, waiting for Harold's response, hoping he'd confirm what Tony had said.

"Not really sure, to be honest with you. She lives at a resort. I assume you saw the place?"

All Amanda could do was nod. Just because Harold didn't know Alicia's reason didn't mean Tony had lied. Harold might not even know Alicia had been planning to sell the business, but Amanda would get to that. "Do you know what's going to happen to the business now?"

"I suspect everything will go to Tony."

Trent leaned forward. "Why is that?"

Harold tucked his chin in, and his brow pressed down. "He is her husband, and those two were nearly inseparable."

"They had a strong marriage, then?" Amanda asked.

"Yes. As far as I could tell. Though you never know what happens behind closed doors."

Her parents' marriage sprang to mind. "I overheard a woman at reception asking for Tony and saw his parking space. I assume he works here?"

"Absolutely. He started here the week after they got married." He angled his head. "You didn't know that?"

"Is he in the accounting department? Or does he manage it?" Amanda went with what was logical given Tony's career background.

"I heard that's what he was doing before, but no, not here. Alicia had him enroll in marketing courses. He oversaw our marketing department."

Tony had loved his work as an accountant. It would have taken a lot for him to change professions. "And you're in distribution. Do the two of you work closely together?" She could imagine that the two departments would need to consult at times. For instance, an advertising approach in one demographic or region may not work in another.

"Ah, yes and no. I'm more about expansion, opening new locations around the United States and even globally. Tony oversaw the models and ad layouts. He seemed to enjoy the work."

What hot-blooded American male wouldn't? she thought, hating the stereotypical judgment. But now she knew why the woman in the lobby had looked familiar. She'd been in the ad layouts at the cabin. The model and Tony could have had something business-related to discuss. Though Amanda was pretty sure a person in marketing wouldn't need to speak directly to a model—not unless they were on the set of a photoshoot. But if there was an affair going on, why would she come to his work? The questions had Amanda wondering if Tony had strayed from his marriage. Had it been rocky, despite his claims otherwise? The nuptials had certainly happened fast enough. And Tony had told them Claudia had been unfaithful, but was that the true story? If Alicia's death turned out to be murder,

Amanda would need to pry into every nook and cranny of her former friend's life. For now, though, she'd return focus to the deceased. "How was Alicia recently? Was she anxious or depressed, for example?"

"Not at all."

"Was her getting away for a few days normal for her?" This thought had just occurred to her. The urge to hole up somewhere may indicate a change in behavior and possibly suggest she rented the cabin to kill herself.

"Not really. I don't think she knows—*knew*—how to relax."

"It sounds like she was very dedicated to her work," Trent said.

"She was. New Belle was her heart and soul. She started this company when she was still in college."

Amanda fought the desire to glance at Trent. Harold wasn't describing a woman who would sell her business. "Then if we heard that Alicia may have been planning to sell New Belle, that would come as a surprise to you?"

"A surprise? More like an absolute shock. Why would she just walk away? And now of all times. The business is growing monumentally."

There could be a reason that Harold hadn't been pulled into the loop on Alicia's plans. They'd have to ask Tony. "You talk like you knew Alicia well."

"I might be responsible for distribution, but I acted more as Alicia's right hand. I've been here right from the beginning."

She'd sensed pride in Harold's words, as if he took some credit for Alicia's success. "And when was that?"

"She was about to graduate college and was looking for investors. She'd come up with this most revolutionary cream, a night serum, to be more precise. Reborn. You might have heard of it, though it is for ladies older than you are." He nodded his head toward Amanda.

"Impressive," Trent said.

"Alicia was, in every sense of the word. A role model for young women who aspired to achieve great things. No doubt you're aware of how much the media loves her?"

"Did you invest in her idea?" Call it a gut feeling, based on his earlier phrasing.

"I did. One of many who saw the future. Everyone else has since moved on, though."

"Do you own shares in the company?" Amanda asked.

"Oh, no, Alicia could be fiercely independent. She insisted on buying me out years ago."

"And she never took on other shareholders or opened the corporation to public trading?" Trent asked.

"No, she didn't."

"But her husband had shares?" Trent kicked back.

"Not that I know of. Besides, they were quite new as a couple. She might have given him some shares eventually, but as I said, 'fiercely independent.' Having full control of her company was important to her."

Yet she had practically run down the aisle and wasted no time getting Tony to start a new career. Amanda didn't like the direction of her thoughts and how they possibly gave Tony motive. He'd given up his job—for Alicia—and then she decides to close up shop? "What do you think of Tony?" Just asking felt like a betrayal of her old friend, but this was a potential murder investigation.

"Mr. Bishop." Harold drew in a deep breath, set down his glass, and tugged on his suit jacket. "He's a nice guy."

"But...?" Harold's posture had tensed. She tried to relate, set him at ease. "It would make sense to me if you had a hard time accepting him. You were there from the start; he just shows up, marches in here." She bit back saying *and replaced you as her right-hand man.* She went on. "You could have thought he was taking advantage of her, or maybe you had a personality conflict with him?"

Harold shook his head adamantly. "None of that. I admit I was a little suspicious at first. Their romance was a bit of a hurricane, and they got married so fast. Most people these days take their time and don't rush in. Some don't get married at all."

She didn't miss Harold's imagery of the union between Alicia and Tony. Hurricane winds usually destroyed everything in their path.

Harold clasped his hands on the table and continued. "Let's just say it had me wondering about the guy's angle. You must realize that Alicia was worth a lot of money. But he seemed to make her happy, and he did whatever he could for her. Bending over backwards, changing his career, all because that's what Alicia wanted."

All this talk about Tony getting married quickly had it coming back to her. Tony used to be fast at giving his heart. But Tony changing careers wasn't something Amanda saw him taking lightly. And what did Tony plan to do if New Belle was sold? Maybe just become a kept man, but Amanda doubted Tony would be happy to retire at age forty-one, still so young. He'd always liked to work and had been so driven. "How did others in the company feel about him?"

"We welcomed him because of Alicia."

Not really an answer, but she'd move on. "Do you know if Alicia had any enemies or received any threats?"

"As I said, she was a role model. The media loved her, and she'd been awarded Entrepreneur of the Year a few times, among other adulations. Of course, she attracted haters like any public persona does."

"Did these haters ever send her anything in writing, say in emails or by postal mail?"

"There were a few."

It may be a stretch to think one of them had acted upon their words, but they'd have to first see the letters to determine the threat level. "Before we leave, we'll need to get those from you."

A subtle nod. "She put them in a special spot on the server. She named it File Thirteen, as in garbage. She had a great sense of humor. She's really going to be missed."

"So you can print those out?" she asked, placing more emphasis on the request she'd already made.

"Absolutely." Harold made no move to leave but leaned back in his chair and swept his gaze from her to Trent and back to her. "You have an awful lot of questions for not knowing what happened to her. Should I be concerned that someone killed her?"

"The investigation is ongoing," she said. "In some cases, manner of death is not immediately apparent."

"Manner...?"

"Natural, accidental, suicide, murder," she explained.

Harold shuddered. "I can't imagine suicide, but if someone killed her... She deserves justice."

"We agree," Amanda said. "Would you mind telling us where you were last night between nine and midnight?"

"Not at all. I was home with Mags, my wife. Well, Maggie. Margaret is her given name."

Trent jotted the information in his notepad.

Amanda noticed Harold's sudden urge to ramble, which made her assume the conversation made him uncomfortable for some reason. "Do you know if Alicia planned to have any visitors at the cabin while she was there?"

"Ah... do you mean, was she cheating on Tony?"

She hadn't meant that, but... "Sure."

"No, I can't see that."

"What about meeting up with any friends or business acquaintances?"

"I wouldn't know if anyone popped by while she was there."

He scratched his wrist, sliding his fingertips under the cuff of his shirt.

They thanked Harold for his cooperation, and Amanda gave him her business card. Before they left, they were shown to Alicia's office with the request that they not touch or take anything with them until they had a warrant secured.

The space was plush and luxurious with a crystal chandelier that hung over her desk. Alicia had certainly admired the finer things in life.

They also spoke to a Scarlett Dixon, who worked as an assistant to Alicia and Tony. A kind young woman with a big heart. She seemed devastated by Alicia's death.

"This is all that was in File Thirteen." Harold stepped into Alicia's office, a folder in hand. "Not much but hopefully it aids the investigation."

"Thank you." Amanda took the file and opened it. The stack of papers inside was at least a quarter-inch thick.

Harold dipped his head and left, and Amanda and Trent followed soon after. She was fixed on the fact that Harold hadn't known Alicia was planning to sell. Having professed himself to be Alicia's right hand, shouldn't he have been privy to that? Also, Harold had invested start-up capital because of his belief in Alicia and New Belle. He certainly wouldn't want to find his faith misplaced. What if Harold had lied to them to protect himself? Could he have killed Alicia Gordon?

SEVEN

Amanda was just getting into the car when a text chimed on her phone. It was a message from Rideout to call ASAP.

She did just that, and put the call on speaker so Trent could hear. "It's Detective Steele," she said when Rideout picked up.

"You take ASAP seriously. I just sent the text."

The wait was killing her. "You have something for us?" she rushed out.

"Oh, do I ever. First, cause of death was cardiogenic shock, respiratory arrest second. Now, a microscopic evaluation of her lungs showed a hypertrophy of the smooth endoplasmic reticulum of hepatocytes."

She and Trent looked at each other. His expression of absolute confusion confirmed she wasn't alone in feeling that way. She was hearing everything but only understood about half. Rideout normally kept his speech to the level of a layman.

"And in simplified English?" she asked.

"The cells that process protein in the liver are enlarged."

That she could understand. "Do you know what could have caused the enlargement?"

"Pentobarbital poisoning."

"The stuff that's used to put animals to sleep." She'd known that since losing the family dog when she was sixteen. Her father had laid out what was going to happen to Rosco as a matter of fact, without any sugarcoating.

"That's right. Now, I would still like to wait on the blood-work to be absolutely certain—and that's if it's detectable. Pentobarbital usually remains in the body anywhere between fifteen and fifty hours, depending on how fast it is metabolized."

"So we may never know for sure?" That possibility sank like a stone.

"Let's think positively."

It was harder to do than say. "How much is needed to be fatal?"

"Anywhere between two to ten grams. But I want to be upfront. Pentobarbital is sometimes prescribed to treat anxiety and depression—small doses, short-term, it's safe. But as you know, Alicia Gordon was only prescribed birth control."

Cold blanketed Amanda's shoulders. "The sleeping medication. There was a bottle of Sleep Tight on the nightstand. It's available over the counter."

"I'll make sure it's tested for contamination."

Amanda was starting to rethink her preference that Alicia's manner of death was murder. The dead always had secrets; some they took to the grave. But a murder investigation had a way of exposing everything, even what loved ones didn't want found.

"What are the side effects if someone ingests too much pentobarbital?" Trent asked.

"Dizziness, nausea, weak and shallow breathing, a rapid pulse, low blood pressure and body temperature. She also could have been drowsy, confused... There are a lot of ways the drug manifests itself."

"The woman who owns the cabin mentioned confusion," Amanda said. "Is it possible Alicia had pentobarbital in her system for a while and some of the symptoms showed up in the day or two before she died?"

"It is possible."

Amanda had been hoping it wasn't. "Alibis in this investigation are going to be useless."

"At this point, yes," Rideout agreed.

"When will we have the toxicology results?" she asked.

"Probably looking at Monday, at the earliest."

"Okay, call me the second you have them." They would have to wait for answers a little while longer—and so would Tony.

"I assure you that I will." With that, Rideout was gone.

"Murder or suicide?" Trent put out there, his voice slicing the brief silence that had fallen between them.

"Could be either, but I'm thinking there might be an easier, faster way to go."

"And there's Pamela Zimmerman's take on things. Alicia Gordon struck her as dazed and confused."

"Yeah." Amanda chewed on that. "The day before Alicia died. I think someone drugged her with pentobarbital without her knowledge. If she wanted to kill herself, I don't think she would have spread it out over days."

"Murder then," Trent said.

"And with alibis out, that leaves us with means, motive, and opportunity unanswered. The opportunity part is especially dicey. We don't know for sure where or how she consumed the pentobarbital." She stopped talking there. If it had been added to Alicia's sleeping aid, where would that leave Tony? He'd certainly have access.

"You all right over there?"

"I'm fine," she pushed out. *Does he read minds and energy now?*

Trent held up a hand. "Excuse me for asking."

She pinched her eyes shut a second. Sarcasm and snippiness weren't working for her or Trent—and he didn't deserve it. He'd as good as told her he didn't have feelings for her. She should let whatever budding ones she had for him wither and die. "Sorry, I'm a little on edge."

"Just a guess. It has to do with Tony?"

"Yeah." She kept asking herself if she'd have the fortitude to arrest Tony if it came to that. But she had turned in her own mother over a year ago to face a murder charge. If Amanda was going to break the law or look the other way for anyone, it would have been for her own flesh and blood, not an estranged friend.

"It can't be easy when a friend's involved in something like this."

"Again, calling him a friend is stretching things."

"Ready to elaborate more on that?"

"I already told you we met in high school."

"Yeah, he married Claudia, you married Kevin..." He was peering into her eyes, hungry for more than the meager offerings she'd doled out so far.

"We remained friends as adults. The four of us hung around often—that being Tony, Claudia, me, and Kev. After he and Lindsey died, Tony and Claudia pulled away, and I let them. We fell out of touch, and yesterday was the first time I've seen Tony in years. Well, in six-plus years, say."

"Wow. And then you have to tell him that his wife is dead. That's shit."

"Hey, don't pity me too much. I'm a tough cop."

Trent smirked. "No one's denying that."

"Good. And I'll do my job. If Tony Bishop was involved with his wife's death, I will arrest him." She drilled that point home with solid eye contact.

"No reason to believe you wouldn't, but..."

"I know. I need to tell Malone about the connection, and the longer I wait to do that, the messier it will be."

"Yep."

"I'll let him know. Right now, though, you and I need to focus on Alicia's life and who might have had motive to kill her."

"The tried and true are jealousy, money, revenge..." Trent tapped the steering wheel. "What am I missing?"

"Love. You'd be surprised what people will do in the name of it. But we can't forget that Alicia was also a very wealthy woman. Who stood to benefit from her death?"

"It is said: follow the money. Tony is going to inherit New Belle, and that place has to be worth a mint."

"Something he'd never get his hands on without her death." Again, putting that out there made it all the more real—Tony had motive. "I'm sure there's far more on the line than her business too—investments, bank accounts, property holdings... We should get our hands on her will."

"I agree. We might want to look at anyone who was interested in buying New Belle too. Maybe Alicia was a hard negotiator, and someone felt with her out of the way, they could take over the company from her successor for far less."

"Also, was Harold Armstrong really in the dark about Alicia's plan to sell New Belle like he claimed? Or did he actually know about it? He was obviously vested in the company—at first financially, but he stuck by Alicia all these years. It likely became more than a business relationship. Maybe even beyond friends. A father figure? I just wonder where he'd be left if Alicia sold."

"It would have been a major life change for him, and the guy's not getting any younger."

There was so much to investigate, and they'd barely scratched the surface. For the people they mentioned, the primary motivating force would conceivably be money. Where did that leave jealousy, revenge, love? "Well, I think our next step is clear," she said. "We need to talk to Tony again, find out more about Alicia."

"Here I thought you were going to suggest lunch." Trent smiled over at her.

She appreciated that he was trying to set her at ease, accounting for her feelings. "Okay, but something from a drive-thru that we can scarf down in the car."

"I'm not fussy. Just hungry." He laid a hand over his flat stomach as if to emphasize the point.

"All right."

He drove them to Petey's Patties, Zoe's favorite place to eat. Though her preference might have been swayed by the boxed meals that included a small toy—a marketing ploy they'd obviously copied from McDonald's. But, as they say, don't fix what isn't broken.

Amanda ordered a bacon cheeseburger, cutting out the fries, and a Coke. Trent did the same except he kept the order of fries.

They munched it down in the parking lot.

"Zoe can never find out that I ate here without her." Amanda bit off a chunk of cow, pig, and carbs... *Delicious!* She'd never be a vegetarian.

Trent looked over at Amanda. "She likes this place?"

"She *loves* this place."

If Amanda knew they were going to stick to talking about personal matters, they could have gone inside and sat at a table instead of balancing everything on their laps and the dash. When she'd suggested dining in the car, she imagined them either discussing the case or eating on the move. But as much as she was in a hurry to talk to Tony, she wasn't.

It was going on one thirty in the afternoon when they pulled into the Gordon/Bishop driveway. Tony answered the door wearing jogging pants and a fitted tee.

"Mandy?" His gaze danced over her to Trent, back again. "You have some news?"

She cringed at him calling her by her nickname and thought of correcting him. For the purposes of their interactions, he should be calling her Detective Steele. But she let it go for now. "Can we come in?"

"Of course." Tony shook his head as if he were remiss for not already making that offer. He added, "I was just on the phone with my dad. Mom's gone. Did you know that? She died of a stroke three years ago."

"Sorry for your loss."

"Seems you're saying that to me a lot lately."

An awkward silence fell for a few seconds, in which Amanda became curious about something. "Alicia's parents must be having a hard time," she said, an inquiry enclosed as she'd heard nothing about them.

"They both died a couple of years back. Car accident," he added at a near whisper and turned his gaze briefly away from her. "Anyway," he went on. "I'm just trying to make arrangements."

"Has her body been released already?" Amanda put that as delicately as possible, but typically Rideout would notify her of such things. And the autopsy had just been conducted. Heck, Rideout could still be finishing up.

"Not yet. I'm just trying to get ahead of things."

What he was doing was pushing through, like a robot performing its duties. Keeping busy to feel needed. She remembered the feeling. He probably feared if he halted mission mode everything would collapse on top of him. And he wouldn't be wrong. Then again, there could be another reason motivating him. The faster Alicia's body was in the ground, the faster evidence of her murder could be buried along with her. She stiffened. "Didn't Alicia have preparations already in place?"

"Some, yes. Come, let's sit." He took them to the sitting room where she'd served notification the previous day.

Once everyone was settled, Amanda spoke again. "She had some 'end of life' matters sorted but not everything?" She found that hard to believe about a highly successful business owner. Most of them were organized and ready for all contingencies.

"She had a will but didn't have her funeral arrangements planned out. That would have been too much for her. Alicia was about living... *Life!* She was a businesswoman through and through, but she was also somewhat of a daredevil. She was a fresh breeze as far as I'm concerned. She loved skydiving and white-water rafting."

"Oh, I enjoy that too," Trent chimed in.

Amanda looked over at him and raised her brows. She wouldn't have guessed him to be the adventuresome, outdoorsy type. She'd rather have a tooth pulled without drugs than barrel down a rushing river that swatted her around, eager to capsize the boat and drown her. *No thanks!*

"She is... *was*... a lot of fun." Tony's eyes glazed over—the reverie alive for the moment.

"We have some more questions we need to ask you," Amanda said. She wasn't going to mention pentobarbital until it had been confirmed with absolute certainty as playing a role in Alicia's death.

"Sure. Fire away. However I can help. I just want all this..." He swallowed roughly, his Adam's apple heaving. "I just want all this over with for the kids' sakes."

"I imagine this has been very hard on them." The empathy slipped out, being a part of her, but she had to reel herself back and remain objective. "My partner and I are considering different angles, and one thing that may help us is to see a copy of her will."

"Her will." He tossed that out like it sat as bile on his tongue. "Like one of her beneficiaries is behind her death?"

"I didn't say that."

"That's exactly what you're saying, Amanda."

"Detective Steele," she corrected sharply.

Tony sat back like he'd been physically struck. "Detective Steele, am I a suspect?"

"I'm not sure why you're getting so defensive."

"You're sitting here, in my house, insinuating that I might have something to do with my wife's death."

"I'm not," she said. "We do, however, need to consider all angles, all the evidence."

He bunched up his face. "Yeah, sure, I can get you a copy of her will. Just remember I volunteered. Would a killer do that? And from what I understand, you don't even know what caused her death. Do you?"

She chose her words carefully. "Not yet." The truth without leaving room to tear it apart.

"Huh." Tony worried his bottom lip, his eyes staring into space. "So you don't even know if she was murdered?"

"We don't." She wanted to tell him the investigation was steering them that way but had to be careful how she played this. "There are other possibilities," she added. She'd explore the path of suicide more for due diligence. Rideout hadn't been able to say if Alicia had ingested the pentobarbital in one large dose or little by little over the course of a few days. Heck, he wasn't even ruling pentobarbital as contributing to her cause of death until he saw the toxicology report.

"Did Alicia ever attempt suicide in the past?" Trent asked, his expression grim.

"What? Absolutely not!"

"Mr. Bishop. I'm just asking these questions to get a better idea of what might have happened to her." Trent's attempt to smooth things over had Tony's scowl deepening.

"You're not even masking what you're getting at, but I can tell you she didn't kill herself."

Amanda gave it a few beats before she inserted, "The signs can be easy to miss."

He clenched his jaw and glared at her. His gaze was so intense it had her insides jumping, but she had a job to do.

"She was in good physical health, but did she have any emotional wounds, lost relationships that weighed on her?" She thought of Brad and Leo and how neither was Tony's son.

"We all have relationships that don't work out."

The way he said it felt leveled at her. Personal. She pushed on. "Was Alicia acting differently? Withdrawing or antisocial? Having a hard time sleeping?" Again, Amanda thought of the sleeping aid on the night table at the cabin.

"Not any different. She's always been a light sleeper, but she had a lot on her mind."

"Did she take something to help her sleep?" Amanda didn't want to assume Sleep Tight was a nightly occurrence.

"Yeah. Sleep Tight."

Amanda nodded. "And that was something she took every night?"

"She did."

Amanda was suddenly desperate to know whether the sleeping aid at the cabin had been tampered with. She'd need to wait to find out. But she was feeling satisfied for the moment that Alicia hadn't killed herself. If she had, she'd exhibited no signs of wishing to do so beforehand. Maybe she could find out more about Alicia's health in the days leading up to her death—something to disclose whether she had ingested pentobarbital over time or not. "Did Alicia complain of nausea or shallow breathing?"

"No."

"Have low blood pressure, a rapid pulse, dizziness?"

He shook his head.

"Difficulty concentrating or confusion?"

"Some I guess, but she had a lot on her mind, as I told you.

So, yeah, sure, her thoughts would stray some. She'd sometimes lose track of what day it was."

Was that a coincidence or indicative of being poisoned over days? "Did that happen often for her?"

Tony seemed to give it thought. "More often recently, I guess."

"Could that be because she was under a lot of stress wanting to sell the business?" Trent asked.

"Yes, probably."

"We spoke with Harold Armstrong," Amanda began. "He didn't even know that Alicia planned to sell."

"That's because she hadn't told him."

"He was her right hand," Trent pointed out.

"That's why. Alicia had no idea how she was going to break the news to him."

"He'd be devastated?" She could find motive for murder in that. She and Trent had already hypothesized about this very thing.

"I think he'd be disappointed, but he's going to have to accept it. I'll be telling him."

"You've decided to sell the business already?" Amanda thought it was rather fast to have come to a decision of that magnitude overnight—in the wake of losing his wife, no less.

"That's what she wanted, so..."

"Where was Alicia in the process? Was she already entertaining offers?" Amanda asked.

"She was in talks with Eve Kelley, the owner of Pixie Winks. No idea why she even gave that woman the time of day."

"Why is that?"

"Eve claimed that Alicia stole the formula for Reborn from her in college."

This was the second time hearing about that serum, but the first hearing about the allegation.

Tony smiled, though the expression was small and fleeting. "You've never been a girlie-girl. Admired that about you."

She wasn't sure how to react to that—roll with it as a compliment or take some offense. She suddenly had the urge to look at herself in the mirror. At least she put on foundation and smeared on lipstick most days. "Thanks... I guess?"

"Reborn is a restorative night serum. It's where New Belle got its start. Investors took notice and gave Alicia the seed money she needed to get things rolling."

"Yes, I know what Reborn is." Her pride wouldn't admit she'd had no clue before Harold Armstrong had mentioned it. "If there was this history between the two women, why was Alicia considering selling New Belle to Eve?"

"You'd have to know my wife to even somewhat understand. She never let the money go to her head, but she treated everyone kindly. Even Eve, despite her lies."

Amanda wasn't going to say it out loud, but to her, it sounded like Alicia may have been living with a guilty conscience.

Tony continued. "You know Alicia memorized every one of her employees' names from the head office in Woodbridge? Think we're up to twelve hundred now."

That was impressive, though almost unbelievable. "She knew all of them?"

"She did. She also opened her door to every new hire to meet with her for an hour during their first month. She operated on the motto that employees should believe not only in the product but the person behind it too."

"It sounds like she was an amazing woman." Amanda was conflicted, and the whole Eve allegation was gnawing away at her. Could Eve finally have had enough and killed Alicia? But what would be the motive when she was close to obtaining New Belle? That is, unless things had changed.

"Mandy, she was. You would have loved her. As for Eve,

Alicia wanted to make things good between them. That's why she was giving Eve the opportunity to make the first and final offers."

"Meaning...?"

"Eve extended an offer, and while Alicia would gather others, before she made a decision, she was going to return to Eve to see if she could match the offer."

Huh. That seemed to wipe out motive for Eve. Again, unless things had changed. But it certainly sounded like a confession of guilt on Alicia's behalf. And depending on how much interest was drummed up, the purchase price could have climbed to a point that wasn't affordable for Pixie Winks. "Did Alicia have other offers?"

"Think she did. I'd have to dig into that and let you know."

"She squeezed you out of this process?" Amanda asked.

"It was her business."

"That didn't bother you at all?" Trent's voice sounded skeptical.

"Why would it?"

"You changed careers for her, and then a few months down the road, she's ready to disregard that? That didn't bug you in the least?" Trent was being antagonistic—far more than Amanda deemed necessary.

"She wanted to spend more time with Leo. How is that a bad thing? And look around. I have no need to work, whether she kept the business or sold it."

Amanda could breathe a little easier with those words. It could clear Tony of financial motivation—that is, unless he was unhappy in their relationship. And what if Alicia had wanted out of the marriage? She was stretching things here, but it was something to consider. Could Tony have been left with nothing? Frustration knotted in her chest. Any relief disappeared. But Tony wasn't the only one whose world and existence was affected by Alicia's decisions. How disappointed would Harold

Armstrong be about the sale of New Belle? Enough to kill Alicia if he had known, possibly in the hopes of preventing the sale from happening? "What are your thoughts about Mr. Armstrong? Let's revisit how you think he'd have reacted if he knew about Alicia's plan to sell."

"He's been with her from the beginning. He's a good guy."

"And financially, how would he make out if Alicia sold?" Amanda was thinking Harold was older and recreating himself at that point in his life wouldn't be easy.

"She'd have made sure he was taken care of. Besides, he's old enough to retire. He should have a beautiful nest egg set aside ready to pull from."

Though not everyone was wise with their money, and Harold could have built up debts. "Forward whatever you find on other bidders as soon as you can."

"Will do."

"We'd also like your approval to access her computer and phone records," she said.

Tony's face hardened. "I feel the need to protect her privacy. For now. I mean, you don't even know for certain that someone..."

"No, we don't. But a look at her correspondence could help with that determination."

"I'm sorry. I want to help in whatever way I can, but I have to draw the line somewhere."

She'd asked him out of respect for their previous friendship, but they probably had enough to get a subpoena approved for her electronic devices. She didn't care for the wall he'd erected. "We'll get a judge involved, then. We'll also petition for her financials."

"Do whatever you have to."

"We will," Trent said firmly, stepping in.

She was steaming at Trent's interjection. She didn't need

him adding any more weight to what she'd already said. "We should go, but if we could get that copy of the will..."

"I'll go get it now." Tony went upstairs, and while they waited, Amanda couldn't even look at Trent.

A few minutes later, Amanda and Trent were back in the car, a copy of Alicia's will in hand. She clicked her seat belt into place and faced him in the driver's seat. "What was up with you in there?"

"Up with me? You can't be serious?"

She hadn't expected him to snap back, and it took her off guard. "You overstepped. He just lost his wife, and you had no reason to show such aggression."

"Someone had to do it."

"Argh." She used to find herself respecting Trent when he showed his temper, even found it attractive. When it was aimed at her... not so attractive. "You don't speak on my behalf. Do I have to remind you that I'm the senior detective?"

"Apparently you feel the need to."

"Just drive us back to Central." She glanced at the clock on the dash. 2:30 PM. Too bad it wasn't closer to five, and she could head home.

"He calls you Mandy."

She nudged out her chin. "What about it?"

"You are the detective investigating his wife's death. There has to be a line."

"I couldn't agree more." She pushed her butt into the seat and faced forward. Through her peripheral vision, she could see him watching her, but she couldn't face him right now. As much as there were times having Trent as a partner was a blessing, she was starting to revert to her previous thinking. Partners got in the way of getting the job done.

EIGHT

Amanda and Trent arrived at Central, and she headed straight to Malone's office. Trent went to his desk with Alicia's will.

She rapped her knuckles on the doorframe.

Malone motioned her in with a wave. "Just the person I wanted to see."

She offered him a small smile as she entered and shut the door behind her.

"Oh, whatever you have to say must be serious." Malone sat up a little straighter.

"It is." Her mind kept throwing around whether it would be prudent to tell him about the friction between her and Trent, as well as her connection to Alicia's husband. She dropped into the chair across from Malone. "I'm here about a few things." Her intention was out, leaving her little choice but to proceed. "Trent and I have our hands on the victim's will. Trent's starting to look it over as we speak."

"Great. It could shed light on a suspect if her death was motivated by financial gain."

"Yes. Trent and I are considering that as one angle." She

held back telling Malone that they already knew Tony Bishop stood to inherit.

"As I'd expect." He spoke slowly, watching her. "Something else? You have things under control from what I'm hearing, and I appreciate the play by play on the case, but I have a feeling there's more to why you're here." He studied her face. "Am I right?"

She let out a deep breath. "Yeah. There's no easy way to say this other than to come out with it, but I used to be friends with the victim's husband, Tony Bishop." She expected an animated reaction, a declaration that it would be a conflict of interest for her to investigate. He gave her none of this.

"I was wondering if you were going to come to me."

"What...? You knew?"

"Uh-huh. From the start."

Amanda leaned back in the chair. "And you never said anything."

"I knew you'd tell me."

She was touched by his faith in her. "I would have told you sooner, but I didn't know how far I'd be going with this investigation." She went on to update Malone on Rideout's findings.

"Oh, sounds like it could be murder."

"The way Trent and I are leaning."

"All right, can you remain objective with this case? Say, if the evidence mounts and you're led to the husband?"

"I haven't seen Tony for the better part of seven years."

Malone nodded. "So there's definitely some separation there."

"I'd be lying to say I don't feel empathy for him, but it's not going to affect how I do my job."

"Suppose I can trust that. You've already proven yourself in that regard. You know what it feels like to be in his position—from the standpoint of..."

Then why had he questioned her ability to do just that a second ago? "So you're not going to remove me from the case?"

"Nope. I have faith in you."

"Thank you."

"Now, when you came in here, you said you wanted to talk to me about a few things. Was that just the update on the case and your confession, or is there something else?"

She'd been hoping he wouldn't ask. She wasn't sure she really wanted to bring up the friction with Trent. Another thing occurred to her. "We could benefit from getting authorization to look at the victim's phone records and her computer." She left out Tony's refusal to hand them over.

"Yeah, that's going to be a no-go right now. Until we have a ruling or strong reason to prove murder."

"Rideout is quite certain that—"

"Pentobarbital was in her system. Yes. I heard you, but we still don't know how the victim came into contact with it—or that she did. I'd prefer to wait until the tox results are back or the investigation gives us more to go on."

She chewed on that. Hated the flavor. Nodded. She wanted to help him see he was being ridiculous, but she wouldn't win any argument with Malone once his mind was made up.

"I have a feeling there's more you wanted to say."

There's a lot but... "I'm not sure if Trent and I are quite seeing eye to eye these days." There, just like ripping off a Band-Aid. Just as painful as when the sticky strip yanked hairs from the roots.

"Probably just a spell. From what I can see, you two work very well together. You've closed a lot of cases—in record time, I'll add."

She tried to think of a counter, something to defend her position. But he was right; she and Trent did get the job done. Her issue with Trent was rooted in her personal feelings—ones that shouldn't exist. Just as she had thought before. She'd shove those feelings down deep inside until they ceased to exist. She'd proven before she could be an ice princess when she'd shut out her parents and siblings after losing her husband and daughter. Not that it was any real way to live. She jutted out her chin, nodded. "You're likely right. Just a spell." She attempted a smile but didn't trust the expression showed.

"Whatever it is, I'm sure you'll figure it out. Now, you might recall that I said I'd wanted to see you."

She thought back to her arrival. "Ah, yes." She'd since assumed it was to talk about her connection to Tony Bishop.

"Word about Alicia Gordon's death has reached the new chief, and he wants answers *lickety-split*—his words. Says the people of the county deserve as much since Gordon was a prominent member of the community. She brought jobs to the area, supported local charities, etcetera."

The new police chief was Jeff Buchanan. He was initially put in as an acting chief last November until a new one could be given the permanent position. But he'd quickly impressed the County Board of Supervisors and they made the appointment official in February, dropping the "acting" part from his title. Amanda didn't know Buchanan that well, but his reputation had reached her. An outsider but a decent man, committed to the job, the community, and his family. That all sounded good if it was true. She'd reserve opinion until more time passed. "Trent and I are doing all we can," she said.

"I trust that. I just wanted to keep you apprised that the chief has his eye on the case and interest in its speedy resolution."

Doubt he wanted it resolved faster than she did. "Is that all?" Amanda put her hands on the arms of the chair to get up.

"Yep."

She left his office. The closer she got to the warren of cubicles for the Homicide Unit, bringing her nearer to Trent, she felt a jumble of nerves. *Stuff it down, Steele!* She lifted herself taller, back straight. As her dad would say, "Appear confident, become confidence itself."

Trent lifted his head but didn't say a word.

"You should know that the police chief wants us to do everything we can to resolve this case quickly." She was too proud to get into how she'd told Malone about knowing Tony Bishop and having been his friend in the past. If Trent really wanted to know, let him ask like a big boy.

"Can't say that surprises me. While you were with the sergeant, I googled Alicia Gordon."

"Okay. I thought you were going to be looking at her will."

"I'll get there," he said coolly. "Her career path and all her accomplishments were incredible. She started New Belle while she was in college, as we know, but she wasn't shy at all about approaching big-name investors to help her get things rolling. Reborn, that cream, established her in the women-over-forty market."

"She was certainly impressive." *And she seemed to have it all...* Until she didn't. So who would want to strip that from her? "In your time playing on the internet, did you get a chance to look into Eve Kelley and Pixie Winks, by chance?"

"Playing?" he volleyed back.

She smiled. "Just giving you a hard time."

"Well, the answer is while I was *working*, I did look into Eve and her company. I never found any public allegations against New Belle from either."

"Huh. Why would Eve have kept quiet about that?" If it had been Amanda in Eve's place, she'd have hired lawyers and gone to the press.

"I think we'll need to ask Eve Kelley. As for her company, Pixie Winks, it serves a younger market than New Belle. Their focus is women in their early twenties, even teenage girls. They offer bright colors and glimmery shades..."

Amanda stifled a laugh.

"Something funny?" He cocked his head.

"You talking about *glimmery shades*. Sorry, continue."

"That's about it. But why would Alicia Gordon want to sell the business she worked so hard to build to Eve Kelley when they didn't even have the same target demographic?"

"Another good question. One we'll need to ask Eve. After all, she wouldn't have experience with the more mature market." She refused to say *older* market, as she was creeping toward forty now that she was on the other side of thirty-six.

"Something else you should know. I flipped through the threats sent to Alicia. I'll need to go through them in more detail, but one already stands out to me. 'How dare you sell what isn't yours to sell? You'll pay for this.'"

"Whoa. Interesting, given what we know now about Eve. Did she send the threat? Possibly kill Alicia?"

"She could have motive."

"But Alicia was in the process of giving Eve the opportunity to get it all back."

"What Eve probably already saw as hers, and she was being forced to pay for it."

"I see where you're going with this. No doubt we need to pay Eve Kelley a visit. First, since we're here, let's look at Alicia's will." She walked over to her cubicle, sat down, and thumbed through the paperwork—one hundred pages long. She found where the beneficiaries were listed, along with what they inherited. She split it up, handing half to Trent over the low divider. "Make a note of who stands to inherit what. I'll do the same with this." She held up her equally high stack.

"Wow. That's a lot to leave behind."

"That's a lot of potential suspects," Amanda mumbled as

she dug in. She finished her half by quarter to five. Trent lifted his head and looked over at her. "Highlight reel?" she asked.

"The listing of her business assets: the company and all its holdings, vehicle fleets, its buildings, a few warehouses, etcetera."

"A few warehouses?"

"Three throughout the US."

"My portion covered her personal assets," she said. "Vehicles again, the residential property in Woodbridge, a vacation home in the Bahamas, investments..."

"The value of all of this must be in the tens of millions. If not more."

"So hit me with some names of beneficiaries."

"Tony Bishop, Brad Slater, Leo Rossi."

"Her family. Not surprising. What I found too. Leo stands to inherit a vast sum, which won't be accessible until his twenty-first birthday. Then there is money there to be distributed as a monthly allowance for the rest of his natural life. Same provisions were made for Brad Slater. Alicia also left donations to numerous charitable organizations."

Trent nodded. "Now I did find one particularly interesting clause relating to the business. And I'm guessing that given Tony has plans to sell New Belle, he may not be aware of it."

"What is it?"

"We'd do well to ask the executor of this will to be sure, but it reads to me like Tony would have no right to sell the business."

"Yet he sounded like that's what he planned to do."

"Exactly. So I don't think he was familiar with this clause."

"We'll need to meet with the estate lawyer to get clarification. I have a feeling there's something we're missing." She glanced at the clock, and it told her it was five. She had a shot of getting home to Zoe on time. She stood. "We'll start up again tomorrow. We'll visit the executor of the will to get some clarification on that clause you found and have a chat with Eve Kelley at Pixie Winks."

"Sounds good."

"Night." She offered him a smile before leaving. Tomorrow was a new day, the opportunity for a fresh start.

NINE

Friday morning, and while most people would be on a countdown until the weekend, Amanda was counting down for a break in the case. Was it too much to hope that Alicia's toxicology results would return sooner than next week? Even if they only heard back the sleeping aid at the cabin was contaminated, it might feel more conclusive that they were looking at murder.

It was just after nine, and she and Trent were sitting in a stylish lobby, waiting on Chester Morton, an estate lawyer tasked as the executor for Alicia Gordon's will.

"Detectives?" A man in his late fifties with a pleasant demeanor came over to them. "I'm Chester Morton. Follow me." He led them to an office and grabbed another chair so there'd be one for her and Trent. He sat behind his desk. "How can I help you?"

"We have a question or two about Alicia Gordon's will."

Chester winced. "I can't discuss the details of a client's will without authorization from the main beneficiary."

Amanda produced the copy of the will. "We received this from Tony Bishop, Alicia's husband. I suspect that's enough authorization right there."

"Not exactly."

"He shared this with us. There's no other way we'd have possession of it otherwise." She heard the desperation in her voice.

"All right," the man dragged out and leaned back in his chair. He narrowed his eyes and steepled his hands beneath his chin. "I will do my best to be cooperative." He gestured with an open palm for her to proceed. She motioned to Trent.

"So New Belle passed to Tony Bishop, her husband. But it reads as if Tony wouldn't have any rights to sell the business for three years after her death. Am I reading that clause correctly?"

"Yes and no. It was very important to Alicia that her eldest son be guaranteed the business, even upon her death."

Amanda glanced at Trent, back at Chester. "I'm not sure I understand."

"The clause stipulates Tony Bishop can sell only after three years, but if Brad Slater is still alive at that time, Mr. Bishop must ensure Brad receives the fair market value equivalent. Whatever he cleared above that would be his to keep."

"All right, but who would pay more than market value?" Trent asked.

"It can happen in cases of a bidding war," Chester said.

"And just to clarify, Ms. Gordon's other son, Leo Rossi, wouldn't be guaranteed anything from the sale?" she asked.

"That's right."

"So, she was ensuring that her business proceeds landed with her eldest son?" Trent pushed.

"Precisely."

Yet, Tony planned to sell. Did he not know about the limitation in that clause? Was that just something he'd told them? To what end? To cast the light of suspicion away from him? "So Tony was essentially fixed into running the business for at least three years?"

"That's right. Now, another section of the will gives me the right to step in should Mr. Bishop be driving New Belle into the ground."

"To protect Brad Slater's interest," Trent surmised.

"Correct."

Amanda didn't understand why Alicia included that clause when she was planning to sell the business herself. "We've come to the understanding that just before her death, Alicia was looking to sell New Belle. Is the will we have the most recent one you have on file?" Amanda handed the paperwork over to Chester, who studied it with a quick eye. Though the man had probably been through its pages so many times he'd likely memorized a lot of it.

"This would be the most recent, yes." He gave the file back to Amanda. He rubbed his trimmed beard. "I will disclose something, though. Alicia called earlier this week and requested a meeting to review some aspects of her will."

Amanda stiffened, inched forward on her chair. "Do you know what?"

"No, we never got that far."

Alicia could have planned to cut someone out of the will, then that person found out and wanted to prevent it from happening.

"Is there anything else, Detectives?" Chester danced his gaze over the two of them.

"Don't think so." Amanda stood. "If we have more questions, we'll be back. And if anything comes to your attention, please call me." She gave the estate lawyer her business card, then she and Trent thanked Chester for his cooperation and left.

Back in the department car, Amanda started the conversation.

"We need to find out what she planned to change, but I realize we can't ignore that Tony benefited financially regardless. Running New Belle in a managerial capacity, he'd draw money in. Then there were the personal assets he was set to receive, such as the house." Saying this, she felt like she'd put a knife into Tony's back.

"Don't go there yet."

She looked over at Trent, confused. First, he seemed to push Tony into the position of prime suspect, and now he was backing off.

Trent went on. "There are other people who benefited financially."

"Yes, and you heard the lawyer. Alicia was planning to change something in her will."

"Well, it doesn't mean she was taking someone out of the will."

"Okay, another motive then. Possibly someone with a personal motive or vendetta—Eve Kelley." Hers was the first name on the edge of Amanda's brain.

"Poison or drugging is more a woman's method of murder."

"Statistically. But real life doesn't always conform to statistics. We could be looking at a man."

He smirked. "Playing devil's advocate, I see."

"We have to argue every point until one sticks."

TEN

Trent parked in the lot for Pixie Winks. It was a much smaller outfit than New Belle, but the building and grounds were still rather impressive. A sizable pond with a large fountain sat on the front lawn next to a sign that spelled out the company's name in large, metal letters. A little pixie was perched on the *W* in Winks, its wand touching the dot on the *i*.

"Any closer, and they could be looking at a lawsuit from Disney for copying Tinker Bell," Trent said, echoing Amanda's thoughts.

The main reception area was colorful, and Trent's words about *glimmery shades* ran through her mind. The brand certainly didn't shy away from a flashy presence. A couple of people swished by them on Segways. Others were on Heelys and rolled past, gliding across the floor. The lobby had several beanbag chairs among the eclectic spattering of furniture.

"Haven't seen one of these since college." Trent was smiling as he lowered himself into one of the beanbag chairs.

"Ms. Kelley is ready for you." The chipper receptionist who had greeted them when they came in was standing in front of them.

Amanda wasn't sure if the young woman heard Trent's groaning upon standing up, but Amanda had. Beanbag chairs were best left to those under thirty.

The receptionist led them to a room labeled *Think Tank*. It had a red wooden table surrounded by chairs in all the primary colors. Amanda would quickly go crazy shut up in here for long. The table alone fired up a bit of rage within her. It felt like a rather confined space too, with boxy windows. The redeemable quality was the view of the water feature out front.

Amanda and Trent got comfortable at the table facing the door just as Eve Kelley walked through. She looked like her driver's license photo, which Amanda and Trent had pulled up just before coming.

She was slender, and despite the playfulness of her brand, she appeared quite serious. Even more so than in photos Amanda had seen of her in business magazines. The only thing currently fun about her image was her short pixie cut.

"Detectives," Eve purred, a smug aura of arrogance oozing from her. She held out her hand for Amanda and Trent in turn, and the introductions were made. Eve dropped into a chair across from them. "It's such an awful shame about Alicia. I've known her since college."

Though her words painted the picture of a tragedy, her tone and inflection didn't hint toward sorrow over the loss. Grief didn't touch her olive-green eyes either. "We heard that you two go way back," Amanda said.

"Do you know what happened to her? The papers are saying she was found dead, but details are being withheld." Stiff, rigid. Not striking Amanda as being too affected by Alicia's death at all.

"We can't say at this time. Her death is an open investigation. But you may be able to help us." Amanda hoped the appeal to human nature would work.

"If I can. Sure."

"When did you last see Alicia Gordon?" She'd build up to what they'd heard about Eve's allegations against Alicia. She'd also reserve mention of the threat to Alicia for now. No sense putting the woman on the defensive and causing her to clam up.

"It would have been two weeks ago."

"You seem quite certain," Trent said.

"I have a memory for things that matter."

"And why does this matter?" He volleyed her words right back to her.

"You may have heard that Alicia was planning to sell New Belle..." She paused there for a few seconds, scanning their faces. "I was in open negotiations with her for its acquisition. I submitted my offer to her in person, Monday, two weeks ago."

"Why were you interested?" Amanda asked. "Her products target women over forty and your line seems more geared to twentysomethings."

A tight smile. "It's called diversification."

Eve Kelley was certainly a businesswoman through and through and had built a successful company herself. Any perceived arrogance was ill-worn confidence. "That's smart thinking."

Eve gave no reaction that Amanda's compliment meant anything to her. "I thought it only made sense, and when Alicia came to me—"

"She approached you?" Trent jumped on that. Amanda was equally curious. If this were true, it would seem Alicia was eager to sell her business.

"Yes. She wanted to give me first dibs on buying New Belle."

"That must have come as a welcome surprise," Amanda said.

Eve's eyes flickered, indicating what, Amanda wasn't sure. "We had an arrangement," Eve said.

Amanda noticed Eve hadn't touched on the *welcome*

surprise comment. "Which was?" Amanda was playing coy, interested to see if her response would match what they'd learned from Tony Bishop.

"The deal was I would make an offer, and it would be valid for one month. During that time, she was open to consider bids from other companies and investors. Then she'd circle back to me with her best to top."

"Do you know who else was interested in New Belle?" Amanda asked.

"No. The other offers were blind—meaning the only one aware of the figures would have been Alicia and whomever she decided to share them with."

That was a new tidbit. "My partner and I were surprised to hear of your interest. We've learned you two had a rocky relationship."

"Not sure I'm following."

"We heard that she stole the formula for Reborn from you," Amanda said. "The serum upon which she founded her company."

"Where did you hear such a thing?" There was a marked irritation in Eve's tone.

"Not at liberty to say."

"Well, I don't know where you heard that."

"If it is true, Alicia really didn't have a right to sell what wasn't hers." Amanda let the similar wording from the threat to Alicia hang in the air.

"She built her business on many products. Besides, Alicia and I were moving past that."

"So, she did steal from you?"

Eve pursed her perfectly painted lips together. Her jaw tightened. "I can't say anything about this."

"You can't?" Trent pushed. "Is that why there's nothing public about your claim?"

"It's not just a claim," Eve spat. She took a few seconds

composing herself, pulling down on her shirt, nudging out her chin.

"Help us understand," Amanda said.

"I never went to the media because I signed a nondisclosure agreement."

"Come again?" The response was out before Amanda could filter it. "Why would you do that? Why would Alicia offer you one?"

"She knew what she'd done. And I was desperate when I signed."

"You did it for money?" Trent countered, sounding somewhat disgusted. Possibly because Eve had sacrificed her own value for a payday.

"There are worse ways to earn it. But, yes, she paid for my silence. Not that I was compensated for anywhere near the amount I deserved and what would have been mine if she hadn't taken the formula in the first place." A slight scowl.

"I'm sensing some animosity," Amanda said as Eve's cheeks flushed.

"Wouldn't you? She took what was rightfully mine. We were roommates, and both of us were chemistry majors. She was working on this serum, obsessing over getting it just right. It was me who came up with the solution. Not her. Without my input, she never would have figured it out."

Trent clasped his hands on the table. "Is that something you can prove?"

Eve scoffed. "If I could have done that, I never would have signed the NDA."

Proven or otherwise, it was what Eve believed to be true. Had the contention festered over the years and served as motive for murder? Eve was obviously still heated about the matter.

Eve knotted her arms. "Why are you both looking at me like I killed her?"

"Did you?" Amanda countered.

"That's absurd."

"Alicia received a threat, part of which made it clear the sender didn't think Alicia had any right to sell New Belle, that it wasn't rightfully hers and was built on a lie," Amanda said. "Did you send that threat to her?"

"No."

"She did wrong you, badly. Maybe you wanted to make her pay." Trent shrugged. "It would be understandable."

"I didn't kill her. Why would I? After all this time, she was going to make it right. And now she's dead."

"You could benefit from her death," Amanda put out there.

"How's that exactly?"

"For starters, maybe you could buy New Belle for less money now," Trent said, answering in place of Amanda. "Assuming Ms. Gordon's beneficiary is interested in unloading the company."

"Good idea," Eve said. "Something worth trying. Did it fall to her husband?"

"We can't say," Amanda replied.

Eve waved a hand. "I can find out."

"It's also possible Alicia Gordon changed her mind about the arrangement with you," Amanda said.

Eve flashed a cold smile. "I've done quite well for myself without that night cream, if you take a look around."

"We have," Amanda said stiffly, noticing Eve hadn't addressed the suggestion that Alicia had changed her mind. "And based off quick impression, it's hard to believe your company could afford to buy New Belle." A tad harsh, but Amanda hoped it would goad a reaction.

Eve glared at her. "We are in the process of expanding distribution to several states throughout the country. I invested a lot of the profits, and it's time to diversify—not just in product line but in customer base too."

"Fair enough." Amanda supposed it was possible Eve had

been squirreling away money, not just cycling it right back into the company.

"Fair enough," Eve mimicked. "As I've said, I have no reason to want Alicia dead. Buying New Belle would have been incredible for my company and the growth of both brands."

At face value, Eve seemed to present a convincing defense for herself. "If you were to point us in anyone's direction, assuming of course that Alicia was killed, who would that be?"

Eve's chin trembled just slightly, so slight in fact it could have been easy to miss.

"You know of someone?" Amanda prodded.

Eve sat straighter, but vulnerability crept into her eyes.

Amanda inched forward on her chair. "Are you afraid of someone, Ms. Kelley?"

Eve swallowed roughly. "Should I be worried about my safety?"

"I don't see why." Amanda was hesitant to dismiss Eve's concern, but she needed more information.

Eve rubbed the back of her neck. "Alicia was a powerful businesswoman and often in the media. I am too, and I receive threats. But I think something about us being successful women fosters more enemies."

"What sort of threats?" Trent asked.

"I've received many over the years, and there are a number that refer to me as a bitch and that I don't deserve what I have. Threats that what I have will be taken away."

"Did you receive any recently? Say, since you made an offer to buy New Belle?" Maybe the bidding wasn't as *blind* as it was supposed to be. Things did have a way of leaking out. Could it be that other bidders found out about the arrangement Eve had with Alicia and killed her because of it?

"I usually get at least one a week, but yes."

Goosebumps danced across the back of Amanda's neck,

shoulders, and down her arms. "Send those threats to us, please." She gave her card to Eve.

Eve's face paled, and she nodded. "I'll have Joanne compile them for you now. You can take them with you when you leave."

"And Joanne is...?" Amanda asked.

"My assistant. Be honest with me. Do I have reason to fear for my life?"

"There's nothing to indicate that at this point. None at all." Amanda did her best to be reassuring, but she wasn't a fortune teller. And she'd been wrong before.

ELEVEN

Amanda snapped her seat belt into place, and Trent drove them back to Central. They were armed with a folder of hate mail addressed to Eve Kelley—some were printed emails, and others were snail mail. Eve's assistant had clipped the ones from the last week together, and it was about an eighth of an inch thick. *So much for Eve's claim of receiving a threat a week...*

"Here's what struck me from talking with Eve Kelley," she began. "One, I don't think she's behind Alicia's death, at least right now. But what if one of the people who made an offer to buy New Belle found out the auction was essentially rigged? Could there be motive in that?"

"There could be. Also the threats Eve received may be coincidental, like ones sent to Alicia. Eve did say she received threats on a regular basis. It was nothing new."

"Yeah, and the same goes for Alicia. She had a folder on the server dedicated to them." The admission deflated her. The hate mail could be entirely irrelevant.

"We need to figure out how blind the offers were."

"Has Tony sent the names of the other bidders?"

"Not yet." She hated that Tony hadn't provided the information already. She didn't want to have to poke at him, but he should have done it by now. Her phone rang, and caller ID prepared her for CSI Blair. Amanda answered on speaker. "Detective Steele. With Detective Stenson."

"We have some findings you'll want to know about." Brisk, to the point. Why should Amanda expect anything else?

"Hit us." Amanda's heart was racing. *Did they find something in the sleeping aid?*

"We lifted prints from a wineglass in the cabinet that don't belong to Alicia Gordon."

Amanda deflated. Not exactly the news she was waiting on. "Ms. Zimmerman rented out the cabin. The prints could belong to anyone."

"They could, except the same prints were also lifted from the glass on the table next to Alicia Gordon and an empty wine bottle in the recycling bin."

"So Alicia had company, and whomever that was had a drink with her," Trent summarized. "So much for *no* company."

"Was the wine drugged?" Amanda asked.

"Not from what we've found."

"Strange that they'd presumably wash their glass, though not very well, and put it back in the cupboard," Trent said. "And who was this person? One of the bidders there to sweet talk Alicia into accepting their offer? Or was she having an affair?"

"Nothing to confirm either, just that she had a mystery visitor." Amanda's stomach soured. *Had Alicia been looking to cut Tony out of the will, and he found out and went to talk with her outside of the house?* Again, it was all hypothetical. "What about the sleeping aid? Did you check to see if it was contaminated?"

"I was getting there. And the answer is yes. The liquid sleeping aid found at the cabin contained pentobarbital."

Who had known Alicia took the medicine *and* could get

close enough to tamper with the bottle? "Was there much missing from it?"

"It's down about half."

They'd have to find out how much she normally took each night to know how long she had been getting dosed.

Blair went on. "Rideout might be better able to answer any other questions you have about the drug, but I do know that pentobarbital is primarily metabolized by the liver and kidneys, and the effects are made worse when paired with alcohol. Not to mention the pentobarbital is addictive in and of itself. She could have taken more than the recommended dose on the Sleep Tight label."

There was no way of knowing how long she'd been taking the drugged sleeping aid or who had added it to the bottle. Amanda's head spun. But surely, her former friend wasn't a killer. "Where would a person get pentobarbital?"

"It's sometimes prescribed. Other than that, off the streets or through access to a medical or veterinary clinic."

More options than desired... There could be one way of narrowing things down. "Were you able to get any prints off the Sleep Tight bottle?"

"None other than the victim's."

"Whoever messed with the liquid wore gloves to cover their tracks," Trent said.

"Like any half-intelligent killer would." To CSI Blair, Amanda said, "Thanks for all this."

"Oh, there's more. CSI Donnelly and I found shoeprints outside one of the cabin windows."

Hairs rose on Amanda's arms. "Someone was watching her from outside?"

"They were facing the right direction to look through the window into the living room. Can't know with certainty when the prints were left but with the rain and the mud... probably Tuesday night."

"Can you tell the brand of shoe or...?" Amanda was being optimistic, but she was aware of databases that catalogued sole impressions. She also knew that shoeprints were almost as unique as fingerprints, specific to the owner and history of the footwear. Wear patterns varied—the distribution of weight—and terrain can affect the sole with nicks and the like.

"Not yet, but that's in the works. Though I can tell you they'd be a man's size eleven. A diamond pattern on the sole. Possibly a running shoe. We also found tire tracks in the cabin's driveway that don't coincide with vehicles we know were there."

"Did those shoeprints also lead to whatever vehicle left the tire marks?" she asked.

"No, they led to the road and disappeared."

"So whoever left them had parked on the road and walked in," she suggested.

"Seems so."

That doesn't sound at all suspicious. "Excellent work. Let us know the minute you have more."

"Will do."

"Thank—"

Blair was gone. "Goodbye to you too," Amanda mumbled.

"She really doesn't like you."

"From her viewpoint, for good reason."

"Why? Did you have the affair with her, get her pregnant, and decide to stay with your wife?"

"Ouch." She'd told Trent a while ago about her father's affair and her half-brother—not long after she had found out, in fact. Hearing it put so straightforwardly took emotion out of the equation.

"Maybe I was too blunt?" Trent winced.

"You could have used more tact, but you're right. And I understand why you said it."

"You're taking this on yourself and making excuses for her rude behavior."

"True. And like you said it's not like I'm the one who wronged her."

"Right."

She didn't add anything else to the topic, but as she'd thought before, at some point she'd have to have *that* conversation with CSI Blair. It would be extremely uncomfortable, but maybe a single moment of awkwardness would be better than what was happening? Then again, maybe talking with Blair about the affair, etcetera, would make things between them worse. *Enough about Blair...* "Alicia had a visitor who poured her wine, possibly tried to clean up after themselves."

"And a stalker? Someone waiting for her to die, for the drug to take effect?"

"Not that they'd necessarily know when that would be."

"True enough, and if her mystery visitor was her killer, why leave the tampered sleeping aid for us to find?"

"They might have been hoping we wouldn't look at it? Or that we'd take it to mean she did this to herself? Hard to say." Amanda massaged her forehead. "But we need to stop with all the questions."

"Hard to get answers, then." He smiled at her, and she relented, returning the expression.

"I know, it comes with the job," she said. "And here's another one. Who all knew that Alicia took a sleeping aid and would have motive to add the pentobarbital?"

Trent opened his mouth to talk, snapped it shut.

"You don't have to say it. But expanding our horizons beyond Tony and keeping an open mind, who else might know?" She paused there, realizing how rhetorical it was at this moment. "At least we have one answer. Alicia Gordon was murdered."

"How do you figure that?"

"If she laced her own Sleep Tight with pentobarbital, why not down the entire bottle? Ensure death."

"Good point."

Not that it sat well with her. Her former friend just became the prime suspect.

TWELVE

Amanda and Trent grabbed a quick bite to eat and gulped back a coffee before going to Tony's house. Both were churning in her stomach like laundry in the wash. The detour had been more of a delay tactic than anything. But there'd be no more putting this off.

Trent turned into the paved driveway.

Her phone rang. Malone. She answered on speaker.

"Any updates on the case?" he asked.

She filled him in on the tampered bottle of Sleep Tight.

"Her sleeping aid was drugged, but have you confirmed the poisoning with Rideout?"

"He won't have toxicology results until early next week." She'd already told him that, and it wasn't like him to forget.

"Huh. Still, until we have proven she ingested it, I'm not sure where that leaves the investigation."

"Rideout was fairly certain she'd been poisoned after looking closely at her liver." She'd told Malone that before too. "The tox results were for confirmation."

"Right, confirmation."

"And unless someone was trying to kill Alicia, the sleeping

aid wouldn't have been tampered with." Amanda could feel her redhead temper firing and gearing up to full throttle. Why was Malone being slow about this?

"It's possible she planned to take her life."

"Possible, but not likely. If that was the case, why didn't she just swallow a bunch at once?"

"Can you prove that she didn't?"

Why is he being so difficult? "Sarge, we need to move forward with this investigation. We need access to her phone records, computer, and financials."

"Can't do it, Steele. Not quite yet."

With the use of her surname, the chances of successfully appealing to him were made slim, but she wasn't going to let that stop her from trying. "Why not?"

"I believe I've been clear. After the toxicology results return *and* if they show pentobarbital poisoning, I will make sure you get subpoenas approved for all you require."

"But—"

"No, I'm done listening. Speak to the husband again. Maybe he'll let you poke around her phone and computer. But we can't get a warrant for those things just yet. And you might not want to hear this, but you told me the woman's sleeping aid was poisoned. Someone close to her could be responsible. You need to take a good, hard look at the husband. Friend or not."

She was speechless, and her mouth dry. Trent was looking at her profile. "We're at his house now. I'll keep you posted." She ended the call and held her phone so tightly the edges of it bit into the sides of her hand. She could try going straight to a judge, but if it got back to Malone—and it probably would— there'd be hell to pay.

"You told him about Tony," Trent said.

"He already knew, but yes, I tried to."

Trent slowly nodded. "He's acting strange. Not allowing us

to apply for warrants until we have the toxicology results? Seems over the top, considering what we have."

"Yep."

"Wow. All right, well, we press on. We talk to Tony Bishop and go from there."

She had her phone to her ear.

"What are you doing?"

"A workaround." She got CSI Blair on the line and asked for a list of names and numbers recently in contact with Alicia —incoming and outgoing. Trent stared at her open-mouthed the entire time. A few seconds later, she hung up. "CSI Blair is heading out for the weekend soon, but she'll delegate this to someone in the lab. Latest we'll receive the list is tomorrow." While the forensics building wasn't open to walk-ins on the weekend, people would be there working.

"Do you think you should have done that?"

"Probably not, but it's done now. As they say, better to beg for forgiveness..."

"Not when you've already had permission denied."

It took two rings of the doorbell for someone to answer. Tony Bishop had dark circles under his bloodshot eyes. Without a word, he gestured for them to come in and led them to the sitting area.

"Tell me you have some answers."

"More questions, I'm afraid," Amanda said dropping onto the dark-gray couch. Trent sat beside her. She went on. "You told us that Alicia had trouble sleeping and took Sleep Tight."

"That's right."

"Does she have any bottles here at the house?"

"Yeah, she usually has a couple on hand."

"Could we get what you have?"

Tony locked his gaze with hers. "Why, Mandy?"

"I'll tell you in a minute. Could Trent go with you and get them?"

Tony glanced at Trent. "No, but you can. I don't want a stranger rummaging in her things."

"Okay." She gave Trent a glance as she stood, and he handed her a plastic evidence bag. She didn't really want to be alone with Tony, possibly in tight quarters.

She followed Tony upstairs thinking the entire time, *Let's get this over with.*

He took her into the primary bedroom, which was massive. The king-size bed and other pieces of furniture were dwarfed in the space. To the far right was a living room flooded with light from large windows. The bathroom was on scale with the rest of the house—lots of open floor space. A shower with seven nozzles. A double vanity that seemed to stretch on forever.

"Beautiful home," she said. The silence between them was awkward and carried a vibration.

He stopped walking and faced her. He was only about six inches from her. His eyes briefly dipped to her mouth, back up to meet her gaze. His breathing was a little haggard. "Our timing has never been right, has it?" He scanned her face, and she stepped back.

She held up the plastic bag between them, annoyed. "No. Including now. Your wife just died."

His shoulders slumped. "I know... I just want to get my mind off of it, how much it freaking hurts."

She could understand how sex could make a person feel alive after a great loss, but it seemed so fast for Tony to even be thinking about it. But everyone was different. "Let's just get the sleeping aid and get back to Detective Stenson."

He stayed put for a few seconds longer, before going to the vanity and opening a drawer. "Here." He gave her a bottle labeled *Sleep Tight.*

"This is the only one in the house?" She put the bottle into the bag.

"One other place I can check." He disappeared into a walk-in closet and came back with another bottle. "Her overstock," he said as he extended that bottle to her. "As I said, she usually has a couple."

She went to take it, but he didn't let go—at first. "Thanks."

"What's going on, Mandy? What happened to Alicia?" He rubbed the back of his neck. His eyes, portals to his grief, glistened with unshed tears.

"Let's go back downstairs, and we'll talk more. Okay?" She could have hit herself for adding *okay*, like she was giving him a choice. She'd do well to remember she was the detective here, and he could have potentially killed his wife. She turned away.

But not fast enough.

He put his hand on her wrist, his palm searing where it met her flesh, and gently prodded her to face him again.

She stiffened. "Don't touch me."

He let go of her. "Just tell me what's going on. I'm going crazy."

"We'll discuss it downstairs." This time, she said it with more authority, and he drew back, angled his head.

"You don't suspect that I had something to do with whatever happened to Alicia, do you?" His voice fractured on the words. Her heart squeezed.

She licked her lips and took a deep breath. "I'm not doing this here."

They stood there for a few seconds in silence, staring at each other. She was hauled to the past, whether she wanted to take the trip or not. There was a time she liked his hands on her, his lips on hers, but that was a very long time ago. And they were never meant to be, their timing off—and now was certainly no different. If she peered too deeply into his eyes, she could see the young man that she'd once cared for. But she had to scrape past the layers of pain and sorrow. "You look exhausted." The words slipped out, their source empathy. Inside, she was waging a war. He was a suspect! But he was also someone she'd been close to.

"I'm not sleeping."

"That's understandable. Oh, you haven't taken any of this, have you?"

"No, but maybe I should have."

"Trust me, best that you hadn't."

"What aren't you telling me, Mandy?"

Again with the Mandy... "Just come downstairs with me." She led the way, and they returned to the sitting area, joining Trent.

Both of them sat where they'd been before. She avoided all eye contact with Trent.

"Time's up. Tell me what's going on, Detective." Just from upstairs to here, he'd transitioned, addressing her professionally. But she knew the other—the personal—wasn't too far behind it.

"Tell me what you know about pentobarbital," she said.

"Pentobarbital? Isn't it what vets use to euthanize animals?"

"One of its uses," she said. "How do you know that?"

"I'm quite sure I heard Beth mention it before."

"Beth? Your daughter?"

"Uh-huh. Never mind. It doesn't matter."

Amanda's heart was picking up speed, and her hands were becoming clammy. What was he holding back? Was Beth a vet or training to become one? Did she have reason to kill Alicia?

"Where are you going with this, Amanda? It has something to do with that, doesn't it?" Tony pointed at the bag with the Sleep Tight bottles.

"Detective, please. Let's keep things a little more formal, considering the circumstances. And, yes, it does."

"And that's what ended up killing her?" Tony swallowed roughly, and his eyes filled with tears.

She stiffened. "We don't know for sure yet." *Though it seems pretty damn conclusive to me!*

He looked up at the ceiling and flailed his hands. "You're talking in riddles. I'd like some clear answers."

"Wouldn't we all?" she fired back and snapped her mouth shut under his gaze. "Please, just trust me. We're doing everything we can." The appeal, the softened tone, even the initial sharp reaction all came because of her past connection with the man across from her. She'd never have spoken to a stranger within an investigation that way. She considered her next words carefully, measuring them in her mind first and trying them on. "Pentobarbital was present in the bottle of Alicia's Sleep Tight found in the cabin."

"Dear God." Tony shook, and he rubbed his arms. "You don't think I poisoned it, do you?"

"Help us rule you out," she said as gently as possible.

"You can't truly believe that I did that... Killed her. You know me."

"Mr. Bishop," Trent started, passing a glance at Amanda, "Detective Steele and I follow where the evidence takes us. We don't make things up or twist things. If you had nothing to do with Alicia's death, there's nothing you need to worry about."

Amanda appreciated how Trent balanced a firm stand with a delicate touch, and his timing was perfect. "He's right," she added.

"We were friends, Amanda. Doesn't that mean anything to you? Don't you know me?"

Anger burned in her chest. She fought the urge to lash out at him. He and Claudia had faded out of her life—not that she'd stopped them, but she had been the one hurting. She was the one who had lost a husband and a daughter in a single blow. Tony Bishop should have made more effort to be there for her. They had a history. "I did know you," she pushed out through clenched teeth, "but that was a long time ago. A lot has changed."

Tony's face pinched, and he frowned. "Suppose it has." He kept looking at her, though, like he wanted to say more, possibly explain his past actions, but now wasn't the time. It was time, however, to get down to business.

"You were to get us a list of bidders," she said stiffly. "Do you have those names for us?"

"I do."

"We'll need them from you. It could be very important to the investigation. We also spoke with Eve Kelley."

Tony rolled his eyes. "What's she saying now?"

"The bidding was to be silent, the identities were to be kept anonymous, but we need to determine if they stayed that way."

"You're thinking one of them might have taken Alicia out. But why?"

"We're still sorting out all the pieces. Did you know the bidding was to be silent?"

Tony shook his head. "I think you might do well to look closer at Eve Kelley."

"You didn't seem to think that when we spoke before."

"She was bitter about what Alicia had done to her."

Amanda could admit that Eve still seemed to carry a lot of angry energy about the subject. But she couldn't ignore the fact that Eve had also received threats, some Amanda felt could be in relation to her offer on New Belle. She didn't want to reveal her entire hand to Tony, though. "If we could just get the names of the companies who submitted offers."

"I'll get them to you."

"Before we leave." She had to lay down the deadline or Trent would.

"Fine. Is that all, then?"

"No. We need to know everyone who could have had access to your wife's sleeping aid," Amanda said.

"Everyone in this house, but it's not like the kids are going to kill their own mother."

It happened, but Amanda wasn't going there until there was cause. "Anyone else? Do you have other people in the house?"

"No. Well, not anyone who would get into the primary suite and her bottle of Sleep Tight."

"What about housecleaners?" Trent asked.

"Sure, I guess."

"We'll need their names."

"Fine."

Amanda wasn't relishing the direction the conversation now had to take. Since poisoning was involved, they had to expand their view to include people in Alicia's personal orbit who might have motive. They'd touched a bit on it on a previous visit, but it was time to circle back. "How were Alicia's relationships with her exes?"

"Fine. Leo's dad comes around. He shares custody with Alicia, and obviously he helped raise Brad too."

"And the relationship between him and Alicia?"

"Amicable."

"And Brad's father?" Trent interjected.

"Not a part of Alicia's life. He just keeps in contact with Brad."

They'd burned through Alicia's side, leaving Tony's ex. "How did Claudia handle your divorce and remarriage?"

"Claudia? Wow, I didn't expect her name to come up again."

"Just answer, please." Claudia could have gained access to Alicia's sleeping aid, motivated because she wanted Tony back. It may be a stretch, but it was a possibility.

Tony's eyes darkened. "She's miserable. The guy she left me for broke it off with her."

Maybe not a big stretch... "It must have been hard for Claudia to see how happy you were with Alicia."

"Perhaps, but not enough for her to kill Alicia if that's what you're driving at."

Trent glanced at Amanda and proceeded to ask Tony, "Has Claudia reached out to you since Alicia's death?"

"Sure. She offered her condolences, even brought over a casserole. I tried to eat it, but ended up throwing it out." He winced. "Like me, cooking isn't her strong suit."

"When did she come by?" Amanda asked.

"Yesterday."

After it had hit the news... If Claudia had been involved with Alicia's death, then she was at least smart enough to wait on the media before coming forward with her sympathies. Was she trying to get Tony back now that Alicia was out of the way, or had Claudia's intentions been pure? And the tougher question, had Claudia poisoned Alicia? To do that, she'd need access to the bottle of Sleep Tight. "Has Claudia ever been here besides yesterday?"

"Ah, yeah."

She raised her eyebrows. "You say that like there's something we should already know?"

"Alicia hired Claudia to come up with designs for packaging and rebranding."

It took a few moments for Amanda to remember what Claudia did for work. "She's still an artist?"

"She is."

Amanda was letting what Tony told her sink in. His new wife had employed his old one. That must have made for an awkward arrangement. "So she came over to the house sometimes?"

"Yes."

"When before yesterday?"

"Uh..." Tony's forehead compressed like trying to recall was a difficult task—either that or he was formulating a response. "Think she was here Sunday...? Yeah, that's it. She had an epiphany and wanted to share a rough mock-up with Alicia, said it couldn't wait for work hours."

Amanda's insides were fluttering—and not in a good way that spoke of excitement but rather dread. "So this past weekend?"

"Yes."

"Could she have gotten to Alicia's sleeping aid?" Amanda asked.

Tony leveled his gaze at her. "You don't seriously think she had anything to do with Alicia's..."

Amanda hoped she didn't. "Just answer the question please."

"Seriously, you'd be fishing in the wrong pond. Why would Claudia kill Alicia?"

"You just told us she wasn't happy, she could have wanted you back."

"But... Wow. That would be extreme."

"I've seen extreme," she said drily. And her mind went back to how Tony had gotten weird at the mention of his daughter, shutting that branch of the conversation down quickly. "How is Bethany, by the way?"

"Beth? She's fine."

"It must have been something for her to deal with. The divorce," she added to clarify.

"Not really. Claudia and I had been separated two years by the time it finalized. Besides, Beth is an adult and married. My split from Claudia was of little consequence to her."

Amanda wasn't so sure about that. "We've asked before, and I am going to again. Could we have Alicia's computer, just in case it lends something to the investigation?"

Tony shook his head. "I can't let you. Not unless I'm forced to by a warrant. It contains proprietary information."

"It could aid the investigation," Trent stressed. "Help us find out who did this to your wife. Don't you want that?"

"Of course, I do, but I still won't."

Trent flipped his notepad closed and clicked his pen. "Alicia was planning to change her will. Do you know anything about that?"

Amanda's mind was such a mess, she cursed herself for not tugging on that particular string.

Tony shook his head. "I don't know."

"So you didn't kill her because she was removing you as a beneficiary?" Trent's eyes were steel, and his gaze was fixed on Tony.

"Absolutely not." Tony's cheeks burned a bright red.

Amanda let a few beats of silence pass, studying Tony, but his body language was closed off. "All right, if we could get those bidders' names, we'll be out of your way."

A few minutes later, she and Trent were back in the car.

He twisted his hand around the steering wheel. Eventually, he looked over at her. "He could have poisoned her. We should look at his vehicle's tires and his shoes, at least find out his foot size."

She could still conjure the feel of Tony's hand on her wrist.

"Amanda?" Trent prompted.

"We will if it comes to that, but do me a favor. Look up Bethany Bishop in the system."

Trent sighed and clicked on the keyboard for the onboard computer. "Bethany Wagner now. Twenty-three, married to Isaac Wagner, thirty-one."

"And what do they do for work?" It was hard to ask, her gut telling her she wasn't going to like the answer.

"One second... Oh."

That *oh* might as well have been a stone tossed to the bottom of her stomach. "What?"

"Looks like they own Paws and Claws. It's a veterinary clinic." He looked over at her. "And Tony knew pentobarbital was used for euthanizing animals."

"So do I. Doesn't necessarily mean anything."

"Yeah, but you take that and how he clammed up after mentioning Bethany. It all seems a little strange."

"I see that."

Trent shifted his body to face her. "I know you're not going to want to hear this."

"Then don't say it." She looked into his eyes. "You don't have to say it."

THIRTEEN

Amanda had barely convinced Trent to leave without interrogating Tony further. He drove them past Paws & Claws, but the clinic had already closed for the weekend. They even swung by the couple's house, but it was dark. Amanda fell back on making a call. When a person needed to be questioned in a murder investigation, she preferred first contact be made in person. *Murder investigation... Bethany... little Bethany.* She used to babysit Lindsey sometimes. Bethany had only been sixteen on her last visit to the house.

The number rang to voicemail. Amanda listened to Bethany's greeting but didn't leave a message. Amanda put her phone in a pocket. "Bethany Wagner is off our list for today. Her voicemail greeting says she's out of town for the weekend and back on Monday."

"Really?" Trent shook his head. "People will never learn, will they? Telling anyone who calls your number that you're not home, you might as well be screaming, 'Feel free to blitz the joint.' They deserve what they get, just like people who use one-two-three-four for their password."

"That's a little harsh." Not that she disagreed with what he'd said.

"Just as bad as when people splash their comings and goings on social media. Actually, that's worse."

"I see you feel strongly on the matter." Amanda laughed.

"You think? All right, so our next stop is Central?"

"Sounds good. We'll get this sent up to the lab." She lifted the bag with the sleeping aid bottles.

Trent drove them to the station, parked, and looked over at her. "Penny for your thoughts."

She was thinking that she could do with some relaxation tonight. Anything to squeeze out the suspicions that Tony had killed his wife—that and how uncomfortable she'd felt upstairs with him. She might even ask her best friend, Becky Tulson, an officer with the Dumfries PD, over to the house to watch movies and eat comfort food. "We'll meet tomorrow morning. You good with that?" She realized she'd brushed off his question, but she wasn't in the mood to talk.

"I am. Do you think Malone will clear the overtime? It is Saturday."

"Just leave it to me."

Trent took a deep breath, seeming to consider his next words. "You sure he won't want definitive proof that Alicia Gordon ingested the tampered sleep aid?"

"Listen, I don't know what's up with Malone lately. Just leave him to me, as I said."

"All right, if you're sure. What are you thinking for tomorrow?"

"Where to start? Tony's ex, the other bidders for New Belle, take another look at the threats sent to Alicia and read the ones sent to Eve. See if we can find any that sound similar."

"Right. And we should also have that list of numbers from Alicia's phone."

"Yep. We'll look at them too."

"All sounds good to me. What time?"

"Nine? I'll need to line up someone to watch Zoe." That wouldn't be a hard feat. Amanda had numerous nieces and nephews, and Ava, one of her nieces, really clicked with Zoe. Then again, Ava was getting to that age when her social life could take priority at any minute, and babysitting might not hold as much appeal.

"Works for me."

The two of them went in their separate directions. Amanda called Becky on the drive home, and her friend said she'd come over at six thirty. Amanda found Libby and Zoe on the couch in front of the TV.

"Mandy!" Zoe dropped a slice of apple onto her plate and ran over.

That greeting would never get old, but Amanda wasn't naive enough to believe it would last forever. Especially once Zoe became a teenager and Amanda, the enemy. Of course it didn't *have* to go that way, despite what Amanda remembered looking back at her own youth.

"Hey, sweetie." Amanda rustled the girl's hair and smiled at Libby who was getting off the couch, at a much slower rate of speed than Zoe had.

"This is a nice surprise. Home early *and* it's a Friday night," Libby said. "Penny will be happy too. We've got plans to go out for dinner."

Penny Anderson was Libby's life partner. "Enjoy! And thank you," Amanda called out as Libby stepped outside.

"My pleasure." Libby closed the door behind her.

Amanda turned to Zoe. "Good news for us... Becky's coming over, and we're going to eat cheeseburgers and french fries and watch movies. How does that sound?"

Zoe squealed and clapped her hands. "Awesome!"

And it was. Becky arrived right at six thirty, and they made the messiest cheeseburgers in the history of mankind. Zoe had so much ketchup dripping down her chin, she resembled a victim of some heinous crime. The thought had Amanda flashing back to the cabin and finding Alicia there, though it had been a rather clean scene.

The hazard of the job was that the ugliness of it could sneak in when it was least expected and most unwelcome. Now wasn't the time. She'd be back on the job tomorrow; tonight was about fun, relaxation, and lightness.

After they ate, Zoe insisted on getting decked out in her Elsa costume and then convinced Amanda and Becky to play *Frozen*. It wasn't hard for Amanda to participate—she'd watched the film with Zoe so many times—but Becky was less familiar. Instead of it upsetting Zoe, it had the girl laughing to tears, which infected Amanda and Becky and had them doubling over.

The party was then moved to the living room where they watched a warm-hearted romantic comedy, not Becky's go-to movie genre, but it was PG for the younger audience present.

By the time it was over, Zoe was asleep on the couch, her head on Amanda's lap, her feet on Becky's.

Amanda held up her index finger to Becky and proceeded to slowly maneuver the girl and nudge her awake. "Come on, time for an adventure."

"Oh, I'm awake." Zoe pouted and rubbed her eyes.

Amanda smiled and kissed her forehead. "You don't look very awake."

"I am. Will you read to me? Then I'll sleep."

It had become a habit for Amanda to read from *Alice in Wonderland* before Zoe went to bed. Amanda looked at Becky.

"Go ahead. I'm not going anywhere." Becky tucked her legs under her, pulled out her phone, and was instantly immersed.

Zoe led the way down the hall to her room with Amanda trailing close behind. She helped the girl out of the Elsa gown and into pajamas. She tucked her into bed with her favorite stuffed toy, a dog addressed formally as Sir Lucky, and read to her.

These small pockets of time were what Amanda had come to recognize as a reward at the end of the day. She had to be tough and strong to the world—her job demanded that—but here in her home with Zoe, Amanda could let her guard down, be herself. Breathe.

While she read the beloved tale, thoughts of Tony Bishop slithered in. First, profound empathy for what he was going through. This was followed by fear that he might have been behind his wife's death. Next, all that morphed into being alone with him and how it had stirred up the past, again emphasizing how their timing had never been right and never would be.

"Man...dy?" Zoe yawned. "I'm sleepy now."

"All right, sweetheart." Amanda closed the book and tapped a kiss on the girl's forehead. "Sleep tight. Don't let the bed bugs bite."

Her eyes sprang open. "The what?"

Amanda smiled. "Nothing. Besides, nothing can get to you. Not with Lucky by your side."

The stuffed dog was tightly wedged under the girl's arm.

Amanda got up and turned on a projector that cast stars onto the ceiling, shut off the overhead light, and slipped from the room. She left the door open a crack.

She grabbed a glass of water before returning to the couch with Becky, who'd refilled her wineglass while Amanda was gone. Her friend's cheeks were flushed in the glow coming from the TV screen. Becky was quick about putting her phone away and exchanging it for her wine. "While you were gone I was just thinking, why don't you ever go out anymore? Why don't *we*? You could have Ava sit Zoe, and we could—"

"Shit."

"Something I said?"

"Something I forgot." She hadn't called her niece to line up babysitting for tomorrow. "Becky, could I ask you for a favor?"

"On one condition."

"You haven't heard what the favor is."

"Doesn't really matter. One condition."

"Which is...?" Amanda would probably be sorry she'd asked. When Becky dipped into the wine, it was often hard to predict what she might say.

"You will get a sitter for Zoe and go out with me. We—well, *you*—will pick up some hot guy and hook up."

Becky was already seeing someone. Brandon Fisher, a special agent with the FBI's Behavioral Analysis Unit. He was growing on Amanda, but she was keeping a close eye on him. Chalk it up to being protective of her friend.

"Nope. I'm not interested in hooking up."

"Think of it as adult fun."

What Becky didn't realize was that Amanda had had enough *fun* to last a lifetime. When she was broken over the loss of her family, one-night stands became a weekly occurrence. In fact, it was the only way she cared to connect with a man— sexual gratification. No exchange of names, addresses, occupations. Best of all, no emotional attachment. She'd clung to it as the perfect elixir for her shattered heart for several years. That was until she discovered it was just a cruel lie she told herself. The toll it actually demanded from her soul wasn't worth it. "Yeah, not really my thing."

"Sex isn't your thing?"

"Who has the time?"

"Seriously? Come on."

"Sleeping around is one surefire way to catch an STD."

"Oh my word. Being a cop's making you dark."

There was no denying that, but it was also all that Amanda knew. She was fine blaming the job. "Possibly."

Becky took a sip of her wine. "Even if you don't *hook up*, what about dating again? You had a nice little thing going with Logan for a while."

Another secret Becky wasn't privy to was that Logan had been a one-night stand that broke all the rules and bloomed into a relationship. He was also the last one-night stand Amanda had —and the last she ever intended to have. "All good things come to an end."

"Wow. Again, very dark."

"Realistic." Logan couldn't handle the risks inherent with Amanda's job. Besides, Zoe was her priority. She did think about him sometimes, though. They did have *a nice little thing* —for the time it had lasted. And she didn't regret it. The relationship gave her a taste of something real and tangible again.

"You have to get lonely sometimes."

Amanda felt her cheeks heat at the thought of Tony, at the thought of Trent even. *Gah!* "When the hell would I have time to date anyone? Please, tell me."

"You make time for what's important."

"We're different people," Amanda said.

"How do you figure?" Becky turned her back to the arm of the couch, fully facing Amanda.

How to put it exactly... "I don't need a guy in my life."

"Hey now, that's a low blow." The words came off as an insult to Becky, something Amanda hadn't intended, but thankfully her friend was grinning. "You're right. I rather like being involved. Friends with benefits." She laughed loudly, and Amanda shushed her. Becky went on. "You're a great mom, and what you've done for Zoe is incredible. Just don't lose yourself."

The sincerity in Becky's tone had Amanda's chest tightening. Until this moment, Amanda hadn't realized how much she'd been functioning in mission mode. Like a train on rails—one set of tracks for work, another when she got home.

"You know I'm right..." Becky lowered her head to meet Amanda's gaze, which had drifted to the couch cushions.

"Maybe."

"All right, so you'll start dating? You said you didn't want to hook up..."

"I'll go out with you for a girls' night, but no promises on the guy front."

Becky bit her bottom lip and eventually nodded. "I'll take it."

"And in exchange you'll watch Zoe tomorrow so I can work."

"Do you ever take a full weekend off?"

"I had last weekend off."

"Huh. And you never even called me. We could have gone out and had some fun."

"Becky," Amanda said, trying to steer her friend back. She could tell from Becky's grin that her mind was still on Amanda hooking up with a guy.

"Fine." Becky held up her hands in surrender. "I'll drop it for now."

"Good." Silence lasted for two seconds, then Amanda blurted out, "I've been reconnected with Tony Bishop."

"What? You—"

Amanda put a finger to her lips. "Just keep it down some."

"Sorry." She was speaking in a near whisper now. "Tony? You reconnected?"

"Maybe that's too strong a word."

"You guys were always just like... well, ships passing in the night."

Amanda bobbed her head side to side.

"Honestly, I thought you and Tony might have ended up together. That is, before Kevin turned out to be the one."

"So did I." Amanda's gaze flitted to Becky's wine. For the first time in seven years, she had a craving. She hadn't even sipped a single alcoholic beverage since the drunk driver had taken out Kevin and Lindsey.

"Tell me all about it. Your *reconnection*."

"Again, not ideal. Never was. Tony and I always had bad timing. Now, though, he's a murder suspect."

"He's what?" Becky slapped a hand over her mouth, self-correcting her volume. She dropped her hand. "You're going to need to tell me more now for sure."

Amanda proceeded to do just that, leaving out the moment when she'd been alone with Tony in the bedroom.

Becky relaxed against the back of the couch. "You really think the Tony you knew killed his wife?"

"The Tony I knew is from years ago. This one, I don't know."

"Okay, fair enough. But still..."

"I don't know what to think, and it doesn't matter anyway. I'll follow the evidence."

"This is crazy."

"Yep. And I don't really want to talk about the case or Tony anymore."

Becky shifted around so she was facing the TV and said, "Well, Zoe's asleep, so how about a violent movie?"

"And I'm the one who's gone dark?"

They quickly settled on a movie. Amanda was certain she'd missed out on the full impact of the opening scene. While blood and guts were flying everywhere, she was lost in her thoughts, her mind a freaking mess. Her time with Logan had made her feel alive as a woman. She'd felt desirable, wanted, needed. Far more than she'd ever experienced with one-night stands. It wouldn't be horrible to experience those feelings again. But with Zoe, she really didn't have time to devote to a relationship. Zoe came with luggage at just six years old. She'd seen her father shot and lost both him and her mother in one night. Amanda's priority as her adoptive mother had to be the child's welfare—mentally, emotionally, spiritually, physically, in all ways. Between that and the job, there wasn't much room for a personal life.

FOURTEEN

Saturday mornings should be full of hope and fun plans. Amanda's wasn't so bright. She was in the car with Trent on the way to see Claudia. The last time she'd seen her, Claudia had been married to Tony, and the real kicker was, as far as Amanda had known, the two of them were happy. But who really knew what was going on inside another person's marriage—or mind, for that matter?

"Tell me about her." Trent looked over at Amanda from the driver's seat.

"Claudia? Well, it's been a long time since I've seen her, but she and Tony were seeing each other some in high school. They were always on and off, but Claudia became pregnant at the end of grade twelve. She and Tony got married when they graduated from college. Beth was just a little girl then."

"I see."

"Must not have been all bad. They were married for a while."

"Until the point Claudia strayed and asked for the divorce. I'm all caught up now."

"Quick study." She smirked at him, but her expression

faded quickly. "Going to see this woman has me stressing some." She hadn't intended the confession and wished like hell she could reel it back in. "Never mind what I just said. We're there because of a murder investigation. That's all."

"That's not *all*."

She was about to snap, ready to defend herself, insist that she could remain objective, but he was smiling.

"Murder is a big deal," he said.

"Oh." She'd thought he was going to stress the personal tie between her and Claudia. "Yes, murder certainly is."

"Though I could handle this alone if you'd be more comfortable." He'd gone serious now.

"I appreciate the offer, but I'll be fine."

"All right." He returned his attention to the road, leaving her with her rambling thoughts.

The conversation she'd had with Becky played on repeat. Amanda could rationalize her feelings toward Trent. He was always within arm's reach. He was a good-looking guy, loyal, and funny. He always had her back. He had a dash of a temper, but it only flared when warranted, often in defense of an underdog. Admirable. Otherwise, he was easygoing while not being a pushover. Maybe she was just imagining that he felt things for her too, because she was lonely. Nothing more.

A few minutes later, she and Trent were on the front stoop of Claudia's two-story house. It was where she'd lived with Tony, and Amanda had to wonder why she hadn't moved. Was she clinging to the past?

Amanda raised her hand to knock, and the door opened. Claudia, all five foot four and ninety pounds of her, was standing there.

"Amanda?" She swept her eyes from her to Trent, back to Amanda.

"Claudia, this is my partner, Detective Stenson. We're here in an official capacity."

"Should have known you weren't here for a personal visit." Claudia spoke low and turned as she did, so Amanda wasn't sure she'd heard her right—more like wished she hadn't heard her. The jab poked like a bee's stinger. Painful.

Trent met Amanda's gaze, his eyes seeming to ask if Amanda was good to proceed. She nodded and butted her head for him to follow Claudia, who had retreated into the home already. Amanda closed the front door.

"You do remember where the living room is?" Claudia called over her shoulder, directed at Amanda.

Another jab, and it had Amanda's temper firing. The friendship had fallen apart because both sides failed to work at the relationship. The separation wasn't entirely Amanda's fault. After all, she was the one who had lost so much at that time. If anything, Claudia and Tony should have made more of an effort. But the sharp remarks reminded Amanda what Claudia could be like. She was a pro at holding grudges. Had she held one against Tony for marrying Alicia so quickly? But how did that reconcile with Claudia working for the woman?

"Amanda, you did hear me?"

"Yes, Claudia," Amanda mumbled. She entered the living room, and it was just how she'd remembered it, almost as if time stood still here. Amanda sat down on a puffy chair and crossed her legs. Trent sat on the couch, and Claudia joined him there.

"You don't look much different." Claudia slowly drew her eyes over Amanda as if she were a vulture sizing up a meal, searching for any weakness in its prey.

"You too." She thought things might be weird between them, but this was even more uncomfortable than Amanda had imagined. "You've heard about Alicia Gordon's death?"

"Of course, but I'm not sure why you're here wanting to talk to me about her."

"What was your relationship like with her?" It was impossible to keep all the snip out of her tone. Blame it on the way

Claudia was treating her. But pain often caused its victims to push others away.

Claudia narrowed her eyes and worried her bottom lip. "Alicia was a strong woman. She knew what she wanted and how to get it."

Amanda sensed one of these acquisitions was Tony as if he were an object to acquire and possess.

"You didn't exactly answer Detective Steele's question," Trent stepped in.

"We got along well."

Amanda found that claim a little hard to swallow. Even if Claudia had accepted that Tony moved on with his life and was making a home with Alicia, it would be hard to discard the history. "And the nature of your relationship with her?" Amanda knew what Tony had told them already, but she wanted to hear it straight from Claudia.

"I worked for Alicia." She squinted, studying Amanda. "I'd be surprised if Tony didn't tell you that."

"He did," Amanda admitted, taking some pleasure in doing so.

Claudia glared at her. "Then why ask about our relationship if you know everything?"

"We're conducting an investigation," Amanda said firmly. "We ask questions; you answer them."

"Not if I get a lawyer," Claudia snapped. "That would shut things down real quick."

"If you feel you have something to hide, then by all means, do that." Adrenaline was pumping through Amanda's body and had her pulsating.

"Just ask what you need to and get out."

"Ms. Bishop," Trent cut in, "were you ever in your husband's home, the one he shared with Alicia and her children?"

"Yes," Claudia hissed.

"Did you ever go into the primary bedroom or en suite bathroom?" Trent asked.

"Of course not."

There was an edge to her voice, which Amanda pounced on. "You're lying to us."

"No, I'm not, and frankly, I'm insulted you'd say that."

Amanda remained silent; Trent followed her lead. Claudia eventually broke the silence.

"Fine. Yes, I was in their room."

"Why were you in there?" Amanda asked.

"You have a lot of questions, and I don't like it."

"We're just trying to fill in some blanks. Nothing more."

"Uh-huh. More like trying to see if I had something to do with Alicia's death. Am I right?" Claudia raised her eyebrows.

"We're just investigating," Trent said firmly. "Please. Answer Detective Steele's question. Why were you in their bedroom?"

Claudia sighed. "I was just curious. Nothing more. No real purpose."

Amanda supposed she could understand that if Claudia was pining away for Tony. But that did nothing in terms of helping clear her of suspicion. "Are you happy in life, Claudia?"

"What does that have to do with anything? And I find it inappropriate that you're here. You lost the right to ask me any questions, let alone these personal ones. We're no longer friends, and I don't see what your line of questioning has to do with what happened to Alicia."

"As I said when we arrived, we're here in an official capacity," Amanda said. "And we're tasked with figuring out what caused Alicia's death."

"Which you believe is murder."

"Technically we never said she was killed," Amanda countered.

Claudia crossed her arms, sniffed out in derision. "No other reason for you to be at my door."

Amanda had about enough of Claudia's attitude. Scratch all empathy. She'd been trying to do a diplomatic dance, but she was done dancing. "It was your idea to end your marriage to Tony because you fell in love with another man. But that man left you."

Claudia's cheeks glowed a bright red. "None of your business."

Amanda shrugged. "Tony told us. That must have hurt. You guys go back to the last year of high school. Throwing away that long of a relationship, and for what?"

"What does any of this matter?"

"You were quite quick to offer your sympathy to the widower," Amanda pointed out. "You were there the day after Alicia's death hit the news, with a casserole."

Claudia pursed her lips. "I worked with Alicia, and I liked the woman. Even though I'm quite sure the only reason she hired me was to stick her relationship with Tony in my face."

"You make her sound vindictive," Trent said.

"She could be. Besides, as you noted, Amanda, I was with Tony for a long time and we share a child. The history, the bond, never goes away." With the last admission, Claudia's tone softened.

Amanda took a few beats before asking, "Do you still love Tony?"

"Yes, but I know it's never going to be like it was between us again."

"Did you find that you were jealous of Alicia?" Trent edged in.

"Yes, but not enough to kill her, if that's what you're implying."

"But you wanted to get back with him. Still do?" Amanda's empathy traveled through her voice.

"I did. *I do.*" Claudia met her eyes, and for a second, Amanda saw her old friend behind them. "I made a huge mistake letting him go, but how could I have known that at the time? I mean, he was all I ever knew. Even when we were younger and took *breaks* from each other, I never had anything remotely serious with another guy."

Amanda nodded. "You two made a good couple."

"We were. Until we weren't. He seemed to have lost interest in me, and vice versa. Life became about taking care of Bethany and making a living to provide for her. Tony was working his way up in the accounting firm, and I was pouring myself into my art, selling some pieces at galleries."

"I remember," Amanda said. "You have a true talent."

Claudia didn't respond immediately, possibly unsure how to handle the compliment. Eventually she said, "Thank you."

"You're welcome."

"None of any of it matters anymore, though. We're different people now. There's no turning back. I'm quite sure of that."

Amanda couldn't offer assurance. She believed it was entirely possible that too much time could pass and make reconciliation impossible.

"He got married to her so fast. But you know what he can be like." Claudia put her attention on Amanda, and she wished she could disappear. Claudia went on. "He just got caught in her web."

"Alicia's web?" Trent asked.

"Her charm, you could say."

Amanda was uncomfortable being wedged between her two former friends. It was made all the more awkward because both of them had motive. It was time to revisit Claudia's trespassing into Tony and Alicia's bedroom. "Have you heard of the drug pentobarbital?"

"Of course I have." She shut her mouth.

"Go on," Amanda encouraged.

"No, I don't think I should."

"What do you know about the drug?"

"Why are you asking me about it? Did Alicia die from it or something?"

Amanda and Trent's silence answered for them.

"Oh. *Oooh.*" A glint of rage flashed in Claudia's eyes. "It's time for you to leave."

"We're not going anywhere until we get some more answers," Trent said.

"You're not getting any unless I have a lawyer. This is police harassment."

"Claud—"

"No. Go. Both of you. And stay away from Beth." She thrust a pointed finger to the doorway.

Amanda and Trent had just cleared the front door when Claudia slammed it behind them.

"*Wow,*" Amanda mouthed, her back to the house, looking at Trent.

"Guess we don't have to worry about objectivity here at all."

"The woman gets under my skin."

"That's apparent." Trent laughed.

"Nothing funny about all this."

"I know. It's just if we don't laugh, we cry, right?"

"That might apply to you," she teased. "Back to business. She was rather protective of Bethany, just like Tony was. Do you think they suspect something there? Like they might believe the daughter poisoned Alicia's sleeping aid?"

"I don't think it even needs to be that. They just might not want her caught up in all this."

Amanda sure hoped not. She still saw Beth as that teenage girl with twin braids and braces. Had she grown up to be a killer?

FIFTEEN

Amanda was fuming, and her mind kept tossing around Claudia's words about her marriage to Tony, specifically the part about them growing apart because life became all about taking care of Bethany and earning a wage. While Amanda's pampering Zoe wouldn't cause her to lose a partner, she could lose something far worse—herself. Something that Becky had pointed out. Drinking Becky always had wise epiphanies.

Trent had put the car into gear, not that she had a clue where he was going.

"Where are you taking us?"

"Figure we probably have a long day ahead of us. Thinking a super-duper large coffee from Hannah's Diner is called for."

"I like it." What she'd really like was to talk to Bethany Wagner, but that wouldn't be happening today with her out of town.

Ten minutes later, the two of them were walking through the door of Hannah's Diner, the bell jangling overhead.

"There you are." May Byrd, the woman who owned the place, had a huge heart and was the pulse of the community—or at least had her hand on the pulse. Her coffee shop was a popular place for locals. It wasn't only because she served the best coffee on the planet—she had a warm spirit too.

"You realize I was just here a couple of hours ago." She'd picked up a coffee on the way to meet Trent at Central.

May waved a hand. "It's Saturday, and you're obviously working." Her gaze drifted to Trent, and she grinned so large, Amanda half-expected her to reach out and pinch his cheeks. *Weird thought...*

"That obvious, eh?" Amanda imagined she must appear ragged after going a round with Claudia. The past was rarely a hospitable place to visit.

"You've got that look. I'm thinking that *you're* thinking about an extra-large coffee. Black."

"Always." Amanda smiled and tapped the counter.

May looked at Trent. "Assume the same for you?"

"Sounds great. Thanks."

"Just a sec." May turned around and poured their coffees.

Trent pulled out his phone. Amanda stared at nothing in particular, seething over how petty Claudia had been—and her nerve in implying that Amanda had been the reason behind their dissolved friendship, like Claudia had nothing to do with it.

"All right. Good news," Trent said. "I checked my email—looks like it was sent to both of us—and we have the incoming and outgoing numbers from Alicia's phone."

"Great. We'll dig in when we get back to Central." The feat would be even easier to tackle with a delicious hot brew in hand.

Once back in Woodbridge, the two of them set up in Trent's cubicle, and he opened the attachment the CSI had sent with Alicia's recent phone activity. They looked at both the incoming and outgoing calls. Alicia had been in regular communication with Tony Bishop and Harold Armstrong. There were also calls with Eve Kelley, Pamela Zimmerman, Seth Rossi—Leo's dad—

and the estate lawyer's office. No unknown numbers or contact with any of the bidders. Claudia Bishop had called last Sunday, and that coincided with what Tony told them about her calling and coming over to the house that day. What really stood out were conversations between Alicia and Eve. Alicia had called Eve Tuesday afternoon, the day she died, and the call lasted fifteen minutes. Then Eve had called Alicia back two hours later, and that call lasted thirty minutes. She pointed this out to Trent.

"They could have been talking about New Belle," he suggested.

"Twice in one day—when their arrangement had already been ironed out?"

"I don't know. We'll have to ask her about it."

"Yep. First thing Monday, we'll find out for sure. We also have that set of tire tracks at the cabin, and the fingerprints on the wineglasses and the bottle. Eve's? Did she go to the cabin later in the day to talk more with Alicia and then tampered with her sleeping aid?" That left the man's size-eleven shoeprints without an explanation, though.

"Possible, but remember Alicia could have been drugged over time."

"*Could have been.* We don't know for sure."

"True. There's this guy too." Trent pointed at Seth Rossi's name. "Leo's dad."

"He could have easily been calling to discuss something to do with Leo. Confirming a pick-up time or something as insignificant as that."

"Whatever the case, there couldn't have been much said in forty-five seconds. That's how long the call lasted. And it was on Monday, the day before Alicia died."

That part was hard to ignore. "Huh. She took his call, but she wasn't happy to hear from him?" she tossed out. "It seems a stretch to think much of the call length, Trent. But I guess it's possible their split wasn't as amicable as Tony made it sound. And really it's hard to believe it could be. Alicia moved on with Tony rather quickly. She'd only been split from her ex for about six months before dating Tony."

"As Mom would say, no moss grew under their feet."

She smiled and shook her head.

"I still find it crazy they'd get hitched so fast. Marriage? That's a huge commitment. If I ever take that step, I'm going to know her like the back of my hand."

"Well, good luck with that. There are so many layers to people, and most are carrying around secrets."

"My woman won't be."

"As I said, good luck."

"You had secrets from Kevin?" His brows raised.

Whoa! The personal question slammed her with guilt. Tony. She'd never told Kevin that just after they'd started dating, she'd kissed Tony. But why would she? It was a moment of weakness, brief, fleeting. Tony had professed his love for her and dared her to deny her feelings. When she fell speechless, he'd pulled her in. The kiss happened. They lingered in each other's arms. But the timing was unfair. There was Kevin and Claudia to consider, though Tony had insisted he wasn't entirely sure about his future with Claudia. They were on a "break" at the time. The fact remained, though, that the two of them had a child together. Amanda didn't want to interfere with that, and she had a sense of loyalty toward Kevin. She put an end to whatever could have started between her and Tony then and there.

"Amanda?"

"No." She could justify that answer, right? She'd held back because nothing good would have come from her confessing the kiss to Kevin. It just would have hurt him for no reason. After all, Amanda had chosen him.

Trent smiled at her. "See? Those women do exist."

She broke eye contact. "Pull a background on Rossi," she said, hoping desperately the course of their conversation was permanently detoured.

"One second..." Trent proceeded to do just that. "He owns a contracting company for new builds... Oh."

She leaned over. "I see it. Seth Rossi has a history of assault. Goes back the better part of eleven years. Looks like a bar fight. Other than that, there's not much detail on file. He served six months."

"Still proves he has a temper. He may like to settle things with physical violence."

Amanda thought of the shared custody arrangement. With Alicia's plans to sell the business, was she going to pursue full custody of Leo? "Let's go pay Rossi a visit, find out why he called Alicia and what kept their conversation so short."

SIXTEEN

Amanda and Trent grabbed something quick to eat before heading over to Seth Rossi's house in Woodbridge. Time had flown as they'd looked at Alicia's call history, and it was after one in the afternoon when they were seated across from Seth in his living room.

"She just decided one day we were through." He snapped his fingers. "Just like that."

"That must have made you bitter," Trent said.

"Ya think?" Seth shook his head.

"So you're not terribly upset that she's dead...?" Amanda raised her eyebrows. She hadn't much cared for the man from the moment he answered the door. He had a chip on his shoulder and wore it for the world to see.

"I loved Alicia until she broke my heart. We were together for over a decade. I talked to her about marriage, and she was having nothing to do with it. I even took in Brad and treated him like my own son—he *is* my son, as far as I'm concerned. Then she marries that guy in what, a heartbeat? Pfft. Ridiculous!"

His feelings toward Alicia sounded more possessive than

loving. "We're aware that you and Alicia spoke on the phone on Monday. What was the conversation about?" No point stressing how the timing of the call fell in relation to Alicia's death or it could get Seth's back up more than it already was.

"She became a royal bitch. It's one thing to leave me, but then she takes my son? She never had a problem with me spending time with Leo until she married that guy. Then suddenly I wasn't good enough anymore? That wasn't right or fair. I was trying to talk sense into her."

"Life is rarely fair." Harsh but true. And there couldn't have been much "sense talking" on Monday as the call had lasted less than a minute. She was struck by how Seth kept referring to Tony as "that guy," like he didn't know or care to remember his name. It also sounded like the two men didn't get along, but Tony hadn't seemed to have a problem with Seth.

"Whatever," Seth pushed out. "Now she's dead, and I've been trying to get ahold of her husband. I want my son back in my full custody now that Alicia's gone. I'm Leo's biological father, and he belongs with me."

"Suppose that's for the courts to decide," she said.

"I know you don't care about any of this. Why would you?"

She took a few deep breaths, trying to calm her temper. Just last fall, a man who turned out to be Zoe's biological father had stepped forward. Thankfully things worked out in Amanda's favor when he didn't want to take on raising the girl. But if it had come down to it, Amanda would have fought for the girl.

Trent glanced at Amanda, then asked, "Were you in a custody battle with Alicia, then?"

"It would have hit the courts soon, I suspect. Not that I have the money or means to fight her with her millions of dollars and an army of lawyers. Not like contracting pays as much as the cosmetics industry."

"Legal proceedings have started?" Amanda struggled to understand why Tony never mentioned any of this. And "amicable?" Not by any conceivable stretch of the imagination. Alicia's relationship with her ex was strained at best.

"We were just about to that point. That's what she told me Monday before she hung up. 'You'll be hearing from my lawyer.'" He shook his head. "I refuse to roll over. Leo is my son."

"But you just said that you don't have the means to contest her." Amanda tossed his earlier words back to him.

"I would have found a way."

Had he? Had Seth felt helpless in the face of a custody battle with Alicia and her money? It sure sounded like it, but enough to kill her? "When was the last time you saw Alicia?"

"She let me pick Leo up two weekends ago. Took begging to get it to happen."

"So it was becoming more difficult for you to get time with your son?" Trent asked. Obviously, she wasn't the only one seeing motive with this guy.

"Yep. Every single day. Heck, the nanny saw him more than Alicia ever did, so where the hell did she get off...?" He scowled and shook his head. "At least I'd have been around for him."

"A nanny?" The question scraped from her throat, and she laid a hand on her stomach. Why hadn't Tony mentioned one? They'd asked if anyone else had access to the house, and he'd said no. Presumably a nanny would have access to Alicia's Sleep Tight.

"Yeah. Tina Nash. Nice enough woman, and Leo likes her."

Amanda glanced at Trent.

"How did Tina and Alicia get along?" Trent asked.

"Fine, as far as I know. Tina did everything that Alicia should have been doing as Leo's mom. But Alicia always threw how important she was in my face. How much stress and pressure she was under. How she ran a cosmetics empire that she had started from nothing. Yada yada. All her choice. And she was stressed, but I wasn't?"

"Stress must have made it hard for her to sleep," Trent said. "Did she have lots of sleepless nights, suffer from periodic bouts of insomnia?"

Amanda loved how cleverly Trent had cued things up to move the questioning forward.

"Yeah, I guess. What about it?"

Trent shrugged. "She probably took sleeping pills to help, then."

"I don't know about the last eighteen months, but she used to take a remedy called Sleep Tight. Every single night while we were together. Too tired for sex most of the time too."

Given this guy's attitude, Amanda couldn't imagine hanging around long enough to procreate. But he'd just done them a favor. He'd confirmed knowing about the sleeping aid. Could they put the contaminated bottle in his hands? "Have you ever heard of pentobarbital?"

"Nope, never heard of it. Why?" Not just his eyes, but his entire facial expression was blank.

Was his response an act to shield himself? After all, Seth Rossi had motive. With Alicia dead, he could be awarded full custody of Leo—if he got away with murder. Amanda wasn't letting that happen on her watch. As the saying goes, *no stone unturned.* "We looked up your background before we came here. An assault charge? Tell us about that."

He clenched his jaw. "It's in the past."

"Eleven years ago," she countered.

"Okay, so, the *distant* past."

"How long were you and Alicia together?"

"Thirteen years."

Two years before the assault charge. "So you and Alicia were together at the time you were charged?"

He nodded. "She was less than two months pregnant."

"What happened?"

"You want to know, dig up the record. It doesn't change the fact Alicia's dead, and I had nothing to do with it."

She'd definitely be digging up the record, and since the file didn't have much to say, she'd be reaching out to the charging officer. His defensiveness on the subject didn't sit well, though. Her mind went to the unexplained shoeprints in the mud outside the cabin window. "What size shoe are you?"

"Eleven. Why?"

Right size. "Where were you on Tuesday night?"

"Are you being serious right now?" Seth flushed and looked at Trent. "She can't be serious."

"Answer her question," Trent said firmly.

"I got home from work at five and was here all night."

"So if we took a look at your shoes, we wouldn't find mud?" Amanda asked.

"I don't have a clue. But go ahead, and look if you need to." Seth threw his arms up in the air. "Whatever floats your boat," he mumbled.

Amanda was aware there was much more to it than just finding mud on his shoes. Even if they found a shoe that had a diamond pattern on the sole, with or without mud, it could just be coincidence. It might not be an exact match to the impression left at the scene. Amanda started to stand, but Trent intercepted.

"I'll take care of it. All your shoes in the front closet?" Trent asked Seth while on the move.

"Yep." Seth knotted his arms and sat back.

Seconds ticked off. Minutes.

Trent returned, shadowing the doorway holding a pair of running shoes in gloved hands. He turned them to disclose the soles. Dried mud in the cracks. Diamond pattern on the sole.

"Looks like we're going to be spending some more quality time together." Amanda stood. "We need you to come with us."

"No way. Because I have mud on my running shoes?"

"Come on, let's go." Amanda motioned for him to stand.

"Please. No." Seth held up a hand to fend her off. "You see my driveway? It's gravel and dirt. Test the mud. You can do that, can't you? Like those crime dramas on TV. You'll know what's on my shoes doesn't match whatever area you're thinking it might."

Amanda yanked him to his feet. "You have the choice. Come with us willingly or make me cuff you."

Seth gritted his teeth. "Fine. I'll cooperate."

"Wise decision."

SEVENTEEN

Today had been more productive than Amanda could have hoped. They might even have the person who'd tampered with Alicia's sleeping aid sitting in the interrogation room. Seth Rossi. Amanda and Trent were watching through the one-way mirror.

They had contacted the charging officer on Rossi's assault conviction and were armed with more details on the arrest. It resulted from a two-man brawl over a woman's affections in a local bar. The other man claimed Rossi had charged at him and that he'd done nothing to aggravate him. Eyewitnesses had backed up his testimony, and it was Rossi who served the time.

"We need to see if we can get more information out of Rossi about his assault charge," she began. "I'd like to know who the woman was, for one. Even just the fact he fought over a woman tells me that he's possessive and willing to go to fists to defend what he sees as his. He might have taken things further and killed Alicia, thinking she was either his or no one's."

"Yeah. Not a good sign."

"Nope. We also need to know what we're looking at regarding his shoes."

"No problem. I can get on that. The crime lab should have uploaded the photographs from the scene onto the server by now. It would be good to get a look at the mystery tire treads and the shoeprints for comparison." They had Seth's shoes and a photo of the tires on his Chevy pickup.

"All right, you go do that, and I'll get in there and start asking some questions. No time to waste."

"You got it." Trent left the room for his cubicle, and she went to the neighboring room.

Seth Rossi was slumped in his chair, but he moved quickly to sit straighter.

"I don't have anything to do with her death. I swear to you."

At least he wasn't saying, "You have to believe me." She'd heard that once too many times in her life, and *once* was enough. She didn't *have* to take anyone's word at face value. She set the folder with Seth's background on the table. It also included some pictures of Alicia Gordon from the cabin. If nothing else she said or did managed to elicit a reaction, these likely would—and it would be telling.

She relaxed her body language, and Seth mirrored it, his shoulders lowering. "Why don't you tell me about your relationship with Alicia?" she asked, deciding to start off on less volatile ground than poking at his assault charge.

"When we were together or after?"

"Either. Whatever you feel like talking about." She said it casually, as if she were relinquishing control of the conversation to him.

"Ah, okay... Our relationship was all fire, until it wasn't. We'd been living together for a few months when she became pregnant with Leo."

"He wasn't planned?"

"No. But I was happy about the prospect of being a father. Still love the job."

She nodded. "What happened to break you up?"

"New Belle."

Amanda drew back. "Her business did?"

"How I see it. We'd been drifting apart, but she put in crazy hours. Even after Leo was born. She let a lot of the responsibilities of caring for him and Brad fall on me."

"Did you resent how much time she put into work?" Amanda asked.

"Ah, yeah. We had a long talk when she became pregnant. She promised she'd be around more, that she'd do her part."

"And she let you down."

"Yeah, but she brought in a nanny to help some."

"Still, it sounds like you're prepared for full custody. You were used to doing all the work before," she said. Sometimes it was advantageous to portray herself as an ally, someone who understood.

"Exactly." His eyes met hers, questioning her sudden empathy. "Do you have kids?"

Amanda hesitated for a second. Not because she didn't count Zoe as her kid, but because images of Lindsey entered her mind. "I do."

"Then you understand how important it is to be there for them."

Amanda opened the folder, more as notification of a nonverbal shift in power. She was taking the lead from here. "I need to ask you about that assault charge." She glanced at the page in front of her—it didn't specifically have the arrest record on it, but Seth didn't know that.

"What about it?" The question was riddled with exasperation.

"It was in a bar, over some girl. That right?"

"Yeah." Seth put his hands on the table, fidgeted with them.

"Who? What was her name?"

Seth pulled back, his face darkening. "What does that matter?"

Amanda hadn't been sure the woman's identity had mattered at all—until Seth's reaction. "Please, just answer my question."

Seth snapped his mouth shut and stared through her.

"If you're not going to talk to me, I'll have no choice but to pay a visit to"—she shuffled to another page in the file, completely for show, elongating the silence, hopefully building up the tension—"the guy you fought with. I'll ask him about this woman, see if he knows her name."

Seth slumped in his chair. "It was Alicia."

"He was making moves on her or something?"

"He was being all pawsy. He wouldn't listen when she told him to back off. I stepped in. End of story."

Maybe Seth wasn't the monster she was building up in her mind. After all, Alicia had stayed with Seth even after his arrest. But Amanda had to see this through, see if her first instincts about the guy were right or not. "Given all your history, and spending some time in jail—because you defended her—it must have been really hard when she left you. And then she gets together with Tony five or six months after that. *Marries* him not long after."

He glared at her but said nothing.

"I'm thinking if you fought to possess Alicia in the past, you might have lost it when she took up with another man."

"Why would I? I'd lose Leo forever."

"Not if you got away with it," she stamped out, watching his body language, but it wasn't giving her anything. She let some time pass in silence, and it sank in how he never said anything much about Brad. He'd only said he'd raised him like his own son, but he would have known Brad for most of his life. Had he just let Brad go? She clasped her hands on the table. "You told us that you went to pick Leo up a couple of weeks ago at her house."

"Yeah, so what?"

"Is this the house you two shared?" Amanda was thinking he'd know his way around and where Alicia kept her Sleep Tight. Seth had motive: jealousy. *And* he'd likely gain full custody of Leo with Alicia dead. He had opportunity, possibly: he knew Alicia took Sleep Tight and could have followed her to the cabin and watched from outside. But when did he get the Sleep Tight bottle to tamper with it? As for means, where did he get pentobarbital?

"No. We both found new places."

Amanda nodded. "Did you go into their bedroom, though? Either a couple of weeks ago or another time. You know, maybe just out of curiosity?" She suggested that, thinking about Claudia's justification for trespassing.

"No."

"And you're absolutely sure of that?"

"I'd have no reason at all to go in there."

"All right. You said Alicia took Sleep Tight every night when you were together. You know if she still took it?"

"Like I said earlier—wouldn't have a clue."

The calm manner in which he'd replied had Amanda believing him. Still, she said, "Pentobarbital." It was one word that would hopefully get him to talk.

"You brought that up at my house. Why are you asking about it? Did it kill her?"

"Alicia's Sleep Tight was contaminated with the drug."

Seth swallowed roughly.

"Do you see where I'm going with this?"

He met her gaze. "You think I killed her, but I swear I didn't. Was I freaking pissed that she was trying to take Leo from me? Absolutely, but I didn't kill her to stop it. I was prepared to fight her in court if it came to that."

"Which you said you couldn't afford."

"I would have gone broke if it meant getting my son back."

"Only the real world doesn't work that way. You'd need to prove to a judge you have the means to care for Leo."

Seth was staring at her, and a single tear slid down his cheek.

There was a knock on the door. She closed the folder and answered. It was Trent, and he was shaking his head. She stepped into the hall with him. "Talk to me."

"The shoeprints from outside the cabin." He handed her a colored photo. A diamond-grid pattern, and there was one distinct slash in the middle of the sole, across the width, like the shoe had been cut by something.

"All right...?"

"The soles of Rossi's running shoes." He gave her another picture. Another diamond-grid pattern, but not the same one.

"Not a match," she huffed out.

"Nope. And the same for the mystery tire treads from the cabin. This is what they look like, FYI." He gave her a picture, and she committed the grooves to memory. Trent continued. "I went a step further, and the fingerprints lifted from the wine-glass and bottle aren't a match to the ones on file for Rossi either."

"We need to cut him loose."

"He could have used another vehicle or worn another pair of shoes."

She shook her head. "He's jealous and hurting, but I really don't think he did this. If he did, we have a lot more to prove."

"Back to square one."

She looked him in the eye. "That being Tony Bishop?"

"I didn't say that."

"No, but I am. He's not been forthcoming about much of anything. Lying about the state of Alicia's relationship with her ex. Things are far from amicable."

"We could question the nanny," Trent suggested.

Amanda flailed a hand. "Another thing that Tony failed to

mention to us, and we even asked who else was in the family home." Her heart was thumping rapidly as anger flushed through her system.

"There could be an explanation for his—"

"Lying," she cut in.

"His omission."

"Whatever you want to call it, we need some answers."

Trent took the photos back from Amanda. "Why not start with Seth Rossi? I know we need to cut him loose, but he might have some insight to provide on the nanny."

"Short of talking to the woman herself, he might be the closest we come to finding out the truth." She turned to go back into the room, glanced over a shoulder. "You can join us if you'd like."

Trent did. Seth looked up at him, at the photos in his hand. "What's going on?"

She sat down across from him while Trent remained standing. "What can you tell us about the nanny? You said her name was Tina Nash?"

"Yeah, like I told you, she was nice enough, qualified, and I trusted her with my son. Just figured it was best that he be with his actual parents."

There was an unmistakable bitterness toward Tony, but that could be understood. "Do you know what her relationship with Alicia was like?"

"They got along fine as far as I know."

Not exactly an expression to bank on, but they had no further right to detain him. She scooped up the folder and stood. "You're free to go."

"I'm... You're letting me go?"

"Yes. Thank you for your cooperation."

"Not that I had much choice," he mumbled and left.

EIGHTEEN

The first thing Amanda and Trent should have done after releasing Seth Rossi was pay another visit to Tony, but she couldn't do it. Rage was blinding her judgment, her objectivity.

"Maybe Tony didn't mention Seth because he didn't figure him for a suspect," she said. "Could be why he never brought up the nanny either." She was trying to find justification for Tony. Surely, he wouldn't lie right to her face. Or omit—the same thing. The latter just whitewashed dishonesty.

"Don't hate me for saying this—and I'm not disagreeing with the point you made—*but* I think he's hiding something about the nanny," Trent said.

She studied him. "You're suggesting maybe Tony was cheating with her or something?"

Trent pressed his lips together.

She could conjure no defense. Tony had made a move on her when he was seeing Claudia, claiming they had hit pause on their relationship at the time. The two of them were on and off a lot during high school and college, though. But maybe he'd taken his "affections" further with the nanny. "Let's just call it a day. A weekend for that matter, and start fresh on

HER FROZEN CRY 143

Monday. We'll talk to Eve Kelley about those phone calls, track down Bethany Wagner, and speak with Tony about the nanny."

"If that's what you want."

"It is." She left the station with the hope that what was left of the weekend would last forever.

No such luck, Amanda thought as she pulled into the lot for Central on Monday morning.

She found Trent at his desk. He held up a Hannah's Diner coffee for her, and she raised one for him. They both smiled.

"Great minds," he said.

"You got it."

They toasted with their paper coffee cups and took sips.

"You want to start with Tony and the nanny?" Trent asked her.

"Nope. Eve Kelley. The phone calls between her and Alicia bothered me all weekend."

He took his time responding. "Sure. We can start there."

She'd obviously surprised Trent with her choice of direction, but she still couldn't face Tony. Besides, where would it ultimately lead the investigation if she freaking ripped his head off?

Eve Kelley's assistant showed Amanda and Trent to Eve's office. Eve was perched behind her desk, cradling a takeout coffee cup emblazoned with the logo from Caffeine Café. She looked exhausted. "Joanne said you needed to speak with me. And that it was urgent?" Lines creased around her eyes as they narrowed on Amanda.

"We do. And it is." Amanda paused. Eve was breathing through her mouth and lightly panting. "Are you all right?"

"Yeah. I'm just tired. It's nothing. What can I do for you?" She massaged her forehead.

"A look at Alicia Gordon's phone records tell us that you two spoke on Tuesday. She called you," Amanda said.

"If that's what it says..."

"You don't remember?" Trent pressed. "You spoke for fifteen minutes, and then two hours later, you called her back. What were you two talking about?"

Eve flushed, and she wiped her brow. It was starting to glisten with sweat. "I... ah... she was going to screw me over again."

She'd tossed it out there like it meant nothing, but the tone disclosed it meant everything. Amanda glanced at Trent. It might be just as they'd guessed, and Alicia had changed her mind on some aspect of the bidding process. "How's that?"

Eve leaned an elbow on her desk and cupped her forehead. "She got some really good offers to..." She paused there like her mind had drifted.

"Ms. Kelley," Amanda prompted.

"I told her to give me a chance. I reminded her of our deal. She told me things change. *Things change.*" Eve shook her head and winced. Her brow was wrinkled like she had a migraine.

"You might have thought to tell us this before," Trent said with a lot more patience than Amanda could have conjured. "Why didn't you?"

"Why do you think? She was going to... what do you call it..." Eve's eyelids fluttered. "Renege on our deal. Now she's dead. I know how that would make me look."

"Are you sure you're okay?" Amanda asked.

Eve waved a hand. "Well, I'm going to win in the end. I'm going to destroy her company. They were served with legal papers Friday afternoon claiming intellectual property theft and suing for compensation."

That was something that Amanda hadn't foreseen happening. "You move fast."

Eve shrugged. "Dog eat dog."

Eve had plenty of reason to want Alicia dead—her nervous, frightened demeanor when they were last here had been an act, it seemed. But could they connect her to pentobarbital and Alicia's sleeping aid? What about the fingerprints or the tire treads? "We're going to need to know where you were Tuesday night last week."

"Oh." Eve's pupils constricted, and she put both her hands flat on the top of her desk. Her body swayed.

Amanda had gotten as far as pulling out her phone and pecking in 9 when Eve's body slumped to the side and landed on the floor.

"What the—" Trent jumped to his feet.

Amanda finished the call and told the 911 operator to get medics there immediately. By the time she hung up, she realized they'd be too late.

Eve Kelley was dead.

The medics arrived about ten minutes later, but only stayed to confirm death. Eve would be taking a different ride. Rideout and his assistant were on the way, and so were crime scene investigators.

Amanda replayed the moments leading up to Eve's death in her head, and her imagination might be on overdrive, but she was sure she was exhibiting symptoms of pentobarbital poisoning. Her death, on the tail of Alicia's, could be a coincidence—but it would be a huge one.

She went over to Trent, who was standing just to the side of the door. "Someone killed her with pentobarbital."

"I think so. Maybe we should have taken the threats more seriously." Trent's guilt was tangible.

"We can't go down that road. We had other leads to follow, and no one can do everything at once." She was doing her best to lift him up, but her own regrets were eating away at her. "And we don't know if the person we're looking for even sent written threats to her or Alicia."

"True. But with Eve, the drug likely wouldn't have been put in her sleeping aid. It's first thing in the morning."

Amanda scanned the room, her eyes landing on Eve's coffee cup. She pointed in its direction. "That."

"We'll get it tested. But who could have wanted both women dead?"

"Someone connected or related to the sale of New Belle, as we thought before."

"Time to speak with the other bidders."

Rideout breezed into the office with Liam trailing him. "I heard this one dropped at your feet."

Amanda didn't find him nearly as funny as he must have thought he was, factoring in his grin. "How it worked out," she responded drily.

"I was actually about to call you when I got your call to come here. I figured I'd give you the update in person. Alicia Gordon's toxicology was waiting for me when I came in this morning. She had a lethal amount of pentobarbital in her system."

Hearing about it now after it had been a strong—and working—theory was anticlimactic. But they had the concrete proof Malone wanted.

"Do you know if she was poisoned with a single large dose or over time?" Amanda asked.

"That's not anything I can tell with any certainty." Rideout looked around the room. "Where's the body?"

"Behind the desk." Amanda pointed, though it wasn't necessary. She added, "She looked exhausted from the moment we walked in here."

"Which was when?"

"Around nine AM, give or take a few minutes. She was breathing heavily, looked like she had a headache."

"Seemed like she was dazed and dizzy too," Trent added.

"Not looking good for her, then."

Amanda bit the urge to say, *Obviously not; she's dead.*

"I'll take a look, see what I can determine. Only thing we can effectively knock off is TOD." Rideout paused there and made deliberate eye contact with Amanda.

"But it does sound like pentobarbital caused this today?" she said.

"From what you're describing, yes, but I'm not leaping to that conclusion without taking the proper measures. If this woman was drugged with pentobarbital, I would wager she ingested some not long before you two arrived." Rideout looked toward the doorway. "No CSIs yet?"

"Probably just a few minutes behind you," Amanda said.

"I'll get started once they've finished taking their photographs, etcetera. Might as well go get myself a cup of coffee."

Coffee... Amanda's eyes settled on Eve's cup.

Rideout and Liam left, and in their place, Sergeant Malone and CSIs Donnelly and Blair filtered into the room. Brief mumbled greetings, and the investigators got to work. Amanda told them to test the cup and remaining coffee for pentobarbital.

Malone stepped in front of Amanda and Trent. "What's going on? And why were you here? I need answers."

"Which we're trying to get, and which we *will* get," she added under his intensifying eye contact.

"As soon as the police chief catches wind of this..." Malone puffed out his chest and tugged down on his suit jacket. "Tell me where you are with the investigation."

She brought him up to speed on why they were at Eve Kelley's office, leaving out the part about getting into Alicia's phone history. She played Eve up as a murder suspect, building off the one threat Alicia had received. "Rideout just confirmed that Alicia Gordon had a lethal amount of pentobarbital in her system. It was likely what caused the heart failure."

"Definitely murder, then? No possibility of suicide?"

"None. Which I tell you with confidence." As far as Amanda was concerned Eve's death removed any doubt.

"Okay. Guess I can authorize you going for a subpoena for her phone and computer records then. And it would seem that Eve's likely off the hook for Alicia's murder. What about your old friend, Tony Bishop? Where is he in all this?"

Amanda had been hoping Malone wouldn't ask. Trent stepped back, though subtly. She caught it, but Malone didn't seem to. Amanda said, "He might be able to get his hands on pentobarbital."

"You can connect him to it? And I'm just hearing about this now?"

"It's a stretch and only in a roundabout way. Means hasn't been established." She filled him in that Tony's daughter and son-in-law owned a vet clinic.

Malone pursed his lips, his patience hitting its limit. "Sounds like it's established to me. The drug is conceivably within Mr. Bishop's reach."

"Yes, but right within the daughter's hand. She is one of our next stops." And she wasn't lying. Even before Eve Kelley had dropped dead, stopping by the vet clinic and speaking with Bethany was on their list of things to do.

"You think the daughter killed these women?"

"Not necessarily, but we can see if she knows of any way Tony—Mr. Bishop—could have gotten any of the drug," Amanda said.

"And hope she doesn't lie to protect her father. Tell me, though, why would Tony Bishop want Eve Kelley dead?"

She wished that Malone hadn't asked.

"Detective Steele?" Malone prompted.

"Eve Kelley had papers served to New Belle for intellectual property theft on Friday. New Belle was founded on Reborn, a restorative night serum, which Eve claims Alicia stole from her back in college."

"People claim a lot of things. If someone murdered Kelley because of this lawsuit, someone is wanting to bury something."

"Could be. Also could be that someone doesn't want New Belle destroyed," she said.

"Or their financial windfall messed with."

She hesitated to agree. Again, it would *bury* Tony Bishop, as the main beneficiary of Alicia's will.

"There's another possibility here," Trent interjected.

Malone faced him. "I'm all ears."

"Alicia made an arrangement that Eve would have final bid on purchasing New Belle. One of the other bidders could have found out and decided to kill both women. Alicia for her dishonesty, and Eve for her participation."

"Not sure about that." Malone adjusted his posture, putting his right leg out in front of himself.

The hate mail. She and Trent had just discussed how they should have taken it more seriously. "When we first visited Eve, she was concerned about some threats she'd received."

"And I'm just hearing about this now?"

Amanda held up her hand, lowered it quickly under his glare. "Alicia received threats too. People in positions of success and authority attract this type of attention. We had other leads to follow before, another mysterious death to unravel."

"The first, it would seem in a long series or...?" Malone's lips set in a firm, straight line.

If he was goading her into saying *serial killer*, he'd be disappointed. "We had no reason to believe Alicia's murder was anything other than an isolated incident. We're still not sure. Eve's death could have been natural." *Not that I believe that for a hot second!* "If Eve was murdered, even poisoned with pento-barbital as well, the killer could be someone within the circle of the two women. The killing could be over. Another theory could be one of the bidders is behind the murders." The only person it seemed to truly rule out was Seth Rossi. He'd have no reason to want Eve Kelley dead.

"How many others are there?"

"Just two others," Amanda said.

"I think it's a long shot, but in case you're right, one might be in danger—or both."

Trent turned to her. "What if Malone is right? And the other bidders aren't safe?"

Her heart bumped off rhythm as adrenaline pumped through her system. She hoped that supposition was so very wrong.

"Sounds extreme, but it is possible," Malone said as if he were agreeing with something he hadn't been the first to suggest. "You mention threats. Go. See if the other bidders received any. Then ferret through them all to see if it takes us to the killer." He waved a hand toward the door. "Go. Mush-mush."

What Malone was suggesting was unorthodox, as normally the suspicious death in front of you received all the attention. Malone was asking them to postpone the usual procedure. She squared her shoulders. "And what about notifying Eve Kelley's next of kin?"

"I'd offer to do it, but I know you prefer to handle those."

She did, and she didn't. But insights could be gained. "We'll do it."

"Figured you'd say that. There are just two bidders, talk to them, get it done. At least you might get a better idea whether you're barking up the wrong tree with them or not."

"And tracing Kelley's last steps?" Trent asked.

"After the notification. Which comes after speaking with the bidders." Malone put it out there with a bite.

Amanda tried to establish eye contact with the sergeant, but he wasn't having any part of it. Something was going on with him, but she wasn't going to find out what right now. And she didn't really want to pick this fight. If she won and her insistence on doing everything by the book resulted in more death, she'd never forgive herself. Though by the time she and Trent finished following Malone's marching orders, they'd probably have to wait until tomorrow morning to investigate Eve Kelley's last movements. "Okay, we're on it." She led the way from the room.

Trent caught up to her, leaned in. "I know Malone's the sarge, and he ultimately calls the shots but..."

"I know." That's all she said, and all she was going to say on the subject. She had a lot of thoughts on the way Malone was acting lately, though. He didn't seem as focused, and he was more hardheaded than usual.

NINETEEN

If only cloning were possible, Amanda would be the first in line. They needed to notify Eve's next of kin, talk to the other bidders, trace Eve's last steps, and those were just the highlights. Assuming Eve ingested pentobarbital, where had she gotten it? But they had their marching orders from Malone.

She and Trent returned to Central to get the information on the two bidders. Before they were going to show up at either's door, they wanted to be armed with some intel. They were in Trent's cubicle.

He sat down and flicked on his monitor. "I noticed in your recap to Malone about why we were in Eve's office, you left out the bit about Alicia's phone history."

"Why go there?" She should feel guilty for going behind Malone's back, but she didn't. "Besides, you saw what he was like back there. Something's off about him." *Like his mind isn't as sharp.*

"I noticed." He started typing. "Okay, so the bidders' names are Rocco Lopez of Smart Acquisitions and Dale Reynolds of Acne Buster Inc. Both companies are in Woodbridge."

"The business names seem straightforward enough, but we

still need to dig." She gestured toward his monitor. "Start with Lopez."

Trent proceeded to bring up the man's personal background and information on the company. "His company acquires failing businesses around the world, makes them profitable, then flips them."

"Just as the name told me. Though New Belle wasn't operating in the red." It made her curious about Lopez's interest in Alicia's company.

He went to the internet and did a Google search. "Ooh." He slumped back in his chair. "Rocco Lopez is *shaaaady*," he said, dragging out the word. "Clean criminal record, but look at these." He pointed to the articles that had come back with his search.

"They allege Lopez kept close company with Congressman Eugene Davis." She drew back, feeling sick. And angry. Just when she'd thought and hoped she'd heard the last of the man, that he'd be rotting in some prison, his name was thrust back in her face. The congressman had been behind a sex-trafficking ring that operated in the Prince William County area. It wasn't even a year ago she had him slammed behind bars. "If this Lopez guy is some perv, I will take him down."

"And I'll be right by your side."

"Just keeping company with the likes of Davis... that makes him a despicable human being. Someone who probably wouldn't have any qualms about killing to ensure he gets what he wants."

"Or hiring someone to do the dirty work."

"Precisely. What about the other bidder, Reynolds?"

Trent clicked away on his keyboard. A few minutes later, he said, "On paper, this guy's rather boring compared to Lopez."

"In this case, boring is good."

"No argument there."

"All right, we start with Lopez, go from there." Just saying his name and knowing his associate's transgression had her redhead temper boiling her blood.

Trent turned off his monitor, and they left for Smart Acquisitions.

Just when Amanda was starting to look at the world with a touch more optimism, Eugene Davis's name regurgitated like a horrid hangover.

"So, being an acquisition company, this Lopez guy could very well have a lot of money at his disposal. Just thinking, how could Eve Kelley be expected to compete with that?"

Trent looked over at her from behind the wheel. "I wonder if Alicia Gordon set Kelley up to fail—putting on a front that she was doing her a favor, but knowing all along that other interested parties could far outbid her."

"Cruel, if that's the case. Alicia Gordon's been painted many different ways—as someone who cares about her employees, wants to sell her business to spend more time with her family, and offers a college friend the chance to get a deal on a lucrative cosmetics company. But there are also the dark aspects to her personality. Vindictiveness. And if she did steal Eve Kelley's formula in college, a thief. If she was backing out of the deal she made with Eve, as Eve told us, then she was also a liar. Not someone to rely on."

"It could be that Eve interpreted her conversation with Alicia as her backing out of the deal..."

"What do you mean?"

"Well, if the other offers were sky-high, out of Eve's reach, Eve could have felt she was being squeezed out."

"Possible."

Trent pulled into the parking lot of a shopping plaza and chose a spot near the front doors of Smart Acquisitions.

They entered the office, a small place that wasn't very

impressive. Basic and functional at best. Bland and cheap at worst. But she supposed the company didn't need to have much space for their work. They just needed a flush bank account. Business didn't need to be transacted in person anymore. Not with online video conferencing, and inherit legalities that could be handled via secure documents and electronic signatures.

"Hello? Can I help you?" A stiff-looking woman in a gray skirt suit came from a hallway into the front area, which consisted of a few chairs and a long coffee table.

Amanda and Trent held up their badges.

"Detectives Steele and Stenson with Prince William County PD. We'd like to speak with Rocco Lopez."

"Do you have an appointment with him?" The woman clasped her hands and leaned her long, lean neck to the side.

"We don't, but it's urgent and imperative that we speak with him right away," Amanda said, measuring her tone with equal parts firmness and respect. "Is he in?"

"He is. I'll see if he can speak with you now." The woman turned slowly and receded down the hall from which she had come.

Amanda glanced at Trent. The place gave her a bit of the creeps, but maybe it was more the fact her mind was tainted against Rocco Lopez before they'd arrived.

"Detectives?" A man emerged from the hall. "I'm Rocco Lopez." He shook Trent's hand and extended his for Amanda's, but she wanted nothing to do with it. He pulled his hand back, showing no sign of being affected by her rejection. "What can I do for you?"

"Do you have a private area where we could talk?" Not that there was another soul in sight. Not even the woman.

"Yes, certainly. This way." Rocco took them to an office, which was as bare bones as the reception area. If this man was wealthy enough to bid on New Belle, he hid it well. His clothing was on the cheap side, and the suit was ill-fitted to his frame. But maybe his affluence shone more in his financial portfolio.

They all sat, Rocco behind his desk, and Amanda and Trent in plastic bucket chairs. *Bucket chairs? Really?*

"What is it that I can do for the PWCPD?" Rocco asked.

"Do you know Alicia Gordon?" Amanda said.

"Yes, of course. Why do you ask?"

"She was murdered last week." She set it out there without tact to see if it netted any reaction.

Rocco slowly leaned back in his chair, swiveled left, right, left, right, left, right. "I didn't realize she was murdered."

It was hard to know what to make of his dry response—a lack of empathy or shock? There was a small widening of his eyes that made her wonder if the latter applied, but could she trust facial expression and body language if Rocco was a scumbag? He'd be good at hiding his true feelings. "Alicia was poisoned," Amanda added. There was no registration on Rocco's face. Good actor or in the dark?

"How horrible. Her poor family... She had a young boy, didn't she?"

Amanda recoiled that he went right there, considering his known associate. "Yes, and a college-aged son. She also left behind a husband."

"I did read this in the paper. It's all so very tragic."

Again, his delivery was so dry, distant, disingenuous. "How did you come to know Alicia Gordon?"

"You're kidding, right?" Rocco smiled. "Everyone knows who she is, or *was*, rather. She was a beacon in our community and someone for young girls to look up to."

Amanda bit her tongue. She couldn't give any thought to this man being involved in the exploitation of children or she'd punch him in the face—and might not stop with one blow. She had to remind herself that maybe the gossip had it wrong. She also had to keep in mind that Rocco could be a killer just as well as another potential victim. Until they knew precisely what was motivating the killer, they had to consider both aspects. "And what was your relationship like with her?"

"We got along well. We met at an entrepreneur brunch last year. It was to raise money for charity."

"And the charity?" she asked, just a quick test to gauge his reliability.

"Children Fighting Cancer."

Sincere, no hesitation. Likely telling the truth.

Rocco added, "It gives children with terminal diagnoses the opportunity to travel or do something they've always wished for."

Amanda didn't know if this man was involved in the disgusting business in which the congressman had dirtied his hands, but she sure as hell hoped not. If he was, the hypocrisy—helping children on one hand while hurting them gravely on the other—was too much to swallow.

"What were your thoughts on her company, New Belle?" Trent asked.

Rocco leveled his gaze at him, a smile slowly leeching its way across his face. "I'm sure we can stop beating around the bush now, can't we? You're here because you found out that I put in an offer on her company. Why exactly you're interested in me because of that, I'm not sure."

"We're just following leads in the investigation," Amanda said. She wasn't going to reveal Eve Kelley's death yet or that they were trying to figure out if he was their suspect or a potential future victim.

"All right." He squinted. "Still not sure how you were led to me."

She couldn't hold back anymore. "You have quite a reputation online, Mr. Lopez."

Rocco met her gaze. "As do you, Detective."

"Oh, yeah? How's that?"

"You brought down the congressman and that sex-trafficking ring."

"With help." Amanda passed a side-glance at Trent.

"Well, I shouldn't need to tell you, but the media blows everything out of proportion. Davis could be anyone's kryptonite. One single picture of me with him, captured at an event *and* out of context, and my reputation... well, it hasn't quite recovered."

Maybe that explained the state of the premises? Business had suffered as a result of the presumed affiliation. Though presumably he had enough money to afford New Belle.

Rocco tugged down on his suit jacket. "I assure you I was not, nor would I ever be, a friend or compatriot of Davis. What he did makes me sick." His complexion paled in support of his claim.

Amanda believed him, but it didn't leave him off the hook for tampering with Alicia's sleep meds or being involved in Eve's death. "When did you last see Alicia Gordon?"

"I went to see her at the New Belle offices two weeks ago now."

"So the week before she died," Trent chimed in.

"Guess that would be right."

"And the purpose of your visit?" Amanda inched forward on her chair, which certainly wasn't made for comfort.

"The offer on New Belle."

Amanda was putting together the image in her mind of Rocco's offer coming in just before Alicia had gone to the cabin to "think." Maybe it was because she was agonized by the enormity and surmised that she could end up breaking her word to Eve Kelley. "What did Ms. Gordon think of your offer?"

"She had a good poker face, but I could tell she was quite pleased with the number of zeroes on the table. Honestly, I'd expected to hear from her to say the deal would be going ahead."

So he says... But maybe he found out about Alicia's arrangement with Eve. "Did she say something to make you think that?"

"No, but it was in her mannerisms and body language. I've been around long enough to know when I've acquired a business or if it's going to fall through. Thing is, I'm not the type of person to take no for an answer, Detective."

"What do you do when someone tells you no?" Trent asked.

"I change their mind. I make them see sense."

Hairs rose on her neck. Rocco might not be a sexual predator, but how far would he go to get what he wanted? "How is that exactly?"

"Nothing like what your face is telling me you're thinking. I just help people see how they would benefit from letting me acquire their business. Talk them back to my side."

"And what do you do with these businesses you acquire, Mr. Lopez?" Amanda wasn't fooled for one second by the man in front of her; he was a cold-hearted businessman out to benefit himself alone.

"I expand them, take them global, turn good profits, and then dump them on the market. I end up making a killing on the resale."

"And you do this for failing companies in any industry?" she asked.

"Many, yes. Obviously, I only pursue ones I'm quite sure I can help."

"From our understanding, New Belle was very profitable. What was your interest in it?"

"I was considering running it myself."

"And you know about the cosmetics industry?" Trent asked.

"Not a lot, but you can pay for expertise. I saw myself closing Smart Acquisitions and anchoring myself to one company. It takes a lot of work to research companies to take over and then figure out how to make them profitable and flip them."

"I can imagine," Amanda said. "And Alicia knew this was your plan for New Belle?"

"I was upfront with her about my intentions. She didn't seem to care what I did with it, though. She said to give her some time, that she'd need to consider my offer."

To Amanda, it sounded like Alicia was undecided, but Rocco took her response to indicate he'd won the bidding. That belief, if genuine, would remove his motive, at least from the angle they were looking at things—one of the bidders exacting revenge on Alicia and then taking out the competition. But what if it was a more tangled web? What if Eve Kelley killed Alicia because of being stabbed in the back *again*, and then someone else killed Eve? That person could have used the same killing method so it would look like one person had murdered both women. Even if there was a copycat, it would need to be someone she and Trent had spoken to about the pentobarbital. "Have you heard of pentobarbital?"

Rocco nodded.

"What can you tell us about it?"

"I believe it's what vets use to put animals to sleep."

"That's right," she said. "And sometimes small doses are prescribed to people. You ever been prescribed any?"

"No."

"Alicia Gordon was poisoned with pentobarbital," Trent deadpanned.

Rocco tugged on the collar of his shirt, loosening his tie. "I had nothing to do with that."

"You seem to know about the drug," she volleyed back.

"I think most people would have heard of it."

"Did you know Eve Kelley?" Amanda decided it was time to change course.

He swallowed roughly. "More *of* her. Owner of Pixie Winks, right?"

"That's right. She died this morning. It's looking like she might have been poisoned the same way as Ms. Gordon. That information is strictly confidential—her family has not yet been informed." She momentarily thought of Malone's orders—why had he insisted they do things backward? It felt wrong talking to Lopez before Eve's family had been notified.

Rocco's eyes filled with tears.

She wasn't sure what to make of his reaction—guilt or empathy. "Mr. Lopez, do you know anything about that?"

"About who killed her and Alicia? No idea." He clamped his mouth shut and blinked slowly. "Do you think I'm in danger?"

"Why would you be?" The question was automatic, but as they'd discussed, one of the bidders could be perpetrator or potential victim. Dread was creeping over her skin.

He twitched like a shiver had laced down his spine. "Let me show you something." His hands were shaking as he opened the lid on his laptop, tapped a few keystrokes, then turned the screen to face her and Trent.

He was showing them an email, the body of which read, *Stay away from New Belle or you'll be sorry.*

The message was timestamped last Wednesday morning at eleven—the day after Alicia's murder and before it hit the news. Had the killer sent it, or was it a coincidence? And the author had obviously still considered New Belle at risk of being sold after Alicia's death, it would seem. "Is this the only threat you've received regarding New Belle?"

"First and last. But now you say Eve Kelley is dead?" He kept swallowing and pressing his lips together like he was going to vomit. "I told myself I shouldn't take the message seriously. Maybe I should?" His wet eyes petitioned Amanda.

Good question.

"Here, take the computer." He thrust it across the desk. "I trust you'll safeguard any confidential information on there, but I keep backups. I'll just get another laptop to work on."

"That won't be necessary." Amanda pulled her business card. "It was just the one email?"

"Yes."

"Forward it here." She pointed to her email address on the card. Rocco did just that, and Amanda confirmed receipt through the email app on her phone. "We'll do our best to track down the sender. In the meantime, I'll get some officers to watch over you."

"Thank you."

She and Trent left and loaded into the car.

Trent turned the ignition and said, "We need to look closer at the threats Alicia and Eve received."

"We do. I'm going to fire this email over to Detective Briggs in Digital Crimes and see if he can track the original sender's IP address. While I'm doing that, you take us to Acne Buster."

"You got it."

Amanda trusted that if anyone could get the job done, it was Briggs. He worked the night shift, but his expertise would be worth the wait. She just hoped his findings would lead them straight to a killer.

TWENTY

Amanda also made the call to Malone to request an officer watch over Rocco Lopez as Trent drove. She really didn't want to think about the possibility of additional victims and tried to push it from her mind. But it was still there when she and Trent were waiting in the reception area of Acne Buster. Given their theory, Dale Reynolds might be behind the murders, not in danger.

"He'll be down for you in one minute," the receptionist had told them.

That had been about ten minutes ago. With every passing second, she half-expected to be told he was dead. But she did her best to distract herself, take in the aesthetics of the lobby. Modestly decorated but with more luxury touches than the acquisition office of Rocco Lopez, which had none. The furniture was comfortable and rather new, though nothing fancy.

"Detectives?" It was the receptionist calling out to them.

Amanda went over to the desk with Trent at her side.

"Mr. Reynolds has asked that I direct you to Conference Room A. He'll meet you there shortly." The woman proceeded to give them directions, which Amanda and Trent followed carefully. The structure was a maze of corridors and chopped up into several small offices. Just a guess, but Amanda didn't think this was the manufacturing location for Acne Buster, but instead a headquarters for the administrative staff.

A man entered the room just as Amanda and Trent sat down at the meeting table. "I'm Dale Reynolds."

"Detectives Steele and Stenson. Please, take a seat." Amanda gestured to the chairs across from them.

Dale dropped into one. "All I know is you're here about New Belle...?" His brow was wrinkled in confusion, his eyes telling the same story.

"You may have heard by now that Alicia Gordon is dead?" Amanda said.

"I have. Very unfortunate. She was a great role model for young women."

Quite similar to what Harold Armstrong and Rocco Lopez had said. "That she was." While there might be some less favorable things they'd uncovered about Alicia, she had founded a cosmetics empire and hadn't let anyone tell her no along the way. "But Alicia Gordon didn't die of natural causes."

Dale's eyes widened as he slipped his gaze from her to Trent, then back. "She was murdered?" The question seemed to scratch from his throat, his voice husky.

Please don't tell us you were threatened too! "She was poisoned. Have you heard of pentobarbital?" Amanda preferred to temporarily, at least, peg him into the hole of killer.

"Quite sure that it's used in putting down dogs."

She nodded. It seemed a lot of people were familiar with that application, probably because they'd lost at least one beloved dog in their lifetime. "That's right, but it's also sometimes prescribed to humans to help with anxiety—small doses, short-term. Would you have access to the drug?" Amanda asked, searching his facial expression and body language for nonverbal answers. Both were saying nothing.

"Me?" Dale laid a splayed hand on his chest. "No, and what are you implying? That I had something to do with her death?"

"We're now investigating two deaths, Mr. Reynolds, and there are certain questions we need to ask," she told him.

"Two murders?"

"We'll get to that. You made an offer to buy New Belle from Ms. Gordon?"

"I did."

It seemed like every word coming from his mouth was forced and thoroughly considered first.

"A generous one, from what we've seen." Amanda hadn't actually seen the bid, but Dale didn't need to know that.

"I really wanted the company. It would have done a lot for us."

"Suppose that leads to the question of why Acne Buster would be interested in a cosmetics line," Trent interjected.

"We wanted to branch out, diversify, that's all."

"So acquiring New Belle would have meant a lot to you?" Trent asked.

"It would have certainly helped our bottom line, but if you're implying I did something to affect the way the bid fell...? I didn't hurt Ms. Gordon. And what reason would I have? With her dead, what happens to her company now anyway?" His focus was back on Amanda.

His genuine inquiry removed him from Amanda's suspicion, but she still had to roll through the questions. "I can't disclose that. When did you last see Alicia Gordon?"

"Two weeks ago, when I made my offer."

"And have you spoken with her since?" His number hadn't been in the list of those Alicia was in recent contact with, but they could have communicated on another phone or in person.

"No."

"Do you know Eve Kelley?" Trent asked, leaping there just ahead of Amanda.

"She owns Pixie Winks. Was she interested in New Belle too? Is that why you're asking about her?"

It would seem he hadn't been aware of the arrangement between Alicia and Eve. "She was, and she'd put in an offer."

"I'm sure Alicia had a lot of interested parties. She built an incredible business."

He certainly didn't sound like the jealous type who would manipulate events to his favor, let alone resort to murder. Still, she wanted to see his reaction. "This is confidential for now, but Eve Kelley is dead."

"Dead?" He undid the top two buttons of his collared shirt.

Amanda took note of his reaction. He was afraid of something, just like Rocco Lopez was. "What is it, Mr. Reynolds?" She didn't want to come out and ask if he'd been threatened just yet.

"I... well, I received a disturbing letter earlier this week." He cleared his throat. "I didn't think anything of it at the time, but maybe I shouldn't have just dismissed it."

"Do you still have it?" Trent asked.

Dale shook his head. "Honestly, I was pissed off and just sent it to the trash."

"It was a hard copy?" Amanda asked.

"No, an email. I deleted it, and my email program then permanently deletes everything when I exit out of it."

There went that lead, but they still had the email sent to Rocco Lopez. "What did it say? Do you remember?"

"I don't remember the exact words, but it was telling me if I didn't forget about buying New Belle, I'd be sorry. Do you think I have to worry? Why was Eve Kelley killed?"

"We're still investigating the matter and whether her

interest in New Belle was directly tied to her death, Mr. Reynolds," Amanda said, remaining calm, hoping it would help him do the same. "But it would probably be due diligence on your part to be vigilant to your surroundings, for your own safety."

"Well, I'd like to have the police watching out for me."

"We'll take care of it," Amanda said.

Dale tugged on the lapels of his suit jacket. "Thank you."

"You're very welcome." Amanda stood, and she and Trent left the building.

"Another bidder who was threatened, specifically with mention of New Belle," she began as they walked through the parking lot. "I think we can safely rule out both bidders as the killer."

"Agreed."

"At least we have the emailed threat to Lopez safely in the hands of Digital Crimes. Hopefully, that helps the case move forward."

"Amen to that."

"We've taken care of what Malone wanted. Guess it's time to notify Eve Kelley's next of kin."

They got into the car, and Trent looked up who that might be.

"Kelley was single, lived alone. Her closest living relative is her sister, who lives in Triangle," he said a few minutes later.

Triangle was a small community within Prince William County. It also happened to be where Zoe had lived with her parents when they were murdered. "Name?"

"Felicity Kelley. She never married either."

"Take us to her. Let's get this over with. Then we'll head back to Central and look at the threats sent to Alicia and Eve."

"You got it."

Trent drove while she made another call to have an officer

sent out to watch over Reynolds. She sure hoped Eve Kelley wasn't dead because she and Trent missed something earlier in the investigation. As it was, they still needed to speak with Bethany Wagner but with everything Malone had them doing first, Beth would have to wait.

TWENTY-ONE

Felicity Kelley was in her late twenties and nothing like her sister by appearance. She was ordinary, more plain Jane. She had long, light-brown hair which she had pulled back into a ponytail. Loose strands fell to her neck and curled around her ears, giving her an elfin look.

Amanda and Trent were standing across from Felicity in the woman's living room—a hectic space with books and papers everywhere in huge stacks. One was over a foot high.

Felicity fussed about trying to clear a seat for them, but Amanda assured her they were fine.

"Please, take a seat," Amanda said gently. She didn't like to stand when delivering notifications in case it came across as intimidating.

"Ah, sure." Felicity looked around and dropped into the only chair that didn't have debris on it. "Sorry about the mess. I wasn't expecting company." She swept a hand over her hair, maybe a self-conscious move to tame the frizz, and let out a deep breath. "I'm just crunching against a deadline, and I fear I'm not going to make it."

"Deadline?" Trent asked.

"Yes. I'm a writer. Mystery." An awkward smile, as if Felicity were far more comfortable with her characters and the worlds she created than existing in reality. "Hey, you two wouldn't mind helping me if I have police procedural-type questions, would you?"

"Not at all." Amanda smiled kindly, wishing she was in this woman's living room for any other reason than the true one. She looked around for a place to sit again. *Guess I'm doing this standing...* "Ms. Kelley, we have bad news about your sister, Eve. I'm sorry to say that she died this morning—"

"She what... she *what* now?" Felicity's eyes widened and filled with tears.

"Eve died this morning in her office at Pixie Winks." Amanda wished she could add that Eve hadn't suffered at all.

"How?" Felicity rubbed her throat, the skin there growing blotchy with every swipe of her hand.

"We need to wait until an autopsy has been conducted to know for sure," Amanda said. "But there are circumstances that lead us to believe her death is suspicious."

Silence enveloped the room as Felicity sat there staring at them, her mouth opening and closing like a fish drawing in breath.

"We appreciate how shocking this must be," Amanda said.

"No." Felicity met her gaze and shook her head. "It's not... well, it is but... You say 'suspicious.' I am quite certain someone killed her." Stated with authority, unwavering conviction.

Amanda glanced at Trent, her brow furrowed. Back to Felicity. "Why would you think that, Ms. Kelley?"

"She... ah..." Tears pooled in her eyes, and she fell quiet for a second or two. "She was sure that she was being watched, followed."

"She told you this?" Trent asked.

Felicity nodded, though it was barely perceivable. "We were close. There's a bit of an age difference between us. Eleven years, but it never seemed to matter. She told me I was an old soul." The hint of a smile toyed on the edges of her mouth, the expression likely squashed by heartache.

Amanda felt for the woman, but her mind was stuck on the fact that Eve had thought someone was following her. Why hadn't she mentioned that to her and Trent when they spoke to her, when they'd asked about threats against her? Had it been pride, fear of being seen as paranoid? "How long did she feel that she was being watched?" Amanda asked.

"Just in the last week, say."

After Alicia's death. Was the person who had drugged her still picking off victims from some sort of macabre checklist? They already knew that Lopez and Reynolds had been threatened, but did they feel watched as well? "She ever find out who it was?"

Felicity shook her head.

Trent shifted his weight. "Where was she when she felt like someone was watching her?"

"Everywhere. At work, home, when she was out."

"Did she ever say why she thought this?" Amanda was trying to read the woman's micro expressions, the ones that would disclose underlying emotional responses, but as of yet had witnessed none.

"She had made an offer to buy New Belle, which you probably know?" Felicity paused there, but continued after Amanda and Trent confirmed they did. "She was starting to think that maybe it wasn't a good idea."

"We spoke with your sister, and she never mentioned any of this to us," Amanda said, knowing it was possible, as she'd thought a second ago, that the sensation had started after their conversation last week. But why not say something this morning?

"My sister was a very proud person, and she lived her life concerned about what other people thought of her. She wouldn't have said any of this to you in case she'd be perceived as crazy."

"We would have taken her seriously." Amanda was certain they would have. After all, when they had spoken to Eve the first time, it was just after Alicia Gordon had died suspiciously. This last week, if she'd brought up the feeling of being watched, would they have taken her at her word? Or would they have viewed it as a ploy to deflect how guilty she looked?

"Did she ever catch sight of a strange car in the neighborhood, anything like that?" Trent must have felt like Amanda—that they needed more to go on than just Eve's feeling she was being watched. But the fact that she was now dead did lend credit to her thinking.

"Not that she told me. She described it more as eyes lurking in the shadows. When she looked, no one was ever there."

Amanda could only imagine how intimidating and violating that would feel. "Do you know of anyone who might have wanted to harm your sister?"

"No one specific comes to mind."

"We're very sorry for your loss." Amanda bridged the gap between her and Felicity and gave the woman her card. "Is there anyone we can call for you?"

Felicity shook her head and sniffled. "I'll muddle through."

"All right. If you think of anything else, don't hesitate to reach out. Or if you have questions about procedure for your books." Amanda pointed toward her card in Felicity's hand. "We can have someone from Victim Services come see you too."

"Thanks."

Amanda and Trent left. Her steps were heavy, laden with fear and regret. If only Eve had mentioned something to them, perhaps she and Trent could have prevented her death. Was there a clue sitting back at the station among Eve's hate mail?

Trent looked over at her once they were back in the car.

"Not liking the sound of that... Eve feeling watched," he said.

"Nope. It would be nice if we had somewhere to go from here, though. A description of the person, even if Eve had only gotten a glimpse of them. Or a vehicle, as you asked about."

"It could go a long way. Felicity said Eve felt followed everywhere. We need to retrace her steps, find out her routine, see if we can get anywhere that way."

"Yes, and another idea—let's go speak with her neighbors and see if any of them noticed a strange vehicle or person hanging around."

Trent put the car into gear, and they proceeded to do just that for the next couple of hours.

Their efforts resulted in nothing.

Next, they called Rocco Lopez and Dale Reynolds. Rocco felt watched but Dale didn't.

Trent was now driving them back to Central, and they were no further ahead on the case. Not really. Sure, Eve had felt watched, but who had been lurking in the shadows and would they be reemerging any time soon to claim another victim?

TWENTY-TWO

Tuesday morning, and they were off to Manassas for findings on another autopsy, two weeks in a row. Two businesswomen dead —one confirmed murder and the other likely headed in the same direction. It would surprise Amanda more if Eve Kelley *hadn't* been drugged with pentobarbital. Not that she expected to have confirmation today. There would be another toxicology report they'd need to wait on. But the circumstances surrounding Eve's death and the symptoms she exhibited just before didn't give Amanda much hope that manner of death was natural.

Amanda and Trent found Rideout in his usual spot, next to a gurney burdened with a cadaver. Eve Kelley's torso was already wide open.

Rideout greeted them with a smile and "Good morning." An exuberance only he could pull off in the face of death.

"Hello," Amanda said, not being able to bring herself to say *good morning* today. What was with all the murder in Prince William County these days? The stats had to be getting worse.

"There are obviously some questions we can take off the

table straight away," Rideout began. "TOD we know was yesterday at approximately nine AM. Cause of death was the same as Alicia Gordon. Cardiogenic shock, followed by respiratory arrest. Now, whether it was aided along by medication or poisoning, again, we'll need to wait on the toxicology report to know for sure. Which, of course, I will be requesting the moment I've finished the autopsy."

"Did you happen to hear from the investigators as to whether her coffee was laced with pentobarbital?" Amanda asked.

Rideout shook his head. "No."

"No? As in you didn't hear, or no, it wasn't tampered with?"

"No pentobarbital in the coffee, but I found this." Rideout pushed a gloved fingertip to the meat of Eve's upper arm. "See that?"

Amanda leaned in. A pinprick. "She was jabbed with a syringe?"

"Yep, I'd say so."

"So if we're looking at pentobarbital again, someone injected her with it," Amanda said.

"Yes."

"Could we assume that Eve Kelley was injected with the drug sometime between her arrival at work and seeing us?" Trent raised his eyebrows at Rideout.

"I'd suspect so, and the reaction would have been fairly swift. It wouldn't have taken the drug long to enter her circulatory system, and that would speed up the metabolizing process. I'd still say we'd be looking at ten minutes, give or take, from the time she was injected. Possibly a little longer, up to twenty minutes. But I don't see it being longer than that."

"Whoever injected her wanted her to die quickly. They didn't want Eve Kelley's death to take days," Trent said. "Our killer is getting impatient."

Amanda turned to Trent. "She could have been injected right at Pixie Winks. We've got to go." She turned to leave but swung back around to ask a quick question. "Were there any signs of struggle or defense?"

"None, but I scraped under her fingernails and will send that to the lab for testing."

"Okay, is there anything else we should know right now?" she asked.

Rideout shook his head. "I'll call if anything comes up."

"Thank you." Amanda was already hustling from the morgue. She spoke to Trent over a shoulder as they went to the department car. "We need to piece together her last minutes—track every single movement."

Trent slid behind the wheel and got them on the road to Woodbridge.

It was noon by the time Amanda and Trent were walking into the lobby of Pixie Winks. A somber and dark energetic residue permeated the place. Death. The presence of a PWCPD officer in the lobby watching everyone who came in probably didn't help dispel the solemn tone. The officer nodded at Amanda and Trent in greeting, which they returned, on their way to the reception desk.

Amanda drew her badge, but the young woman there waved a hand, dismissing her.

"I remember you." Her eyes were wide, and her lashes were wet. "What can I do for you?"

Amanda put her badge away. "Do you always manage the front counter?"

"I do."

"And your name?"

"Jasmine."

"Jasmine, did anyone come to visit Eve Kelley yesterday morning?" It made sense to start at the doors and work their way upstairs.

Jasmine was quick to shake her head. "No one. Well, besides you two."

"Did she receive any deliveries? Maybe a package that a delivery person insisted on handing over in person?"

"No." Jasmine slid her bottom lip through her teeth.

"All right, thank you. We both appreciate your help. Could you get Eve Kelley's assistant for us? Her name's Joanne...?"

"Yes. Joanne Thomson. One minute." Jasmine tapped a finger to an earpiece, and a few seconds later, tapped it again. "You can go up to her office. It's just across the hall from Ms. Kelley's."

Amanda thanked Jasmine for her help, even though she already knew where to go. They'd gone to Joanne's office to collect the threats against Eve. She would likely be the most familiar with her boss's agenda. And there was another benefit —with Joanne's office being across from Eve's, Joanne would likely know if anyone had visited her boss yesterday morning. In fact, Joanne should know a lot about Eve. Including when and how to poison her? But then, what was the motive? And the link to Alicia Gordon? Amanda shook her thoughts aside. She was seeing killers everywhere now.

Eve Kelley's office door was closed, and Amanda and Trent slipped into Joanne's office.

She was at her desk, talking on the phone. "I can take a message for her... Yes... Okay." Joanne's eyes shot up to them in the doorway. Her eyes pooled with tears, and she looked away.

Amanda stepped back into the hall, giving the young woman some space, Trent too. Joanne sounded like she was barely holding herself together, and *take a message?*

"Detectives?"

Amanda turned. Joanne was standing in the doorway of her office, her arms wrapped around herself.

"My partner and I have some questions for you," Amanda said.

They went into the small office and sat across from Joanne.

"Just let me route the line to voicemail." She pushed a button on the phone.

"These are calls for Ms. Kelley?" Trent asked, and Joanne nodded. "I'm surprised they weren't already going to voicemail."

"Bob"—Joanne sniffled—"that's the general manager here, is adamant about my answering every call until her death is made public. But I'm sure with you two here..." Her brow pinched. "Hopefully, he doesn't get upset about it."

"I'm sure he'll understand." That's what Amanda said, though it was a grand assumption as she didn't even know the man. He could have been a tyrant for all she knew. Asking that Joanne answer every call the day after her boss died told her Bob was, in the least, insensitive.

The phone rang once, and Joanne flinched. The call switched over.

"We're sorry for your loss," Amanda offered the sentiment, meaning it deeply, and feeling like she had to compensate for a boss who was clueless. She and Trent would speak to Bob next.

Joanne hiccupped a sob. "Thank you. I still can't believe it happened, ya know? I keep thinking it was a bad dream and that I'll wake up and she'll still be alive. What happened to her anyway? She was here and then she wasn't." Her bottom lip quivered, and she bit down on it. She was doing her best to bury her feelings, it seemed, but she really wasn't in any shape to be at work.

"We're still trying to figure everything out," Amanda started. "You must have gotten along quite well with Ms. Kelley."

"She was my boss, and she always kept that line there, but sometimes she'd let me past it and I'd see the real her."

Trent angled his head. "And what did that look like?"

Joanne flashed a brief smile. "She could be a very nice person, and I admired her for being such a strong, independent woman. She got to where she was by being respectful to others. She didn't sacrifice her values or trample over people to get there."

The woman had set Eve on a pedestal, but Amanda got the feeling the last part was a dig at Alicia. "Eve sounds like she was admirable."

"She was my mentor, truth be told. I don't know what I'm going to do without her." Joanne's eyes glazed over.

"We're quite sure you can help us, Joanne. We need to trace her movements yesterday morning. Can you help us with that?"

"I'll try."

The phone rang, and again Joanne flinched.

"Is there any way for you to turn the ringer completely off?" Amanda felt for the girl.

"Yeah, maybe I will." Joanne pressed on the side of the phone. There must have been a volume toggle there. "Done. It shouldn't interrupt us again." Joanne's shoulders relaxed.

Amanda offered a gentle smile. "Let's start with a simple question. What time did Eve arrive yesterday morning?"

"She always gets into her office by nine."

She and Trent had been walking into Eve's office just minutes after that.

"Like clockwork?" Trent had his pen poised over his notepad.

"Yes. She was a very punctual person. She wouldn't tolerate tardiness. Her assistant before me was five minutes late three times, and Ms. Kelley cut her loose."

Amanda didn't know what to make of that but was happy that she didn't report to such a boss. "I noticed she had a coffee from Caffeine Café on her desk. Did she normally pick one up from there every day?"

"Yep. On the way in. Ms. Kelley had her routines."

That trait would make it easy for a person stalking her—possibly her killer. "Did she have any visitors before us yesterday morning?" It wouldn't seem likely if she'd arrived just minutes before her and Trent. Also that person would need to bypass the front desk, but they could be looking at a Pixie Winks employee.

Joanne shook her head. "You were the first of the day."

"So no one in the office stopped by either—even for a minute or two?" Amanda asked.

Joanne seemed to give that question some thought. "Not that I recall."

"Okay." Amanda was racking her mind. Could someone have injected Eve in the washroom or on the elevator? In the parking lot? But means and opportunity were always linked closely to motive. So who here could check all three boxes? Someone opposed to Pixie Winks absorbing New Belle under its corporate umbrella? "Did you know that Eve Kelley was planning to expand the business?"

"She never told me, but I had that feeling."

"Why is that?" Trent asked.

"Just things I overheard. Alicia Gordon called here for her recently." The way the name came off her lips revealed disdain.

Amanda sat up straighter. "You have something against Alicia Gordon?"

"Yes, no, not really... I don't know. I just know that whenever Eve spoke to her, she was in a foul mood afterward. But it wasn't like she was angry, just that her confidence had taken a hit."

Amanda noted the switch in how Joanne referenced her dead boss by first name now. Joanne seemed to be relaxing—the lack of a ringing phone probably helped. "Alicia intimidated her?"

"I guess you could say that."

Speaking of intimidation, there was the hate mail. "You supplied us with the written threats addressed to your boss, but did anyone ever call to threaten her, that you were aware of?"

"Just the emails and letters I gave you."

"One more thing before we go, did Ms. Kelley ever mention feeling watched or followed?" Amanda asked.

Joanne chewed her lip. "Not that she told me, but she has been jumpy for about a week."

Around the same time Eve had told her sister she felt watched. "Thank you for your time, Ms. Thomson." Amanda stood and gave Joanne her card. "Call me if you think of anything that might help our investigation."

"I will, but I don't expect there will be anything else. I've told you everything."

Amanda nodded, and she and Trent left the office. Once down the hall and out of earshot, he turned to her.

"So if no one visited Eve Kelley in her office, then somewhere in the building just before?"

"Must have been, considering how fast pentobarbital poisoning can cause a reaction, according to Rideout. It's time to talk to Bob, the manager, and find out if there are any surveillance cameras outside or inside the building." They got onto the elevator, and she added, "Someone she shared a ride with on here could have jabbed her."

"Pleasant thought. Or in the restroom."

"Yeah, I considered that too." Every time she thought of Eve getting poked with a needle, Amanda was certain she would have had reacted. A wince. A cry. A swat. Someone could have noticed that—assuming other people were around at the time. Also, Eve herself could have confronted the person, and that could have been witnessed. Then again, if Eve's mind was distracted with personal or business matters, it could be understood why she might not have. But if she was afraid that someone was following her, why had she allowed a stranger to get close?

They returned to the main reception desk and asked Jasmine to get the manager for them.

"All we have is his first name Bob," Amanda said.

"Bob Field. One moment."

A few minutes later, they were being told to take the elevator to the fourth floor—two below Eve's—and Bob's office was the third on the left.

The door was open, and an overweight man sat perched behind a desk, his belly pressed against the edge. "I'm not sure how I can help you with your investigation, Detectives."

It didn't sit with Amanda that he had immediately hedged them off. "Why do you say that?"

"I wasn't even in when this happened. I was off premises in a business meeting with a local pharmacy executive, trying to get Pixie Winks products into all their stores across the state."

He comes prepared with an alibi. That told Amanda all she really needed to know about his relationship with Eve Kelley, but she'd ask anyway. "Did you and Ms. Kelley get along?"

He did a double-take that had the extra weight on his chin jiggling with the movement. "Why ask something like that?"

"It's just a harmless question."

"Not exactly harmless, though, is it? I mean if someone killed her."

"We never mentioned murder," she served back.

He pressed his lips together and angled his head. "Wasn't born yesterday."

"Meaning?"

"You're both looking for someone to arrest for what

happened to her. Just don't look at me." He waved both his hands in front of himself.

"We weren't," she said. "But this is an open investigation, and your cooperation could help us."

"So she *was* murdered?"

"Yes, it appears so." She let out the admission on a sigh. *This stubborn man!*

"Wow." Bob sat back, clasping his hands over his expansive stomach.

"Yes, *wow*," she mimicked. "We're trying to figure out who might have done this and why. We think it might in some way be connected to Eve Kelley's interest in acquiring New Belle. Did you know about that?"

"Ha," Bob scoffed. "That never would have happened. But, yes, I was aware of her interest. I was also aware Alicia Gordon stole the serum that Eve had actually created, and then Alicia proceeded to build her company on a lie. I mean, why would Eve want anything to do with that woman or her brand?"

"New Belle could be seen as not just a company, but a cosmetics *empire*," Trent pointed out.

"Sure. Whatever you want to say. All I know is what Eve planned to do, or didn't, doesn't really concern me."

This guy just rubbed Amanda wrong. Of course, the fact that he was making Joanne field Eve's calls didn't help her impression of him from the get-go. "Have you heard of the drug pentobarbital?"

"Yeah. Wish I didn't. Just had my retriever put down last week."

Dogs were family, but he seemed more upset about his canine passing than he was Eve's death. "Sorry to hear that, Mr. Field. Do you have any access to that drug?"

"No." Bob scrunched up his face. "Why ever would I? Wait —is that what killed her?"

"It's looking that way," she said.

Bob rubbed his forehead, dropped his hand. "I don't know what to say to that."

"What are your feelings toward Alicia Gordon?" she asked, though his earlier tirade made it clear.

"She was a businesswoman. A touch ruthless. I'm behind Eve—or I *was* behind Eve—for filing the lawsuit against New Belle on Friday. Now, that was a wise decision."

"Then you're aware Alicia Gordon is dead as well?" Trent asked.

"Ah... yeah." Bob put it out there almost like he was unsure how he should answer.

"Alicia Gordon was also killed with pentobarbital," Amanda said. "Seems like more than a coincidence. Do you know of anyone who might have wanted both women dead?" *And possibly two other bidders on New Belle?*

Bob, for the first time since they'd entered his office, was speechless.

"Mr. Field," she prompted.

"No, I have no idea. I mean, I can see how Alicia Gordon would have her enemies, especially if she ripped off others the way she had Eve. What would make that person also want to kill Eve? I don't know."

If she ripped off others... Yet another angle to explore, though the investigation hadn't yet led them there. And how would that serve as motive to murder Eve Kelley? Were they making a mistake to assume that both women had the same killer? But she dismissed that as fast as the thought struck. They couldn't ignore that the other bidders had received threats, or the unique killing method that was utilized.

"Eve Kelley received various threats," Trent put out there.

"Oh, I'm sure she did. A person doesn't get to the top of the mountain without them."

"Anyone specific come to mind?" Amanda asked.

Bob shook his head. "No one that jumps out at me, at this moment."

She might as well have been hitting her head against the wall with this investigation. All the cracks and fissures, the misdirection, the lies, the omissions. Tony Bishop. They still hadn't been back to him since learning of the nanny or the fact that he'd held back about Alicia's tumultuous relationship with her ex. *But we're building a case...* Though right now she was quite near her breaking point. They'd spoken to the two people in the building that would have known the most about Eve Kelley's movements, and they were nowhere. Now she was thinking about elevators, stairwells, hallways. If only there was a way to watch Eve's every step. "Does Pixie Winks have any security cameras set up—either inside the building, in the parking lot, both?"

"We do."

Finally, a possible break! "We'll need to take a look at the footage from yesterday morning, from the time Ms. Kelley arrived at the office until we did."

"Sure. Just need a warrant for that."

"We're trying to find out who killed your boss. I'd have thought you'd be a little more cooperative. No?" Amanda angled her head. "I mean we can get a warrant, but that takes time. We might be more inclined to have a closer look at you and others within this company too."

Bob stiffened and jutted out his chin. "I can assure you that no one here killed Eve. What reason would anyone have?"

"A moment ago, you made a point to mention the number of enemies she'd built up. I'd assume some of them would be from right inside Pixie Winks." Amanda watched as her words sank in.

"Fine. I'll make the video accessible to you immediately."

The absence of a denial was unsettling. Nonetheless, Amanda said, "The PWCPD appreciates your kind cooperation in a murder investigation." She mentioned the department name and the word *murder* to stamp home just how urgent the matter was.

"Come with me, and I'll take you to the security office now."

"Lead the way." Amanda waited for Bob to heave himself out of his chair, and she and Trent followed.

TWENTY-THREE

A man in his fifties smiled broadly at Amanda and Trent when they entered the security office, a nine-by-nine, windowless cell. His only glimpses of the outside world were through the six monitors projecting live feeds of the parking lot, front reception, two angles of the warehouse, the back loading dock, and the rear of the building. The extent of coverage was a good sign they might see something to aid the investigation.

Bob stayed long enough to introduce them to the security guy, Mitch Baldwin, and told him to let Amanda and Trent see whatever they wanted and take a copy of what they deemed fit.

"He's never usually that easygoing," Mitch said after Bob left.

"He wants to know who killed Eve Kelley." But Amanda suspected it had more to do with protecting his own ass—not that they had solid reason to suspect him of Eve's murder. She'd bet he was hiding something, though.

"Killed?" Mitch's eyes widened, and he shook his head. "Can't believe someone intentionally did this. She was too young to go. Nice woman too."

"Did you know her well?" Amanda sensed he might, given

his summation. Tony had told them Alicia Gordon made a point to meet all new employees at New Belle's head office. Had Eve Kelley been much the same way?

"Not well, I wouldn't say, but she was always friendly enough when we bumped into each other. She'd always wish me a good morning and ask how I was. So whatever I can do to help."

"Thanks." Amanda smiled. "We need to see whatever footage you have of Eve Kelley from the time she arrived yesterday. As much coverage as possible. Her parking, coming into the building, making her way to her office, going inside." Technically, they only needed Eve's last ten to twenty minutes if the pentobarbital acted as fast as Rideout had told them, but Amanda wanted a feel for what her morning had looked like leading up to that point.

"Ah, sure." Mitch clicked here, clicked there. "I'll see what I can do."

"Do you know when Ms. Kelley arrived?"

Mitch paused his clicking to say, "Ms. Kelley was always in at eight, on the mark."

An hour before she died. What Mitch was telling them also didn't reconcile with what Joanne had told them. "We were told she's at her desk by nine."

"Joanne, I'm assuming?"

Amanda nodded.

"That girl's good at her job and was always attentive to Ms. Kelley's needs. And, yeah, that sounds right. Eve shows up at eight, takes a stroll through the warehouse, drops in on the chemists, has a five-minute meeting with the production supervisor, and takes a walk around the shipping docks. Then she goes upstairs. Like clockwork."

Had Joanne left this routine out intentionally, or did she not know about it? After all, Eve Kelley didn't need to run her every step past her assistant. "All right, show us what you have."

"Look here." Mitch pointed to a screen right in front of him as it lit up. "First up, her arrival." He hit play. "That's Ms. Kelley's BMW." He pointed out the timestamp. "See?" Mitch said with a smile. "Eight AM sharp. Now I'll patch all the feeds together as seamlessly as I can..." The promise was fulfilled when the next segment showed Eve entering the lobby.

On screen, transitions continued to happen as Eve Kelley made her way through the building and into the back warehouse. She smiled and waved at every employee she encountered. Shortly after, she entered a room.

"She's going in to talk to the chemists now."

"They're in early," Trent said.

"Yes sirree, but that's where the magic happens. Magic doesn't sleep. They're in at seven in the morning, leave at three. It's also where a lot of top-secret stuff goes on. I know Bob said to show you whatever you want to see, but I'd feel more comfortable if we skipped that—unless you have a warrant and sign some confidentiality paperwork."

"It's fine, for now." Amanda wasn't concerned because of the timeframe. If someone had poked Eve with a needle in the lab, she never would have made it upstairs.

"But Ms. Kelley visited them every morning?" Trent asked, sounding skeptical.

"Yes, every single workday." The man was smiling, as if proud of his late boss.

Amanda was impressed by the woman's dedication to her business. "Please continue."

Video resumed playing. Eve was in the warehouse shaking hands with a man. His hair was jet black and slicked back. "Who is that?" she asked.

"Gary Adkins. He's the production manager. He and Ms. Kelley would sit for five minutes precisely, and then she would go to the shipping docks and make her way upstairs to her office."

The video played out true to the security guard's narrative. Eve stepped into an office—a room without a camera—and left five minutes later. She did a stroll around the loading dock and went out of sight when she walked behind a truck. She emerged, rubbing her upper arm. The same one that had been poked.

"Stop right there. Back up!" Amanda directed Mitch.

He did as she'd asked, but watching it again revealed nothing new.

"Do you happen to have another angle on this?" she asked.

"Not that will help."

"Show it to us anyway."

Mitch loaded another feed. It was an eagle-eye view but didn't cover behind the truck—where they needed to see.

"All right, go back to the other. Please play it again from the point she goes behind the truck until she reemerges."

Mitch's lips pinched. "You saw something..." He played it again and let the footage go on a little longer. Eve Kelley came out on the right. A few moments later, a person stepped into view on the left.

"Stop!"

Mitch did—immediately.

"Who is that person?" She was pointing at the mystery figure, dark and shadowed under the overhang of the bay. "Is there any way to enhance this?"

"I can some." He proceeded to do that, but it didn't do much for cleaning up the resolution. At quick glance, it was impossible to tell if the person was a man or woman; their back was to the camera. But they wore a white ball cap, and strands of dark hair poked out from under it. Given the length, the person's broad shoulders and narrow hips, Amanda was leaning more toward the mystery figure being male.

"I want to see if we can follow that person's steps from this point on. Can you help with that?" she asked.

"I'll do my best."

Amanda turned to Trent. "You did see what I did?"

"Yep."

To Amanda, it seemed so clear. Eve Kelley had been injected with pentobarbital when out of sight of the cameras, by an unidentified person headed in the opposite direction. The timing was right. 8:55 *AM*. The person must have pulled it off without even alerting Eve, as she hadn't reacted beyond rubbing her arm. "Is that person an employee here? Do you recognize them at all? Their stature, the way they walk...?"

Mitch scratched his head and blew out a breath. "It's hard to say."

"To be in that area, do people need to sign in or have clearance?" Trent asked.

The security guard blanched. "It's probably one of the weakest areas for security. It's where our shipping and receiving offices are. Couriers are in and out all day."

She'd think that would make it more imperative to up the security measures. After all, it didn't even seem like there was much distance between there and the lab. "We're going to need a copy of the footage we just watched. Can you stitch it all together in one video?"

"Of course."

"Also, trace that person's steps, please. If you get any shot of their face, we'll want it. We'll be back in a few minutes to see how you made out."

She and Trent returned to the front desk and requested a meeting with the shipping and receiving manager. She was determined to get to the bottom of what had happened to Eve Kelley, even if she had to speak with every employee in this building.

TWENTY-FOUR

Amanda and Trent were taken to the warehouse, where they were introduced to Ralph Newman, who managed Shipping and Receiving.

"I understand you're here about what happened to Eve Kelley."

"We are," Amanda said. He was larger than the figure from the video, broader shoulders, thicker neck. But he didn't strike her as too affected by Eve's death. Then again, maybe he was striving to keep this meeting professional and leave emotion out of it.

"Please, sit." Ralph cleared two chairs that had been stacked with papers. "There you go."

Amanda and Trent sat down.

"We understand that Eve Kelley made a habit of touring the warehouse every morning," Amanda said.

"Yes, that's right."

"She met with the production manager. Did she meet with you?" Mitch from security hadn't mentioned a morning meeting between the two, but she thought she'd ask anyway.

"No, we didn't speak much. If she had questions about

anything to do with shipping, she took them up with production. It was Gary's head that would roll. Honestly, I was happy for the buffer."

"Did Eve have a temper?" Trent asked.

"She could if things didn't work out the way she thought they should."

There would be no faulting the woman for that. "Eve Kelley didn't meet with you, but did she make it a routine to walk through the loading docks?" She was just trying to gauge what Ralph knew about Eve's movements.

"She did. Not sure what she was really looking for and never asked. She was the boss."

"Did you see her there yesterday morning?"

"Uh-huh."

Every one of Ralph's responses lined up with what they knew. "Do you have an employee with broad shoulders, narrow hips, short dark hair, who might like to wear a ball cap?"

"You mean one of these?" He pulled a white ball cap with the Pixie Winks logo from his desk drawer. "Everyone does when they're on the floor."

Was the mystery figure an employee or an imposter who'd snuck on premises and knew about the hats? "What about the rest of my description?"

"It doesn't sound like any of my guys. Most of 'em are a little heavier set."

"Could it have been a courier dropping something off?" Trent asked.

"Could have been."

She would have liked a more definitive response. "Does the description I just gave you fit any of the regular delivery people? I'm assuming you usually have the same ones who show up."

"We do, but the description you're giving isn't lining up. And they wouldn't be wearing a Pixie Winks hat."

That still wasn't the answer Amanda wanted to hear. The

pixelated image of that mystery figure was clear in her head and the proportions could fit Tony Bishop. But then, wouldn't Eve have reacted to him being in her building? He could have obscured his face from her, though, or have been wearing a disguise. She swallowed roughly, nerves making her tremble, but she pressed her lips into a tight smile. "Okay. Thank you for your time." Amanda handed Ralph her business card, and she and Trent returned to the security office.

They found Mitch perched on the edge of his chair, tapping on the desk. "It will just be another sec— Oh, there we go." He popped a USB data stick from his computer and paired it with a printout. "Got their face, but it's shadowed and very hard to make out. I put the JPEG on the USB drive too."

Amanda and Trent looked at the printed photo, and Mitch was right. The mystery figure might as well be a dark glob. "Did you see where they went or had come from?"

Mitch's lips twitched, and he slowly shook his head. "It's like they just appeared, then vanished."

She thanked the security guy for his help, and she and Trent left his office.

"We'll get this photo to Detective Briggs in Digital Crimes. See if he has any luck cleaning up the image," she said.

"And then what?"

"No one here seems to recognize the mystery person. And Eve Kelley felt like someone was watching her. Whoever injected her with pentobarbital knew her morning routine, probably even familiarized themselves with camera placement. They knew how to reach her without being seen."

"Also, how to get in and out. What do you propose for our next stop?"

"Eve grabbed a coffee at Caffeine Café every morning. We go there, ask around and see if anyone saw this person." She was being rather optimistic, given the resolution of the photo, but hopefully they'd get lucky.

TWENTY-FIVE

Sometimes with this case, Amanda felt like they were spinning their wheels, but surely, they had to be getting closer to a resolution. They had the killer on camera—she was sure of it. But it wasn't enough.

"So this person got to the shipping docks without being seen and left the same way." She shook her head, glanced out the passenger window as Trent drove them to the coffee shop. "Even when people have security cameras that work, it doesn't get us anywhere." She was beyond frustrated.

"We got somewhere." Trent pointed at the photo in her hand. "We're going to find that person."

"The killer. I feel it in my bones. Eve's reaction and the timing line up."

Trent breezed through a yellow to red and pulled into the Caffeine Café parking lot.

"I agree, and for a place with all those security cameras, they sure are weak in the shipping and receiving department."

"Right. Something else the killer must have known about. A former delivery driver or..." She shook her head. "What motive?" She realized as she asked the question there could be so many—and ones they hadn't even yet considered. One they might not even discover until they cuffed the killer.

They got out of the car and went inside. Trent got the door for her, and she noticed a sticker on the glass advertising free Wi-Fi for customers as she passed through.

It was three in the afternoon, and the place was rather empty, though Amanda imagined in the morning during the week, the line went to the door. It wasn't Amanda's type of coffee shop. If she was going somewhere other than Hannah's Diner, she preferred places that served good old-fashioned American coffee. Black. Nothing fancy like this place that offered the gamut—espressos, lattes, cappuccinos, macchiatos, and the list likely went on and on. Considering the crowd they drew, maybe coming here was more of a shot in the dark than she'd first imagined. Even if the mystery person had followed Eve here, would they have been noticed? Would they have even come inside? They could have remained in the parking lot.

Security cameras may be her and Trent's only hope here too.

Amanda stepped up to the counter, her gaze roving the ceiling in search of a camera. She spotted one and pointed it out to Trent, then held up her badge to the clerk, a thirtysomething with black hair and long bangs that poked into her eyelashes. A nameplate pinned to her shirt told them her name was Carla. "Detective Steele, Prince William County PD. I need to speak with the manager."

"That's me."

"We need to talk to you for a moment... if there's somewhere more private?" While the place wasn't packed, there were still people coming in and hanging around.

"Sure. Denise," Carla called out to a woman who was working a fancy coffee machine. "You'll need to handle things for a few minutes."

Denise acknowledged Carla with a wave.

The manager led them to an office in the back. She sat at the desk, but Amanda and Trent remained standing.

"I can't be long," Carla said. "It's just me and Denise today."

"Does this person look familiar?" Amanda extended the printout of the mystery figure.

Carla took the photo and studied it. "There's no face."

"Just look at the shape of the body, height, stature, clothing. Any of it look familiar?"

Carla stared at her blankly, gave the picture back to Amanda. "You do realize how many people come in here in a day?"

"All right, let's try something else. You know Eve Kelley?"

"Of course. An extra-large one-shot red eye, no sugar."

"And that is...?" Amanda just stuck with black coffee.

"It's drip coffee, black, with a shot of espresso. She also liked to add a sprinkle of cocoa."

"Does she ever come in here with anyone?" Trent asked.

"No."

"You ever see anyone tailing her?" Amanda countered.

"Ah, no. What's going on?"

"Eve Kelley is dead." Amanda felt fine with disclosing this, as it would be hitting the news today, if it already hadn't.

"Oh." Carla rubbed her forehead.

"Did you know her... besides her coffee order?" Amanda asked.

"Not really. Just that she owned Pixie Winks."

Amanda nodded, not seeing any other emotion in the woman but empathy for what had befallen a fellow human being. "Does that security camera in the coffee shop work? You have any more out front?"

"It does, and we do. But I'm not sure I can just hand over the footage."

"Would you need to contact the owner to allow us to take a

look?" Amanda was doing her best to balance push with diplomacy.

"I would. And he'd probably want a warrant."

"Even though one of his customers was murdered?"

Carla rolled her eyes and huffed out a breath. "Something you should know about my boss. He's a douche. He's going to assume you're trying to pin Eve's death on the coffee shop." She paused, met Amanda's gaze. "Are you?"

"Not at all."

"Well, I can call him and see what he says." Her gaze dipped to the phone on the desk.

Amanda smiled. "We'll be happy to wait."

Carla licked her lips and picked up the receiver. A second later, she was speaking to the owner. A few seconds after that, she was hanging up. "Yep. Just as I thought, he wants a warrant."

"We'll get him one." Amanda led the way outside, Trent on her heels.

Amanda wasn't going to run the request past Malone. She got on the phone with Judge Anderson, who was known to be quite accommodating and flexible with approving verbal warrants. She ran through what she needed with him in the seclusion of the department vehicle.

"Sorry, Amanda, but I'm not hearing enough to substantiate this request," Anderson said, not standing on formality. "If you had proof that the person you suspect of poisoning Eve Kelley was with her at the coffee shop, that would be one thing. But from what you told me, you don't."

She went silent, stunned but not entirely surprised. She could see his standpoint once he'd echoed the circumstances back at her. "Not yet. Not with certainty, but—"

"Sorry, Detective. Get me more, and I'll approve a warrant for the video."

Amanda thanked Anderson for his time and ended the call.

She shook her head at Trent. "No go. We need more. And I suppose he has a point. We don't know for certain that Eve Kelley's killer even tailed her here." She flailed a hand toward the building.

Trent didn't say anything for a few moments. "That's fine. We have more avenues to explore."

"I'm all ears."

"We focus on who would want Alicia Gordon and Eve Kelley dead *and* have access to pentobarbital. We've never paid Tony and Claudia's daughter, Bethany, a visit. It's a place to start," he added as if an afterthought, but she had a feeling he'd given it a lot of thought.

"Yes, let's do it." With Eve Kelley's murder, speaking with Bethany had fallen down the priority list. It couldn't be postponed any longer.

TWENTY-SIX

The waiting room at the Paws & Claws vet clinic was a zoo. Hound dogs were howling and cats were mewling and hissing. Rabbits and guinea pigs burrowed back in their carriers. One parrot was repeatedly cawing, "Happy Hour."

Trent leaned in toward her. "The bird must be a friend of Jimmy Buffett's."

"Who?"

"Really? Jimmy Buffet. He sings 'Margaritaville.'"

"Country?"

He teetered his hand. "Kind of."

"That's why you lost me."

The woman at the front desk was all smiles when Amanda and Trent walked up to her. Her expression dulled when she realized they didn't have any animals. "How can I help you?"

"We need to speak with Bethany Wagner. Is she in?" Amanda asked.

"She's here. Can I tell her who's looking for her?"

"Amanda Steele." Before coming in, she and Trent decided it might be best to start off using the personal connection instead of going in flashing their badges.

The woman shifted her gaze to Trent. "And you are?"

"He's just a friend of mine," Amanda said. "If you could tell Bethany I'm here, that would be appreciated."

The receptionist seemed to hesitate, but eventually nodded and disappeared down a hallway, leaving the front desk unmanned. She returned a few seconds later, her shoulders slumped forward. Behind her was Bethany—Amanda easily recognized her. The young girl was still in there, as was the family resemblance in her eyes and mouth.

"Amanda?" Bethany motioned for Amanda to follow her, and Trent came along too.

She took them into an office that had a miniature skeleton model of a canine sitting on the desk—at least that's what the gold embossing on the base of the plaque said. A framed diploma on the wall announced that Bethany Wagner had completed the veterinary assistant program. Bethany closed the door but didn't invite Amanda and Trent to sit in the visitor chairs. Amanda was halfway there when Bethany snarled.

"Don't bother. Mom said you might come here, and she told me to get a lawyer if you did."

It was like she had flipped a switch—one way in the public eye, different in private. "No need to get a lawyer involved. We just have some questions."

"Let me be the judge of that." Bethany knotted her arms tightly in front of her bosom.

Amanda gave it a few seconds, hoping Bethany would cool down. "Could we sit and talk? Just for a few minutes?"

Bethany eventually nodded and dropped into the chair behind the desk. Amanda and Trent sat in the visitor chairs opposite. Amanda introduced Trent.

Bethany didn't pass him a glance. "Why are you here, Amanda?"

"I think you know the answer to that."

"You think one of us poisoned Alicia Gordon."

"Us being?" Amanda volleyed back.

"Dad, Mom, me? But none of us did this—not that we wouldn't have had good reason."

Amanda had released suspicion about Bethany being the killer because she couldn't see a motive for killing Eve Kelley, and what would she care about the people who had bid on New Belle? Same could apply to Claudia. "Fair enough. Maybe none of you are responsible, but we have an investigation to see through. We're here because it can't be ignored that Alicia Gordon was poisoned with pentobarbital." Amanda watched as that sank into Bethany's mind and played over her features. Her eyes widened just a bit, but she didn't say anything. "I suspect you have that drug on the premises," Amanda added.

"Of course we do. It's used in euthanasia."

"It's also fatal for humans in certain doses."

"As I'm well aware."

"What was your relationship like with Alicia Gordon?" Amanda asked.

"Pfft. We didn't really have one."

"She was married to your father."

"Uh-huh, and I'm a grown woman who doesn't live at home. But I didn't really like her. Does that make me a bad person? Maybe. I don't care. It's the truth."

Hating her father's new wife might not make her a bad person, but Bethany had left town within days of Alicia's death —a time when she should have been there for her father. Was there tension there? Estrangement even? Or had Bethany already been away when the news of Alicia's death hit? If so, why wouldn't she have hurried back? "You and your dad... How are things between the two of you?"

"He wouldn't take Mom back. Instead, he married *that* woman." Bethany's cheeks flushed. "I shouldn't tell you this because it's not really your business. But unless you've gone through a divorce or are going through one, you can't begin to understand how difficult it is."

"I can imagine it would be very difficult," Amanda said.

"Difficult doesn't begin to cover it."

Given Bethany's volatile attitude toward her father and Alicia, did she not know that the divorce had been Bethany's mother's idea, not her father's? And Bethany hadn't really answered Amanda's question about her relationship with her father. She would guess *complicated* would be the answer. A few moments ago, Bethany was defending him, and now she was angry with him.

Bethany added, "You probably don't think their divorce should bother me so much. It's not like I'm living at home."

"The thought never occurred to me." It might have if she didn't have her own life drama, recently finding out about her father's infidelity. She was surprised by how it had shaken her. And her parents had worked through it all. "Going back to Alicia. Do you have any ideas who might have wanted her dead?"

"How much time do you have? Likely will be a long list, if I really think about it."

"Really?" Trent asked. "From what we hear, it sounds like she was a nice person."

A slight stretch but not entirely untrue. It would be interesting to see Bethany's reaction.

"A nice person? She was all about her business—above everything. She rarely spent time with her sons. Brad, I don't think ever when he was young because she was building her business. Leo, well, he's in the background now."

Trent pressed his lips together, his brow furrowing, his eyes narrowing. "And how do you know all that?"

"They did become a part of my family. I'm not blind, and I saw what she was like. As for the rest, her past, I can piece it together from things Dad has mentioned. Also what I see playing out with Leo."

"We understand Alicia had plans to be more present," Amanda began. "She was in the process of selling New Belle. She wanted out so she could spend time with her family."

"I'd believe that if I saw it." Bethany tilted her head from side to side. "Though I guess it makes sense. Selling now would fit her character perfectly. Selfish."

"I'm failing to see how that would be selfish," Amanda said.

"Me too," Trent chimed in.

Bethany eyeballed each of them in turn, then said, "Dad changed his career for her, just six months ago—give or take—and now she wants to sell? Where does that leave my dad?"

Amanda couldn't disclose that Tony had inherited the business. She did offer, "You can be sure that your father's financial needs will be taken care of for the rest of his life." And really, he could always return to being an accountant somewhere, but the job market wasn't the strongest at the moment.

"Still. Money isn't everything. He had a career he loved."

"He could always go back to it," Trent interjected, saying what Amanda had just thought.

"No. She had her claws into him."

"She's gone now," Amanda said coolly.

"Good riddance, in my book."

Her cold, bitter reaction had Amanda recoiling. "Your father is grieving. Alicia's sons are grieving."

"Grief is something that passes." Bethany set a blazing glare on Amanda.

Amanda gasped, the verbal impact as good as a physical blow. "It doesn't pass," Amanda spat. "It stays with you, becomes a part of who you are. Do you understand that?"

Bethany flinched.

"Do you?" Amanda barked.

"Yes. I'm sorry, I should have been more sensitive."

"Yes, you should have been." Amanda let a few seconds pass before speaking again. "You know, even your mother didn't hate Alicia. She worked for her, which you probably know."

"Yes, it's sad, isn't it? She just took the job so she could see Dad. Quite sure of that. Maybe to free Alicia of some of her money too."

"When did you last see Alicia?" Amanda asked.

"A few weeks ago. Just ran into her at the house when I was there to see Dad. Didn't talk to her much. She just sort of popped into the kitchen, grabbed a coffee, and was off to her home office. She was always on a computer." Bethany made a dramatic show of rolling her eyes.

"It sounds like you knew her well enough. Did you know that she had trouble sleeping at night?" Amanda tossed that out just for due diligence.

"You'd have to ask Dad."

Nothing in Bethany's facial expression or body language indicated she was withholding.

Trent shifted beside Amanda and asked, "Do you know Eve Kelley?"

Bethany nodded. "I've heard of her. She's the owner of Pixie Winks, right? Dad or Alicia might have said her name before."

"She was," Amanda said.

"Was?"

"She's also dead, injected with an overdose of pentobarbital." Amanda would run with that as fact.

Bethany's face was devoid of emotion. "I don't know what to say to that, but I'm not sure why you're talking to me about her."

"How about we circle back to an earlier question? Even if you give us just one name, who would you imagine had motive to kill Alicia Gordon?" Amanda asked. From there they could see if the rest—Eve's murder and the threats against the other bidders—held water.

"If I were you, I'd have a talk with Leo's nanny. The crock about Alicia selling the business to spend more time with her family? Yeah, well, I just don't buy it, but if she was going to do that, then..." Bethany left them to fill in the blank.

"The nanny would be out of a job," Amanda said. She and Trent figured the killer wanted to either prevent the sale of New Belle or drive down the price somehow and get a deal. But would loss of employment be enough motive for the nanny to kill Alicia, Eve, and threaten the bidders interested in New Belle? The nanny would know about Alicia's sleeping aid and potentially have access to the bottles. Goosebumps trailed down Amanda's arms. Then, too, so would the housecleaner that Tony had told them about, but the investigation had steered her and Trent away from following up there.

"Oh, it's not just that; Alicia was a troll to her. I've seen it myself. I was there the one day. Again, to see Dad. He wasn't home yet, but Alicia was, and so was the nanny. I overheard Alicia yelling at her upstairs."

"About what?" Trent asked.

"Alicia was telling her she was incompetent and to get her act together. Actually, now that I'm thinking about it, Alicia told the nanny she better get her act together or she wouldn't provide a good reference."

It sounded like Alicia had told the nanny the need for her services were coming to an end. Motive? The nanny also had opportunity, theoretically. The means wasn't there yet though. And was the nanny the mystery person from the video? Amanda had assumed it was a man, but she didn't know for sure. "Did the nanny ever come here? Is there any way she could have gotten her hands on any of the pento-barbital?"

"I wouldn't think so."

"So if we checked your inventory, it would all be accounted for?" Trent asked.

"It should be. It's locked in a cabinet in a room that also requires a passcode. The drugs are more Isaac's responsibility—that's my husband." Amanda nodded, and Bethany went on. "He never mentioned any inventory discrepancies to me, but..." Her voice trailed off.

Amanda leaned forward. "What is it?"

Bethany met Amanda's gaze. "Isaac and I don't really talk much anymore."

They were married and business partners. "I don't understand."

"We're currently separated and going through a divorce."

That would explain why Bethany had so much heat to infuse into the topic of divorce. "Sorry to hear that."

"Whatever. I keep telling myself people go through it every day. It's no big deal. Except that it is."

"Again, I'm sorry." And in this moment, Amanda truly was.

Bethany's face softened, and for the first time, Amanda caught a glimpse of the young girl she'd known. "Thank you."

Amanda pinched her eyes shut for a second. "Can you find out if there is any pentobarbital missing?"

"Yeah." Bethany took Amanda and Trent down the hall. She unlocked a room and went directly to a caged cabinet with a refrigerated unit next to it. "Both have ten-digit access codes—different by two digits. Only Isaac and I know what they are. If you turn around..." She twirled her finger to mime the movement she wanted them to make.

Once their backs were to her, the machine beeped and the door on the metal cage clanked open.

"Okay," Bethany said, and Amanda and Trent turned back around. She was holding a ledger. "Every time we take anything out, we record it in here, then it hits the computer." She pointed to a small table in the corner with a laptop.

"Who enters it?" Trent asked.

"Isaac. The inventory is checked weekly and verified. But we're a couple weeks behind. I was going to do it later today. Isaac always has some excuse not to get his work done." She flipped pages and dragged her finger down one of them, tapping on a few lines. "Let me just check what the computer says. One minute." She walked to the laptop and looked at some numbers. "Now let me check actual inventory of pentobarbital that we have on hand." She returned to the cabinet and pulled out a black, metal drawer. "This particular drug does best kept at room temperature and out of the light." She opened the lid and did a quick check. "Huh." She glanced back at the computer. "Comparing the written log to what the computer shows, it looks like we're out about fifteen grams."

Amanda looked at Trent. From their conversation with Rideout, it would take anywhere from two to ten grams to be lethal for a human. Hypothetically, there was enough missing to kill more people. Would the killing stop with Eve Kelley?

"No, this can't be right," Bethany muttered, her body quivering.

"Bethany." Amanda put her hands on the woman's shoulders. "Please, tell us. Is there any way someone other than you or Isaac accessed the pentobarbital?"

"I don't see how. I'll have to speak with Isaac."

"We'll wait," Amanda said, tingles running over her entire body. Had she and Trent found the killer's source of pentobarbital?

"He's not in today." Bethany was shaking her head and raking a hand through her hair. "I'll call him." She proceeded to do that on her cell phone, and from the sound of it, she had to leave a message. She lowered her arm, and her eyes were wet when she looked at Amanda. "I'll need to get back to you." She swallowed roughly.

"Okay, as soon as you hear from him." Amanda handed Bethany her business card, and she and Trent left the clinic.

Amanda's steps were slow heading back to the car.

"Missing pentobarbital," Trent said, getting behind the wheel while she slipped into the passenger seat. "Tony did his best to shut down conversation about Bethany. Was it because he was afraid we'd make this discovery?"

"There could be another explanation," she spat and glared at Trent.

"Sure, the nanny, but how do we tie her to the pentobarbital? Bethany said she was never at the clinic."

"All we know is Bethany never saw the woman here. Doesn't mean she wasn't."

"Suppose so."

"And what's to say the inventory discrepancy here has anything to do with the deaths of Gordon or Kelley?"

"Come on, Amanda. Even you must see how this looks."

She most certainly did. Tony Bishop was looking guilty as hell, but she couldn't give herself over to that just yet. "Before we storm into Tony's place, let's build a case against him, make sure we have everything in order first." She felt her expression soften, her words logical and reasonable, but also an appeal.

"Fine. I can get behind that. So the nanny... She could have been privy to what was going on, Alicia's desire to sell, the multiple offers, the bidders' identities. She could have wanted to ensure job security."

"Sure, but that wouldn't explain why she'd kill Eve Kelley or send threats to the other bidders after Alicia's death."

"True. We could probably rule her out as a suspect, but she might be able to give more insights into Tony. You said you wanted to build the case against him."

She hated it when her own words were being used against her. "I do," she pushed out. "Fine, you know what? We'll speak to the nanny, but we still need to talk to Tony again."

Trent scanned her eyes, and if he was good at mind reading, he'd see that she was pissed. Not at him but at Tony for putting her in this position—even if inadvertently. Tony owed her a good explanation as to why he'd withheld mention of the nanny and also why he never brought up the custody struggles over Leo with Seth Rossi.

TWENTY-SEVEN

Amanda called Judge Anderson for verbal approval to collect Alicia's laptop while Trent drove them to Tony's house. When she hung up, Trent didn't say a word, but she could feel that he wanted to. Either that or she was judging herself.

"Spill it. Something's on your mind." She wasn't sure why she was encouraging him to speak because she was quite certain she didn't want to hear what he had to say.

"The unexplained discrepancy with the pentobarbital inventory."

"*As of yet* unexplained discrepancy."

"You can't just ignore that it's very possible Tony got his hands on it."

"From a locked room and a secured cabinet." She heard herself sweeping in to defend Tony when he hadn't earned that loyalty—not by a long shot. First by withdrawing from her life and then failing to mention important information that might have moved the investigation along more quickly. That might have even prevented Eve's death.

"Yeah. A room and a cabinet only his daughter and son-in-law have a passcode for, which he could have gotten his hands on."

"*Could have.* We'll wait to hear from Bethany."

"We need to ask Tony about it when we're there."

"We will," she shoved out.

"Can I say something and not have you jump down my throat?" Trent looked over at her.

No promises... She shuffled toward the car door, eager to put more space between them. "What?"

Trent seemed to hesitate but eventually said, "Just be careful not to let your past friendship with Tony Bishop blind you."

Anger flushed through her. He was treating her like she was inept and incapable of being objective. "We're going to have a talk with him right now. And I just got approval to collect Alicia's laptop." She tried to keep her tone even but wasn't sure how well she'd pulled it off.

"Yeah, I know." He held eye contact for a second longer before putting his focus back on the road.

He pulled into the driveway, and the two of them got out of the car. This was her third time here in less than a week, and from a tough start, the visits were getting progressively more difficult. Today, she couldn't dance around a thing. Tony had some tough questions to answer. And she had to be prepared that she might not like what he had to say.

The door opened before she or Trent had a chance to knock or ring the doorbell. This time, Brad Slater looked like he was getting ready to go out. He was wearing blue jeans, a crisply ironed dress shirt, the top three buttons undone, and black running shoes.

"Looks like someone is going out." Amanda smiled at him.

"Yeah, was about to." He stepped back to allow Amanda and Trent into the house. Brad went on. "Rachel is here. We're going out for dinner, taking Leo with us."

It must have been someplace rather nice, judging by Brad's attire. But it did strike her a little odd he'd be going out in public so soon after his mother's death. To each their own when it comes to grief, though. "And Rachel is?"

"My girlfriend. I wanted to introduce her to Mom..." His voice turned gravelly. "They never had the chance to meet. Guess they never will now."

"Hey—" A young woman with blond straight hair joined them in the entry, Leo sticking close to her. She stopped talking at the sight of Amanda and Trent.

"Rachel?" Amanda said.

"Yeah?" she dragged out.

"This is Detective Steele and Detective Stenson," Brad said. "They're in charge of investigating Mom's murder."

"You two go to school together?" Amanda asked.

"Ah, yeah." Rachel stuffed her hands in her back pockets, swayed, appearing uncomfortable. Amanda appreciated that the situation could be awkward for her. She might be shy too.

"Well, Brad just told us you were on the way out. We don't want to hold you up." Amanda turned her attention to Brad. "We'd like to speak with Tony, though. He's home?"

"Yeah, I'll get him." Brad walked away and could be heard bounding up the stairs.

Rachel went to the closet near the door and pulled out a lightweight blue jacket. "Do you know who did this yet?" Rachel asked, zipping up her coat, her fingertips grazing over a gold pin with the embossed letters *MWHC*. Amanda wasn't sure what it stood for, but didn't think it worthwhile asking—the girl did seem shy.

Amanda shook her head. "Not yet, unfortunately."

Brad returned, jogging toward them. "Tony will be down in a sec. Go ahead and make yourselves comfortable in the sitting room. We just have to get going. We have a reservation for five thirty."

It was after five when they'd arrived. "Sure. Go ahead. Thanks."

The trio left, Brad waving a hand overhead as he walked away.

Amanda and Trent went to the sitting area, dropping down on the dark-gray couch.

"Would you prefer I handle this?" Trent asked her, keeping his voice low.

She shook her head. "I'll be all right to take the lead, but feel free to ask a question if you think of one."

Trent nodded, not getting the chance to verbally respond. Tony was walking toward them with wet hair and smelling of a heady cologne. He must have been fresh out of the shower.

"Do you have news?" Tony took his gaze from Trent and rested it on Amanda. She didn't miss how the attention seemed to settle on her shoulders with the weight of responsibility—her badge, their old friendship.

"Pentobarbital poisoning was confirmed as the cause of your wife's death." She thought it best to start on more neutral territory and work her way up to the half-truths and omissions.

Tony stumbled to the couch and dropped, like a puppet whose strings had been cut. He put his face into his palms and wept.

Amanda's heart ached. The response was so unexpected and raw.

She gave it a few beats, let him cry. Then said, "We're very sorry for your loss." The shallowness of the words, the inability to do anything helpful, chastised her. How she had hated hearing it when she'd been grieving her family. But the sentiment was one she doled out often with this job. She always meant it, but this time, pain burrowed deep within her. "I know there's nothing that can be said or—"

He lowered his hands and lifted his face. "You can find who did this to her."

"There are some questions we need answered." She heard the grim nature of her statement, but it couldn't be helped. There'd be no mask for the seriousness of the conversation they needed to have.

Tony waved a hand as if to give her the go-ahead. His eyes were glazed over, and he appeared numb. Amanda recalled that feeling too well. She also lived through it at times with Zoe, when the girl was haunted by memories of her parents' murders.

"We spoke with Leo's father." She figured she'd start there, considering she'd just seen the boy.

"Seth Rossi. What about him?"

From the cavalier way in which he said his name, it was apparent Tony didn't view Seth as a threat to Alicia. "We understand there was about to be a custody battle between him and Alicia."

"Seth has been threatening that for months, but he's never pursued it. Alicia did her best to work with him."

"That's not what he told us," Amanda said, sickening of the misdirection and lies.

"Let me guess. He told you they were at each other's throats, and Alicia was a bad mom. At least one who was never there for her kids, right? Well, Alicia was a good mom, and that's why she did whatever necessary to keep this from hitting the courts. She didn't want to put Leo through a tug of war, like he was a possession to be fought over."

Was Tony just seeing Alicia as he wanted to, or was the picture that Seth had painted from a warped perspective? Either way, it didn't change the fact there was a dispute between Alicia and Seth, and from Seth's standpoint, he was heated about the custody matter. "I was surprised that you never mentioned the tenuous relationship between Alicia and Seth when we spoke. You told us they were amicable." She didn't come right out and accuse Tony of lying, but it was right there beneath the surface; it would barely take a scratch to sniff it.

"Fine. Things between them could have been better, but like I said, Seth is a big talker." His brow pressed as he met her gaze. "Why are you so interested in Seth? Did he... Do you think he..."

Amanda shook her head, and Tony let out a deep sigh.

"I would have sent you his way if I thought he had anything to do with her death. But he's not a horrible man. Sure, he speaks a big game, but he's a decent person. He loves Leo." Pain wormed into Tony's eyes, and a few tears fell. "He's coming for full custody of Leo now. There, how's that for disclosure?" His face knotted with anguish.

"I'm sorry," Amanda offered, not sure if this would end up working out in Tony's favor.

"I don't know what to do. Would Alicia have wanted me to fight him, or is it better for Leo to be with his dad?" He ran a hand over his face. "Seth isn't a bad person, and I know he'll provide for Leo."

"Make the decision *you* want." Her voice was small as she spoke.

Tony rubbed his forehead. "I don't know. I really feel I need to consider what Alicia would have wanted."

"She's gone," Amanda said softly.

"So days after you lost Kevin and Lindsey, you were able to just move on? You never gave any consideration to, 'Hey, what would Kev think about this?'" he snapped.

She stiffened. "Life for me was a living hell for a very long time." She resisted the urge to point out how things might have been made a bit easier if she had the shoulders of all her friends to lean on. She took a steadying breath and added, "But eventually I came to realize there was no bringing them back. And life moves forward. We just get to have them in our memories."

A tear snaked down his cheek, and he wiped it away. "Excuse me if I'm not there yet."

"You won't be. Not for a long time." Amanda softened her tone. "I just wouldn't want to see you making a decision that will change not only your future, but Leo's, based on what you think Alicia would say. Whatever you decide, it will be something you have to live with for the rest of your life."

Tony dipped his head as if in silent thanks for her concern.

"There's more we need to discuss, though." This was her chance to prove to Trent just how objective she could be—she'd hit Tony while he was already down. "We asked who all came into the house. You didn't mention Tina Nash, the nanny," she said, her insides quaking.

"Well, she wouldn't have access to Alicia's sleeping aid."

"Conceivably, it would be easy enough for her to get to it if she wanted to."

"Oh my God, Amanda."

"Detective."

"*Detective*, Tina would have no reason to want Alicia dead. Just like with Seth. Why would I waste your time—prolong my wife getting justice—by pointing you all over the place?"

"That is something that Detective Stenson and I need to figure out, as part of the investigation." She wasn't going to tell him just yet that they had every intention of leaving here to talk to her, but that was the plan. She'd need to call Libby yet again to let her know she'd be home late.

"Tina's worked for Alicia for several years now. Alicia came to rely on her. Why would she kill her?"

"For one, Alicia was planning to sell New Belle to spend more time with the family. That's what you told us," she said, pausing just a second to see if he wanted to amend that. He was silent. She went on. "If Alicia proceeded with her intention, she'd have been home more, what need would there be of Tina Nash's services?"

"No way. She was still going to need her help from time to time."

"Sure, but most people need more than 'from time to time' to pay the bills. We were told by someone that they'd overheard Alicia yelling at Tina about not giving her a good reference."

"Who?" he spat.

"Bethany."

"You..." He clamped his mouth shut, scowled. "You should leave her out of this."

"Why is that?" she said through clenched teeth. "Did you go into the room where the drugs are stored at your daughter's clinic?"

"Why would I?"

Amanda didn't want to bring up the missing pentobarbital until she heard from Bethany that it was confirmed. But she filed away Tony's response. She might come back around to it. There was more ugly business to attend to. She'd work things a little backward. "Eve Kelley filed a lawsuit against New Belle, suing for compensation regarding intellectual property theft on Friday. Did you know that?"

"Of course."

"Why didn't you inform us of that?"

"Honestly? I never saw that it mattered."

She was starting to feel like a record on repeat. "You need to tell me everything—even if you don't think it's important." She glanced at the ceiling, trying to rouse strength. "Eve Kelley died Monday morning."

"She... she what?" His Adam's apple bobbed heavily, and his eyes widened with panic.

"We believe she was injected with pentobarbital."

"Oh my God," he muttered.

"Two women are dead, Mr. Bishop. Both connected to you." She paused there, letting that sink in. "Is there anything else we should know?"

He blinked tears and shook his head. "No, I told you everything."

"All right, now tell me this. Where were you yesterday morning between eight and nine?" Alibis were useless when it came to Alicia's murder, but they factored in with Eve Kelley, and as much as she didn't want to believe it, Tony could be the mystery figure on the video.

"I was here at the house."

"Can anyone verify that?"

He shook his head. "Rachel came down Sunday night, and she and the boys went out for breakfast yesterday. I just didn't feel like going out in public."

She couldn't get words to form, and her brain was kicking them out in nonsensical order.

"So no real alibi," Trent said firmly. "Did you kill Eve Kelley?"

"No. Absolutely not."

Amanda stood and paced, chilled. "But you have no alibi." She wanted to stress to him how serious that was.

"Am I really under suspicion?"

"Should you be?" she countered, took a few seconds to breathe. No alibi for Eve Kelley, access to his wife's sleeping aid, pentobarbital roughly within reach. There were the fingerprints at the cabin, the shoeprints, the tire treads. "Remind me, when did you last see Alicia?"

"I told you, Monday morning before she left for the cabin."

"You didn't pop up there to see her at all, maybe share a glass of wine, talk?" She was extending him a branch to grab hold of.

"No. She wanted to be alone for a few days, and I respected that."

Only she wasn't alone the entire time... She tried to push that from her mind—they didn't have a clue who the visitor had been—but it could have been Tony. Was he bald-faced lying to her? Or was it more an omission, like with the nanny. Speaking of... "Before we go, we'll need Tina Nash's information."

Tony frowned.

"What is it?"

"I'll get you her info, but there's something you should know before you talk to her."

What now? His forewarning had Amanda's stomach clenching. "Tell us."

He licked his lips. "There may have been an... *incident...* between us."

"By incident, you mean what, exactly?" Amanda asked.

"I kissed her." The confession came out on a long breath. "I'm not proud of it."

"I wonder why," Amanda said.

"Don't judge me. Please. Especially not now. But Alicia could be all about the business. She was gone all hours of the day and night. She'd come home exhausted, drink some Sleep Tight, and crawl into bed. That's if she didn't lock herself in the home office and work."

Amanda momentarily forgot his disloyalty. CSI Blair told them that with the amount added to the sleeping liquid, it would likely have taken days, but she'd been basing that on Alicia taking the recommended dosage. Could Alicia have been poisoned just on the night she died, not over a period of time? "What do you mean she *drank* some?"

"I'm quite sure she took more than the label says to."

"So if a bottle was down about half, how many nights do you figure that would have taken her?" Trent asked, his pen hovering above his notepad.

"Two or three nights?"

Amanda glanced at Trent, her heart racing. "She took that much in one go?"

"Yeah. I tried to tell her it wasn't good for her, but she wasn't hearing it."

Amanda was figuring how this revelation fit with the investigation. It opened the possibility that her bottle had been tampered with before she left home. Someone in this house? And what about the other two bottles they'd collected from here? Were they also laced with pentobarbital? She'd check with the lab first thing in the morning. But now, she had to truly consider that Tony had poisoned Alicia. "What size shoe do you wear?"

"Eleven."

The same size as the print by the cabin window. "Two more things you can do for us."

"If it gets you to go." He glanced away from her after saying this. Any embers of a previous friendship were frayed, possibly never to be stitched back together.

"We need to look at your shoes and the tires on your vehicle."

"Sure. Whatever it takes."

"We will also need Alicia's computer," Trent said.

"No, I told you—"

"We received approval from a judge to take it with us," Amanda said. "I can get him on the phone if you wish."

Tony huffed. "I'll be right back."

While he was gone, Amanda and Trent looked at Tony's shoes. None were a match to the prints left at the cabin. They waited for Tony to return before going into the garage. The tire treads weren't a match, and there was no mud or dirt caked in the grooves. Either Tony had scrubbed them clean or he was never at the cabin, just like he'd told them.

Tony thrust the laptop toward Amanda. "The password to unlock it is 'Abandon'. Now, I'll get you Tina's number, and you can go." Tony pulled his cell phone from a pocket of his pants and rattled off the woman's number. "You can call her for her address." He took them to the man door in the garage, unlocked it, and gestured for them to walk through it. The door shut heavily behind them, sort of a hard stop at any possibility of a reconciliation of their friendship.

She flinched. Trent put a hand on her shoulder.

"Don't take this personally, okay? He's just—"

"Being an ass? Doesn't he appreciate how much I've held back? How, if he were anyone else, I probably would have dragged him in by now?" She looked over at Trent, her expression frozen as her admission filtered back to her ears.

"We don't have enough. Yet. And we need to build that case against him. Remember?"

"Yeah, you're right. But if he is guilty, I want you to know that I'm prepared to do the right thing."

"Who are you trying to convince?" His facial features were soft. "I know you will."

His confidence had her going quiet. She simply nodded.

They got into the department car, and Trent keyed into the onboard system, searching for Tina Nash's address. As the computer worked, he faced her. "Why didn't you mention to him that there was missing pentobarbital at the vet clinic?"

"Not time yet. But I did give him a chance to confess. He didn't. If we find out the pentobarbital inventory is actually short, we'll come back to him. He won't have a leg to stand on."

"I think we should have pushed him harder."

"And what? Have him clamming up and demanding a lawyer? I know what I'm doing."

"I never said you didn't."

"No? Well, it sounds like that over here." She took a few heaving breaths, calming her temper. "We never would have seen his shoes or his tires—or got this." She held up Alicia's laptop. "We'd be stuck in bureaucratic red tape."

Trent raised his hands. "Fine, it seems you have everything figured out."

"Don't be like that. I've just been doing this job longer than you, and sometimes you have to be very careful about crossing certain lines. Once lawyers get involved—as you've probably already seen—everything slows down."

A painful span of silence, and just when she was certain he wasn't going to say anything, he spoke.

"I'm sorry if you took what I said the wrong way."

Not much of an apology, but she reflected back to how the conversation had gotten started in the first place. "You don't need to be sorry. You were just speaking your mind."

"I was," he said as if he were tiptoeing through a minefield.

"Sorry if I overreacted."

"*If?*" He smiled.

"Fine. I did." She rubbed her forehead. She just wanted to believe so badly that Tony was innocent. Was she allowing that desire to cloud her judgment, blind her instincts?

TWENTY-EIGHT

Amanda called Libby on the way to Tina Nash's house to see if she could stay with Zoe a little longer.

It was after six when Amanda and Trent sat down in Tina Nash's living room. They'd pulled a background on her as due diligence before leaving Tony's driveway. No record. Tina was thirty and average height with light blond hair. While she might have conceivable motive to kill Alicia, Amanda wasn't seeing any for taking out Eve. But Tina might be able to tell them more about Tony and Alicia's marriage.

"I don't have long," she told them. "I have another job to get to in forty minutes. I can't be late."

"We have some questions about your employment with Alicia Gordon," Trent said.

"That is a tragedy. Her death, I mean, not the questions. I'll do what I can to help." Tina pressed her lips together and subtly shook her head, and it seemed like a canned response. "I feel for Tony, and that little boy. Leo must be devastated."

No mention of Brad, but *Tony*? Then again, as per his confession, Tony and Tina were a little better acquainted than they should have been. Amanda would get around to asking about the nature of Tina's relationship with Tony, but she wanted to focus on Alicia first. If Tina got defensive and shut down, then they'd already have their other questions answered. "What was your relationship like with Alicia?"

Tina shrugged. "She was my boss. Nothing much else to say."

"And she treated you well, was a good person as far as you knew?" Amanda asked.

"I'd say so. I could tell that she loved Leo..." Tina stopped there, dramatically rolling her eyes. "Just some of her demands were unreasonable."

"Like what?"

"I was to tidy up after Leo *all* the time. He's ten. At some point, he needs to learn some responsibility."

"Alicia didn't agree with you?"

"Nope. She said that's what she was paying me for."

Amanda just wanted to cut straight to it. "Did you know she planned to sell the business to spend more time with him?"

"I did."

"Were you concerned about your job?" Trent interjected, getting there mere seconds before Amanda could ask the same thing.

"No." Tina shook her head. "She was going to still have me in a few hours a week, just not full days."

"The hit to your income couldn't have been something you were looking forward to," Amanda said, careful to keep accusation out of her tone. She really couldn't ignore there was no obvious motive for Tina to kill Eve.

"Alicia had already lined up another job for me. And speaking of a job..." Tina winced and tapped a foot. "I have a part-time one right now to get to. It's a bit of a drive, so I really need to go."

Another job that Alicia had lined up? It must have been after the argument that Bethany had overheard. Why hadn't

Tony mentioned that Alicia had done this for Tina? "We won't keep you much longer. You said Alicia lined up another job for you?"

"Yes, great family too. They even offered me more than Alicia was paying, so it would have been a win."

"Why not leave Alicia before the sale finalized?" Trent asked. "After all, you had this other family lined up who were offering you more money."

"That's not the way to conduct business, and it's called loyalty." She leveled her gaze at him.

Tina's "loyalty" was up for debate if she was willing to kiss her employer's husband. "What is your relationship with Tony like?"

Tina's eyes widened, light sparked in them then dulled. "I'm not sure what you're asking."

Trent leaned forward. "Think it was rather straightforward."

"He was Alicia's husband."

"So no lines were ever crossed?" Amanda pushed.

Tina stuck her chin out. "What did he tell you?"

"We'd just like to compare notes." Amanda gestured for Tina to answer.

"It was nothing serious." She cleared her throat. "It was just casual."

"What was casual?" She really had a horrid feeling about where this conversation was headed—Tony had lied to them again.

Tina narrowed her eyes. "Our relationship."

"Your relationship?" Tony had mentioned *a* kiss.

"Uh, yeah, we are, ah, seeing each other."

"Seeing each other?" The words would barely scrape from her throat.

"We didn't mean for it to happen. It just sort of did."

Trent glanced at Amanda. "So we're talking more than a one-time kiss?" he asked Tina.

"Ah, yeah. We've been sleeping together for about a month."

Amanda could feel Trent still looking at her, but she couldn't bring herself to return eye contact. She was offended and pissed off that Tony had lied right to her face—again. Why would Tony confess to a single kiss and not an affair? He knew they were coming to speak with Tina. Only two reasons Amanda could think of: Tony was too much of a coward to admit this to her face, and two, he'd know how it might make him look guilty. Could Amanda really believe a single word Tony said? "Where were you yesterday morning between eight and nine?" The timeframe to account for Eve Kelley's injection, and Amanda was following a strong hunch.

"I was with Tony." Tina bit on her bottom lip, her eyes darting back and forth between them.

"You were with..." Amanda stood and left. She heard Trent thank Tina for her time.

Back in the car, Amanda couldn't even speak. She was struggling to breathe through her rage. Her vision was red.

"All the lies, the leaving things out... It's not sitting well, Amanda."

"You think?" she spat.

"What do you want to do about this?" He angled his body to face her.

"What can we do at this point? Besides, Tina just alibied him for the time of Eve Kelley's murder."

"She could be lying to protect him. Tony knew we were coming here. He could have asked her to say they were together."

"Not that it makes him look good. And why not just tell us they were sleeping together, for crying out loud?" She raked a hand through her hair and clenched her teeth. "'A kiss, that's all it was, Amanda...'" She mocked Tony's words.

"Yeah, he's not exactly the most forthright person I've met. It doesn't exactly inspire confidence in the guy."

"Again, I agree, Trent," she barked on auto-defense. "Sorry. It's just... You think you know someone only to find out that you don't. I mean, it's not like I've been in Tony's life for years, but I'd like to think I was a better judge of character." For a blink of a second, as a teenager, she'd considered ending things with Kevin to pursue a relationship with Tony. Now she was chockful of gratitude that she hadn't. Tony was a damn cheater.

"Time, relationships, experiences, they change us." Trent put that out there and managed to do so without sounding like some radical new-age guru.

"For sure they do. But Claudia had cheated on him. It ended their marriage. You'd think that would deter him from hurting Alicia in the same way. I'm done defending the guy."

TWENTY-NINE

Before Amanda headed for home, she forwarded the JPEG from Pixie Winks to Detective Briggs in Digital Crimes to see if he could clear the image of the mystery figure. She also left Alicia's laptop at the station to look at tomorrow. Right now, she couldn't get to Zoe fast enough. She was looking forward to salvaging some of the evening. It was bad enough she had to miss pizza night—a meal she and Zoe strived to have every Tuesday.

She opened the front door, and no one was within sight. The house was open concept, allowing her to see into the living room from the entry, with the kitchen behind that, and a hallway to the right that led to two bedrooms and a bathroom. "I'm home," she called out. She headed toward the hall, and Libby stepped around the corner.

"Hey there." Libby smiled. "Welcome home."

"Thanks. Where's Zoe?"

"In her room, but it's not a good night."

"Why? You never mentioned anything over the phone..."

"It happened afterward. She had her friend Maria here. I told you that when you called." Amanda nodded, and Libby went on. "But something was said and..." The woman's lips quivered, but she pulled herself together and nudged her chin out. "I had Maria's mother come pick her up."

"What was said?"

"The girls were acting out *Frozen*, and Maria called Zoe a baby for playing dress-up."

"Oh. Maria's her best friend." Amanda was crushed for Zoe.

"That's probably why it hurt so much."

"And why is a six-year-old teasing another one for playing dress-up? I know kids are growing up faster than they used to, but this is crazy."

"I told Maria's mother what was said. Apparently, Maria's older sister has been making fun of Maria lately, calling her a big baby for putting on costumes and playing with dolls."

"Ah, so that spilled over to Zoe."

"I'd say so. I think Zoe was hurt even more because Elsa and her sister lose their parents in the movie. I think that's why it means so much to her. Zoe can relate. She then sees how strong the characters are and wants to be like them."

Amanda let snippets of the movie play out in her mind. How could she have not realized how closely the story mirrored Zoe's? While Elsa's parents weren't killed, they were both dead —just like Zoe's. "How did Zoe react to Maria's calling her a baby?"

"She started screaming at the top of her lungs. It took a while to calm her down."

Amanda had called about an hour ago. Apparently, a lot could happen in that time. "She's calmer now?"

Libby nodded. "Do you want me to stay, or do you think you can handle this? I'm not meaning to insult you... It's just..."

"Difficult." Amanda put a hand on the woman's shoulder. "It's okay. I've got this. You can go if you wish."

Libby smiled and packed up to go home. The minute

Libby had closed the door behind her, Amanda immediately wished she had stayed. Amanda had taken years to work through her own grief and had moments when she was miserable beyond measure. Sometimes she questioned whether she was the best one to help this little girl through her emotions. But she usually squashed the self-doubt with reassurance that she was, indeed, the best suited for the job. After all, she'd been through it—at least a version of it. She hadn't witnessed her family's actual deaths before her eyes like Zoe, who had seen her father shot and heard her mother's screams. But Amanda had been in the crash that claimed Kevin and Lindsey.

Amanda slowly walked down the hall, gathering her thoughts. Zoe saw a therapist on a biweekly basis, but maybe it would be a good idea to get her in sooner than the next scheduled visit. "Zoe?" Amanda stood in the doorway of the room and tapped the doorframe.

Zoe was sitting on her bed, plucking rhinestones out of the Elsa tiara. She didn't even look up.

Amanda went in and took the tiara from the girl. Zoe still didn't acknowledge her. "I understand your feelings were hurt, sweetheart."

Her big, blue eyes met Amanda's. They were wet but full of rage. "I'm not a baby," she pushed out and scowled.

"No one is saying you are." Amanda eased onto the edge of the bed.

"Maria did."

"She's just a little girl herself. You have lots of fun pretending to be Elsa, don't you?"

"Yeah." The admission came in a tiny voice that was almost indiscernible.

"Then why shouldn't you play?" Amanda hitched her shoulders. "You do what makes you happy." She gently poked Zoe's chest.

She looked down at the tiara that was now in Amanda's hands. "I ruined it."

"We can fix it."

Zoe sniffled. "She's right. I am a baby." She crossed her arms in a huff.

"Not by a long shot. You're a smart girl, way ahead of her time."

Zoe was scanning her eyes like she wasn't believing a word.

Amanda didn't want to bring up the murders of Zoe's parents, but given what this girl had been through, she was leaps ahead of others her age. Zoe had already been forced to face the gut-wrenching reality that life could throw her way—death of loved ones. "I mean it, Zoe." Amanda set the tiara on the bed and reached for the child, wanting to scoop her in for a hug.

Zoe pulled back. "I miss my Mommy."

"I know you do, sweetheart."

"She watched *Frozen* with me a lot." Her bottom lip quivered just a mere second before she started to cry. She pawed at her cheeks, as if angered by the tears and her display of emotion.

Amanda's heart squeezed. Zoe had never told her that before, but it provided another reason why she had such a fondness for the movie. If it had anything to do with Zoe relating to Elsa's loss of her parents, that was a subconscious thing. Zoe watched and immersed herself in the film because it made her feel closer to her mother. Amanda blinked back tears, and when she trusted her voice, she said, "You don't let anyone stop you from doing what you love. Ever."

The girl continued to sob, and Amanda made another move to hug Zoe. This time, the girl allowed the embrace. If Amanda had her way, she'd never let go.

THIRTY

There wasn't enough pizza in the world that could mend a broken heart. Only time was capable of that—well, maybe desire and resiliency too. When Amanda dropped Zoe at school the next morning, the girl was only a shadow of herself. It was about eight thirty when Amanda called the therapist's office and left a message.

She was currently at her desk down at Central, sucking back on a coffee from Hannah's Diner, wishing it could somehow perform a miracle and soothe the ache in her chest. But she was worried about Zoe. And criticizing herself. Did she have what it took to help Zoe face her demons?

Work was the only elixir that stood a chance of distracting Amanda today. Last night, Detective Briggs from Digital Crimes had sent an email to her and Trent. He had no luck cleaning the image of the mystery figure from Pixie Winks, but Briggs wasn't without good news. He had successfully tracked the IP address on the threat to Lopez. It tied back to Caffeine Café, so that could be anyone who took advantage of their free Wi-Fi. Hopefully, video surveillance there would show them something useful.

Amanda tapped a foot waiting for Trent to get in. Not that she had nothing to keep her busy. She already had a verbal warrant for the coffee shop's surveillance cameras. She even had time to call the lab, but there was no update on the tire treads or shoeprints—no match to a brand yet. Better news when it came to the bottles of Sleep Tight Amanda had collected from Tony. The foil seals on both bottles had been broken—something Amanda hadn't noticed because of the lids—and both had tested positive for pentobarbital.

Next, she turned her attention to Alicia's laptop and logged in using *Abandon*. She went straight to the email program and watched as some messages filtered in. So many were marked as spam.

Amanda looked at the senders and subject lines, but none made her curious enough to open the emails. An appointment reminder flashed up. It was for this past Monday and must have been set-up before her death.

F/up with change to will

Amanda opened the appointment, hoping there would be more details in the notes section, but nada. They might never know what Alicia had intended to change.

Trent walked in with a cheery "Good morning."

"Hey." Amanda signaled for him to come to her desk.

"Oh, Alicia's laptop?"

"Yeah. She had a reminder to follow-up on the change to her will."

"Do you know what that was now?"

She shook her head.

"All right, let's think like a CEO." Trent pressed his lips together. "She had a lot to balance and remember. I'd think she'd note everything down. Did you try looking at recently opened files?"

"Ah, no." Amanda wheeled her chair aside to allow Trent access to the computer.

Trent set his coffee on her desk and opened the file manager. He arranged the files so they listed in date order, the most recent at the top.

"Right there." Amanda pointed at a folder called *Will*. Inside was a copy of the current will as well as a Word document. It was dated about a week before her death.

Trent opened the file, and they both read it quickly. There wasn't much there but the impact was significant.

Trent was the first to speak. Amanda couldn't form words. Every time she tried to rally to Tony's defense, something else led her right to him.

"Alicia was going to take Tony out of the will," Trent said, speaking slowly.

"You don't need to say any more. I know how this makes him look." *Guilty as hell.*

"I know you want to build a strong case against Tony, but we're getting there."

"He still has an alibi for Eve's murder." She was still grappling to see him as innocent.

"One that could be contested."

She hated how true that was. There was also the fact Tony had been unwilling to hand over Alicia's laptop. Was it because he didn't want them finding this? But if he knew the file was there, why hadn't he deleted it? She and Trent hadn't hidden the fact that at some point they'd be coming for Alicia's computer. Tony would have had time. Amanda shut the lid. "Let's go."

Trent trailed her at first but quickly caught up. "Are we bringing him in?"

"Not quite yet. We're heading to Caffeine Café." As they walked to the lot, she updated him on the verbal warrant and the bottles of Sleep Tight.

"Every bottle? The killer wanted to ensure Alicia took the drug," he said. "And it would prove that the killer had access to the primary suite."

The summation had her chest tightening. That put Tony squarely in the frame again. But it could also be Tina, Claudia, or Bethany. Even Brad. She hadn't really considered the son much, and he could be dismissed—from a financial angle anyway—couldn't he? He was well provided for financially with Alicia alive.

They loaded into the department vehicle, and Trent drove, foot pressing the pedal to the floor. They were parked and heading into the coffee shop in no time.

The place was packed this morning. Carla was at the counter and sighed heavily when she saw them, then turned her back to them.

"Carla," Amanda called out.

The woman's movements stopped, and she spun again and came over. "I don't have time for this today." She flailed a hand toward the mass of people waiting to order some fancy concoction.

"We are here with a warrant for your video footage. Authorized by a judge," Amanda said. "I can get him on the phone if you want to hear it for yourself."

"It's fine," Carla mumbled and took them into the office. She sat at the desk, clicked on the keyboard, and got up. "Have at it."

"You're not going to help us?" Amanda was expecting the woman to assist them, not give them access to the computer and leave.

"You saw out front, right? I've got to get back. Besides, it's a rather simple program. I'm sure you'll be able to figure it out." She gestured to the now-vacant chair and swept out of the room.

Amanda stared at the empty doorway. "Unbelievable."

Trent smiled. "Don't worry. I'm sure I can figure it out."

"I've got it." She was determined to give it a try. She sat down, and Trent leaned over her shoulder. Cologne. She hadn't noticed it in the car, but he smelled like cedarwood with notes of citrus and the sea. *Focus, Amanda!* Live video was playing out on a split screen. One feed was from the camera she had spotted the other day behind the counter. Its line of sight went all the way to the door. The other camera was directed at the parking lot. "Here goes nothing..." She clicked on a few spots and was impressed by how user-friendly the system was. "Okay, as Carla said, the program is rather straightforward." She spotted folders along the side that were labeled with dates. "The email to Lopez was sent...?"

"Last Wednesday at eleven oh five," Trent told her.

She picked that day's folder. "Looks like there are two sub-files beneath that." She clicked one, then the other. "They're divided based on which camera—interior or exterior."

"We're interested primarily on inside first."

She turned her head to look at him, the movement putting their faces to within a few inches of each other. "Thanks, Sherlock."

He smiled. "I'm here for you."

She turned her attention back to the monitor and played the interior video from the day Lopez's threat had been sent. She forwarded to the time of the email and paused the playback, her eyes scanning the tables. "Are you seeing anything, anyone, who stands out?" She was searching for a person with a laptop but supposed it could just as easily be someone using a tablet or a phone.

"Nope."

"Me eith— There." She pointed to a figure seated at the table near the window. Their back was to them, but given the way their shoulders were curled forward... "Looks like they're holding a tablet, but for all the good the camera does us. We can't see their face."

"Notice the white ball cap?" He put his finger next to Amanda's, and they both pulled back when they grazed each other's hand.

The hat, issued to Pixie Winks employees, was on the table, almost out of sight.

"Who are you?" Amanda mumbled. If only she could reach through the screen, grab this person, and turn them around.

"Let the video play out, and we'll see if we can see their face. If that doesn't work, we'll go backwards."

They did both, but it seemed the person knew exactly where the cameras were positioned and how to avoid them. They'd entered the coffee shop, head down, and beelined for the table. The outside camera didn't give them much either. The person walked while looking at the sidewalk, never glancing up, and then went off camera.

"Huh." Trent stood back. "Okay. Well, maybe we're not completely out of luck. Go back to the point when they're leaving. They walk out of the shop standing up straight. It's only coming in that they're all hunched over."

"All right." She wasn't sure where he was going with this until she finally saw the answer right there on the screen. "The mystery person is about six feet tall," she said.

"Yep." He smiled and traced a finger down the monitor, highlighting the height chart decal on the doorframe. "You know, in case someone robs the place..."

So simple. Right in front of me. "I should have thought of that."

"You should have." He smirked. "But if you thought of everything, why would you need me?"

She had nothing to say to that. Best she just keep quiet on that subject. "Okay, well, not everything is lost, then. We have the height. This person is also the same shape as the one we saw on the video from Pixie Winks. The person who poisoned Eve? Now, this could be a shot in the dark, but what if this mystery person sent the other emailed threats from here too? If we go back and dig through the messages that Alicia Gordon and Eve Kelley received—ones we feel are similarly worded to Lopez's— we can look at the video from those times too. Maybe this person slipped up?"

Trent's eyes lit and widened. "We can hope. Great idea."

"We'll see. There's also the less attractive option."

"Which is?"

"Well, assuming the mystery figure in the Caffeine Café video is both the killer and the person who was stalking Eve Kelley—which we could assume, as they had a white ball cap— we could watch every weekday morning around the time Kelley gets her coffee. But we could be here all day and night if we do that."

"We might end up being rewarded with the killer's identity, though. It's worth the sacrifice."

She took a deep breath. If watching hours of video led them to the killer, then it would absolutely be worth it, but there was the chance they'd come away with nothing but lost time. "Fine. We'll need to take the video footage with us from at least the last week, maybe two, just to cover it. That should be enough." She asked and answered her own question.

"I'll get Carla."

"Thanks. We should see if there's anything she can tell us about this mystery person."

"All over it," he said and left.

Amanda leaned back in her chair, breathing a little easier now that Trent was gone. What the heck was going on with her? Trent was her colleague, nothing more, and never would be. Any feelings she had for him were exaggerated and to be left unexplored. Besides, she had much more important things to keep her busy—starting with finding a killer.

. . .

Back at Central, Amanda took the threatening messages that had been sent to Alicia Gordon, and Trent took the ones to Eve Kelley. The manager from Caffeine Café had said she'd never seen the mystery person. Amanda had also shown her Tony's photo, but she didn't recognize him either. Her responses didn't really mean much, though. Carla told them she was too busy to keep tabs on every customer. Amanda and Trent had spoken briefly with the other girls on staff at the time and the result was the same.

Amanda's mind was on the threat sent to Alicia Gordon—the one that had originally made Eve Kelley sound like their killer.

How dare you sell what isn't yours to sell? You'll pay for this.

Amanda pulled the printed email threat from her folder, noticing again the crease in the page caused from the printer. She tried to smooth it out to no avail but noted the date. It had been sent the Friday before Alicia died.

She compared it to the email address used to send Lopez's threat, and though it was different, that didn't deter her. The killer could have set up multiple email accounts.

She set about looking at the other threats sent to Alicia, but there weren't any others that really got the hairs up on the back of her neck. They read more generic and were a few months' old. None of them were sent from the email address used to send the threat to Lopez.

While she concentrated on the ones sent to Alicia, Trent read the ones sent to Eve. They'd been studying these emails for a few hours when he looked at her over the divider.

"I've got something here." Trent held up a piece of paper,

drew it back, and read, "'You are a liar and deserve nothing! Go back to school.'"

She was hoping for wording far more menacing than that. "Okay, how do you think it applies to what we're looking for?"

"Eve Kelley says Alicia stole her serum. This person is claiming that is a lie and that Eve deserves nothing—as in, she shouldn't have been paid off or compensated for something she had no claim to."

"Or given the right to purchase New Belle," Amanda added but wondered if they might not be stretching things a bit.

"Exactly. And the 'go back to school' part is a direct reference to where the lie had originated—a lie, in the sender's point of view anyway."

"Or they're trying to draw our attention to that time period. Possibly a rabbit hole we could get lost exploring. Regardless, whoever sent this message might have known Alicia and Eve had gone to the same school. That's also when Eve claims Alicia stole the serum formula," she recapped.

"See why it has me excited now?"

"Yes, I kind of do. So who knows that?"

"Could be anyone close to Alicia or Eve, who also had an interest in the future of New Belle."

"Tony Bishop and Harold Armstrong pop to mind."

"What about Brad Gordon, Alicia's son? We haven't discussed him before but he had a stake in the company's future."

"Tony and Brad could be the person from the videos, but I'm not seeing a motive for Brad. How can he know who the bidders were, and why would he care about the business one way or another? Given all the stipulations in Alicia's will to ensure Brad benefited financially from the business, it would make sense she'd compensate him generously if she sold it. And it's not like he wasn't being financially provided for before Alicia's death."

"What if we've been pigeon-holing the investigation, making motive all about money and the company when it isn't?"

"The threats all point in that direction."

"Sure, but if you look at the murder method, poisoning, that's more personal in nature."

His words landed like a rock, but could it reconcile at all with the rest of what they'd learned? Her phone rang, and caller ID told her it was Zoe's therapist's office. "Amanda Steele," she answered and proceeded to ask if there was any way to squeeze Zoe in for an appointment today.

"We have an opening that just became available," the woman said. "If you could get her here for four?"

Amanda looked at the clock on the wall. *12:07 PM.* "I can."

"We'll see you then." The woman hung up, and Amanda sent a quick text to Libby to let her know she would be getting Zoe from school today, then she tucked her phone away.

"Everything all right with Zoe?" Concern filled Trent's voice.

"She's just been through a lot, as you know." She and Trent had been assigned the investigation into Zoe's parents' murders last September. In some ways, that felt like a lifetime ago; in others, like yesterday.

"I can't imagine being in her shoes."

"Me neither. Seeing your father murdered right in front of you—how do you recover from that?" Amanda left it there, but she recalled that not long after the incident had happened, the police psychologist had said children processed trauma differently than adults. They didn't have points of reference to rationalize what they'd seen to start making sense of it. Processing was more about acceptance.

"At least Zoe has you," Trent said, his facial expression tender and his eyes full of confidence.

"Thank you."

"Don't mention it."

Moments like these, when Trent was so compassionate and understanding, reassuring and expressing faith in her, she found it hard not to cross *that* line. As Becky had suggested, maybe it was time for her to start dating and enjoying adult company, but Trent was most certainly off the table. He had to be.

THIRTY-ONE

The voices in Amanda's mind were noisy as hell. There were ones from the investigation that sounded out theories as to how everything stitched together. They also begged for the killer's identity to just reveal itself. Others were of a personal nature and accused her of failing Zoe and falling short in caring for her needs. Romantic notions about Trent also crept in, despite her efforts to dismiss them.

She had rolled her chair into Trent's cubicle, and they spent a couple of hours watching video from Caffeine Café. First, they'd focused on the timing of the emailed threats that they had flagged. Second, they started watching the feed from weekday mornings to see if they could spot the mystery figure stalking Eve Kelley. No luck on either count. And time had run out for Amanda.

"I've gotta go, Trent." She stood and pushed her chair back to her desk. "You're good to keep going here?"

"Absolutely. You'll be back after?"

Amanda nodded. She'd get someone lined up to sit with Zoe, and then she could put in a long night on the case—as long as it took. At least that's how she felt. But was that the right thing to do for Zoe? Somehow dropping her off after the events of last night and an appointment with the therapist felt wrong.

She parked at the curb out front of Dumfries Elementary, waiting for school to let out. Amanda stretched and passed the time standing outside the car and leaning against it.

She texted Libby to ask if it would be possible to drop Zoe at her house at around five and for her to stay the night. The only part alleviating any of Amanda's guilt was knowing how close the two of them were.

Her phone chimed with a message. *Let's talk in person.*

Amanda looked up and saw Libby walking toward her with Zoe at her side. Zoe wasn't waving or smiling. Her little mouth was set in a frown. Amanda helped close the distance.

"Hey, Zoe."

"Hey." A mumble with zero enthusiasm.

Libby pressed her lips together when Amanda looked at her for an explanation. Amanda turned to tell Zoe to get in the car and that she'd be there in a minute, but the girl was already on her way to shutting the door.

"What's happened?" Amanda asked Libby.

"I don't know exactly." Libby was squinting in the afternoon sun. "She's out of sorts. I spoke to her teacher and was told that she was quiet all day."

"That's not like her."

"No, it's not. The teacher's not concerned yet, but she's watching the situation. I'm sure if things continue or get worse, you'll be receiving a call to come in for a meeting."

Amanda put a hand over her stomach. She'd only been Zoe's adoptive mother for a few months, and she was already screwing it up. "She had that episode last night that you know about. She's having a really hard time right now with her grief."

"Yes, I gathered as much. It's too bad we can't just suck it out of her."

"Oh, I wish that was possible. Anyway, I made an appointment for her with her therapist for four o'clock."

"You really need to get moving, then."

"I do." Amanda took a step toward the car but still faced Libby. "Are you able to take her tonight and keep her for a sleepover? I know the timing of this isn't ideal but..." In that moment, Amanda was ready to forget all about the case and returning to Central. Zoe took priority, but there was that thing called balance, and sometimes her job also needed attention—especially when it felt like she and Trent were on the cusp of figuring things out.

"Of course I can. Don't worry about it. She's good with me, Amanda."

She nodded. "Thank you."

"Don't mention it." Libby waved at Zoe, who just looked blankly back at her.

Amanda got into the car, not even prepared for what lay ahead. She had to dismiss her negative thoughts and trust her intuition that she was the best person for Zoe—for the girl's sake. After all, without Amanda, Zoe could be who knows where, and Amanda was quite sure that no one else could love her as much as she did.

THIRTY-TWO

The therapy went about as well as could be expected, possibly better. Zoe had opened up to the doctor, and she was in a better mood when she left. It broke Amanda's heart that she had to leave the girl again, but Zoe seemed to understand. That didn't mean it hurt Amanda any less to drop her at Libby's and turn in the direction of Central.

Trent was holed up behind his desk, and based on his expression, Amanda didn't think he had good news to share. The shake of his head confirmed it. He followed her into her cubicle.

"I sent a note to the lab to forward Eve Kelley's computer to Detective Briggs in Digital Crimes. I also took a look at Alicia's laptop, and there weren't any of the printed threats on it. But I called and had Harold Armstrong forward the emails on Alicia's computer in the office to me. In turn, I forwarded the messages to Briggs."

"Okay, great job."

"Let's just hope he can track the emails and find where they were sent from."

"Did you watch the Caffeine Café video again for the times the threats were emailed?"

He bobbed his head. "I did. But nothing."

"All right. Well, whoever this is—and assuming the threats we're looking at all originated from one person—they are doing their best to cover their tracks. They didn't want to take the chance that if the emails attracted police attention, the messages could be traced to their home by IP address. They were also careful about keeping their face off camera."

"Not entirely sure how brilliant this person is, though. If they were really smart, they'd have used a VPN or something to completely hide their IP address."

"Well, look at you." She smiled at him.

"I know some things. It also helps when your older sister is a bit of a computer nerd."

He'd mentioned he had sisters before. Mostly he talked about the one younger than him, but she didn't know much about the rest of his family. To ask would make their partnership even more personal, though, and she needed to steer away from that.

Trent went on. "But I don't think we should ignore that the threat to Lopez was sent from Caffeine Café—a place Eve Kelley frequented. Maybe the others were sent from places where Alicia Gordon or the bidders made a habit of going."

"Could be, but what a shot in the dark."

"They've been known to pay off. Anyway, if there's something to find, Briggs will uncover it."

Amanda shared Trent's faith in the digital crimes detective. "You brought up the possibility that the killer may have had a personal interest or relationship with Alicia and/or Eve. But I want to stay focused on the business angle. I feel it's likely the strongest link between the two women."

"So, as we've been thinking, the killer is probably someone

who has something at stake when it comes to the sale—or purchase—of New Belle."

"Exactly. And we need to remember whoever this person is would also need access to pentobarbital."

"Have you heard any more from Bethany about the missing inventory?"

"Nope, but it's past time we follow up." She rushed to leave her cubicle, and her cell phone rang. She raised her eyebrows at Trent, curious if it just so happened to be Bethany Wagner calling with answers, but it wasn't. It was her mother. She didn't have time for personal matters right now—not when two women were dead and other people's lives were threatened. She sent her mother to voicemail. "Let's go," she said to Trent, and they hustled down the hall to the lot, got into the department car, and headed for Paws & Claws. They'd check there first, and if the place was already closed for the day, they'd go to the Wagner house.

Her phone rang again, and she checked the screen, cursed under her breath. She answered with, "Mom, I don't have time to talk right—"

"Scott Malone is in the hospital, Amanda," her mother cut in.

"He's... he's what?"

Trent looked over at her.

Her mother continued. "He passed out, and the doctors aren't sure why. He hasn't regained consciousness yet. You have to get here. Now."

"Yeah, yes, of course." Amanda gestured with flailing fingers and directed Trent. "Take us to Prince William Medical Center."

He turned the car in the direction of Manassas where the hospital was located.

"We're on our way. Should be there in half an hour or less."

"Come to the ICU."

Intensive Care Unit. The words rang in her mind and made her feel like vomiting. Amanda ended the call and held her phone, staring out the window. *This can't be happening.*

"Amanda...?" Trent prompted her.

She licked her lips and had this dreadful feeling whirling through her belly. *Passed out... hasn't regained consciousness...* "It's Malone. Something's happened to him."

"Do we know what?"

"Not exactly. Just that he passed out and was rushed to the hospital. That's all I kn-ow." Emotion cracked her voice. She was shaking. Nothing could happen to Malone. Not now, not ever. He was like a second father to her.

"I'll get us there as quickly as I can."

The car shot forward. Colors in various shades outside her window, blurred. She was numb. In shock. Sickened. How unfair that life could take such violent twists and turns.

Come on, Malone. You have to be okay.

Amanda spotted her mother, Jules Steele, in the busy waiting room. She was there with Amanda's dad and Ida, Scott Malone's wife, and Paul, the Malones' youngest son—two families that were really one. Others within the police department must not have heard the news yet or the hospital would be overflowing with the brothers in blue.

Her mother swept Amanda into a bear hug and then corralled her down a side hall.

Amanda swiped at a tear that hit her cheek and looked into her mother's wide, wet eyes. "Tell me everything," Amanda said. "What exactly happened? Where was he?"

"From what we can tell, he was driving home and lost control of his car."

Amanda's stomach tightened at the thought of a car accident. She knew firsthand just how deadly they could be. "You said he passed out." She was grasping for logic and reason, but she couldn't find purchase.

"He did, honey. That's what doctors believed caused the accident."

"Was anyone else involved?"

Her mother shook her head. "Thankfully not. He drove through someone's yard and hit their gazebo. The air bag deployed, and he's banged up and bruised, but thankfully he survived the wreck." Her mother went solemn, then added, "His car may be written off."

"Vehicles can be replaced." What her mother was telling her didn't sound so horrible, not the life-or-death prospect that Amanda had in mind. But there was a knot in her gut. "There's more, though. There has to be. What caused him to pass out?"

"You're trembling, sweetheart." Her mother put her hands on Amanda's arms.

"Please, Mom. Is he going to be okay?" She could barely get the question to form, not wanting to consider for an instant that Malone wouldn't be.

Her mother's chin quivered. "It's too soon to know. All we can do is pray and wait."

Amanda hated that answer. Waiting around was not her strong suit. "So they have no idea why he passed out?"

"Not yet. Once he regains consciousness, doctors will conduct tests to figure that out."

"He... he hasn't..." She rubbed her throat, her voice and sense of reason vacating.

"Stay positive, Mandy," her mother stressed. "The doctors believe he will wake up."

"But they can't know for sure."

"No one can predict the future. We must assume all will be well. You hear me?" Her mother met her eyes. "We must. Now, walk with me. Your father needs you, and so does Ida."

Amanda wiped away more tears that fell. But she wanted to

be strong for her father, Ida, and the entire Malone family. Amanda wondered where the second son was, but he was probably on his way. Both sons lived in Washington, about an hour from Manassas.

Her steps were heavy as she returned to the waiting area. She observed that Trent had made himself comfortable and appeared to be one of the family. Amanda went to Ida and gave her a huge hug and spoke assurances she had no right to promise and feared putting faith in herself.

"Thank you for coming, Amanda. It means a lot to me," Ida told her.

"Nowhere else I would be right now." And with that, she thought of Zoe. It was probably best that the girl was with Libby tonight.

"Means a lot to all of us." Paul hugged Amanda.

"Long time no see," she said, aiming for some lightness.

"It has been. Just wish it was under better circumstances."

Amanda touched his arm and asked after his family—Paul had a wife and two children—and he said they were fine and at home. His wife would get there as soon as she found a babysitter. Paul added that his brother, Sam, was on his way and should be there any minute.

Sam, unlike his brother, was single and seemed happy that way, from what Amanda knew.

Amanda went over and hugged her dad, possibly a little tighter than normal. It was hard to comprehend how she'd pulled herself away from her family after losing Kevin and Lindsey. But for the longest time being around her parents and siblings had just seemed to burrow the pain even deeper. She regretted her choice. After all, who knew how long any of them had? "Love you, Dad."

His response was to pull her in tighter, as if he couldn't find the strength to speak. It just confirmed how shaken her father, the rock of the family, was.

In this moment, any hurt she felt about her father's dalliance with CSI Blair was forgotten and forgiven. She continued to remain by his side as the group awaited word on Malone.

Time had never moved so slowly.

THIRTY-THREE

Amanda had a kink in the side of her neck that was shooting pain into her skull. No matter how she angled her head, trying to stretch it out, the damn cord in her neck bit. Guess that's what happened when a person slept in a waiting-room chair—but she hadn't meant to fall asleep. Honestly, she could hardly believe she had. She was only stirring now because she heard the words, "He's back."

She cracked open her eyes, barely establishing her bearings when she saw her parents, Ida, Sam, and Paul with a doctor.

She fumbled to her feet and joined them.

The doctor dipped his head subtly to acknowledge her arrival but carried on with what he had been saying. "Good news is he's aware of where he is and what's happened. And he's asking for you." The doctor leveled his gaze at Ida. "I'll be conducting tests this morning to see if we can uncover what caused your husband to pass out, Mrs. Malone. These answers are not always easy to detect, and getting to the bottom of it may take a while. Just want you to know that, so you don't expect immediate answers."

"I... I understand." Ida put an arm around Paul, and Sam squeezed his mother's hand. "Can I see him now?"

"You can, but it's best that we keep the visiting short. And limited to as few people as possible." He swept his gaze over the group. Some brothers in blue had filtered in over the night as the news of Malone's accident and medical condition reached them. Amanda's siblings had shown up at various times too, but none of them were there now.

Amanda looked around and saw Trent in the corner of the waiting room, keeping his distance and giving the family space. She looked back at the doctor, who was telling Ida and her sons to follow him. Amanda met her father's gaze. He briefly glanced away, as if he didn't want her to read the emotion in them, the fragility.

"He's in good hands, Dad."

Her father simply nodded, gave a pressed-lip smile, and dragged himself toward a chair.

The doctor had mentioned they'd be conducting tests that morning. *What time is it, or day even?* Amanda pulled out her phone. Thursday, seven AM. *Seven!* Last she knew her eyelids had been growing heavy around three thirty.

She went over to Trent. "You didn't have to stay."

A flicker of irritation sparked in his eyes. "This is where I wanted to be, where I was needed."

If she wasn't concerned about crossing any lines, she'd throw her arms around him. It pained her to resist the urge. But his staying wasn't any sort of declaration of romantic feelings for her. He was being a supportive partner, and Malone was his boss too.

She was so exhausted that all her bones ached, not just her neck. And if she felt that way, her poor father couldn't be faring much better. "Just a minute," she said to Trent and returned to her father. "You should go home, and get some rest. I'm sure the doctor will call you when there's more to tell."

Her father shook his head. "Your mother and I aren't going anywhere until we know more."

"You don't know how long that might be. You heard what the doctor said."

Her father's facial features shadowed and took on hard lines. "Not leaving, Amanda. We're here as long as Ida and the boys are."

Amanda gave him a small nod. There was no talking her father out of something once his mind was made up. She hugged her parents and went back to Trent. She caught him in a yawn. "Did you catch any sleep?"

"Not really. You did, though. Did you know you snore like a drunken sailor?"

Heat crept into her cheeks. She was mortified. "Why didn't you wake me?"

Trent was grinning. "Gotcha."

She shoved him in the shoulder, and he reached for her hand to help keep his balance. His palm was warm and soft. She pulled her hand back. She would endeavor to ignore how her skin felt scorched from his touch—and not in a bad way.

"What are you wanting to do now? Wait around or...?" he asked.

The only thing that had helped her at all after losing Kevin and Lindsey was throwing herself into the job, and that was all that was going to save her now. Her body begged for sleep, but she doubted she could rest at all. She'd likely just lie in bed, tossing and turning and staring at the ceiling. Such a waste of time when there was a killer out there who could strike again— not that they'd heard from the officers watching over Lopez and Reynolds. No news would mean nothing had flagged as concerning. Still, cops were human, and things could be missed. Yet she had more than herself to consider. "Up to you. You're probably dreaming of your pillow."

"I am, but I don't think I could sleep right now."

"Tired-wired?"

"One way of putting it, if you mean you've passed the point of exhaustion and looped around to being fully awake. There's just too much going on. We're getting closer to solving this case, though, I'm sure of it. And how could I possibly sleep knowing what everyone is going through here?"

She admired how Trent was more concerned about others than himself. After all, Trent would be emotionally invested in Malone's diagnosis. "How I feel too," she said.

"Hey, catching a killer has to be a good way to distract the mind."

"I've found it effective."

Trent frowned, and she could read the sympathy in his eyes. It was like it was just sinking in for him how she'd been in a hospital in the past due to a car accident when her family had died. She led the way out of the waiting room before things could get all soft and mushy. She was running on less than fumes by this point, and her nerves were shot. It wouldn't take much to get emotional, and there was a job to do. "What do you say we grab some jumbo coffees from Hannah's Diner, then hit up Paws and Claws?" she asked him.

"Sounds good to me."

They didn't say much more as they drove to Hannah's Diner.

May Byrd met them at the counter, a grim expression eating her face. "How is he?"

Amanda shouldn't be surprised that May had heard about Malone. Rumors in this town hit May's ears at a shocking speed. "Scott Malone?"

"Who else?"

"Doctors don't know yet."

May put a hand over Amanda's, which was resting on the counter. "We stay positive, and we pray. We leave the matter in God's hands."

Amanda pressed her lips but said nothing. From her experience, God wasn't too hands-on. "They are going to be conducting tests on him today to see what caused him to pass out. I'm not sure how much you heard." Amanda was comfortable sharing all this with her, as May was a long-time friend of the Malones.

"Just that he careened up onto the Lamberts' lawn and hit their gazebo. People thought he was drunk at first."

That word *drunk* had anger curdling inside her. "There's no way he'd drink and drive."

"No, I'd say not, and when it became apparent who was behind the wheel, everyone knew it had to be a health issue or mechanical failure that caused the accident." May filled two extra-large cups with coffee. "Here. They're on the house today. Looks like you two could use all the caffeine you can get."

"Pretty much. Thank you." Amanda lifted her cup toward May.

"Just be careful on the roads yourselves, eh? Neither of you look like you've gotten much sleep."

"Hence, the caffeine." Amanda smiled at the woman, hoping that would be enough to assuage her concerns.

Trent and Amanda each ordered a bagel with cream cheese before they left—not that she thought she could get it down and keep it there.

They both knocked back their coffees as they drove to Paws & Claws in Woodbridge. Trent munched on his bagel, while she left hers in the bag.

He seemed about as preoccupied as she was, and they didn't talk much on the way. He parked in the lot of the veterinary clinic, and she was as ready as she ever would be to face this day.

"Let's get some answers." She led the way inside the building.

THIRTY-FOUR

At eight thirty, the clinic doors were unlocked, and the sign said they were open, but the parking lot and waiting room were empty. No one was at the front desk either. It was shockingly quiet, unlike the first time they were there.

Amanda pressed the bell on the counter and called out, "Hello?"

No one responded, and Amanda looked at Trent. "Where the heck is everyone?" An anxious feeling was spreading over her skin. Had something happened to Bethany Wagner and/or her husband? "Hello?" she repeated.

There was some thumping, and Amanda glanced at Trent again as if to visually confirm he'd heard it too. She ignored the protocol of waiting at the desk and went behind it, heading to the source of the noise. Trent moved with her. It led them to the room where the drugs were stored.

Bethany Wagner and a man who Amanda assumed was Isaac, Bethany's husband, were rummaging in the medicine locker.

"Stop what you're doing. Right now," Amanda barked.

The Wagners stopped.

"Step away from the locker." Amanda danced her gaze over the couple. "Disappointed that I haven't heard from you, Bethany."

Bethany licked her lips. "I was going to..."

Amanda made eye contact with the man. "You're Isaac Wagner, I presume?"

"I am."

"Detectives Steele and Stenson," she said more for Isaac's benefit. "Can you tell us what you're doing?" The scene playing out in front of her and Trent wasn't looking good. The couple had drugs spread out on a table and wore this expression that screamed they were guilty as hell of something.

Bethany's shoulders sank. "I should have called you. I apologize that I didn't."

"I'm not looking for apologies, Bethany. I want to know what you two are up to right now and what happened to the missing pentobarbital." Amanda wouldn't be leaving until she had the answer to both questions.

"I'm... We're—"

Isaac put his hand on Bethany's shoulder. "We've done nothing wrong."

"I'll decide that," Amanda pushed out.

"We're just here trying to review the inventory logs," Bethany said.

The front door opened and thumped shut.

"I need to go and..." Bethany jabbed a finger toward the hallway.

"Stay here." Amanda motioned for Trent to see who had arrived, and he left the room. "Go on," she said to Isaac and Bethany, not caring which one of them wanted to pick up the storytelling.

"Nothing much more to say," Isaac said, his voice somber.

Trent returned and informed them it was the front-desk clerk who had arrived.

"I have a feeling your initial assumption that some pentobarbital is missing was correct?" Amanda was quaking. They were here trying to cover up the missing inventory, it seemed. There could only be one reason for that—they were trying to protect someone. Tony?

"It was," Bethany admitted and rushed to add, "and I realize how my not calling might make things look."

"How is that?" Amanda countered, playing stupid.

"Like I'm trying to cover something up."

"I hate to say it, but the thought crossed my mind." Amanda didn't see a point in lying. "Do you have any idea what happened to the missing inventory?"

Bethany glanced at Isaac, and it was so subtle it could have been easy to miss.

"Bethany," Amanda prompted her.

The woman hugged herself and rubbed her arms.

Amanda could hardly believe she was heading down this path, but she had to keep an open mind. "You didn't care much for Alicia. That's what you told us." She gestured toward Trent. Back to Bethany. "Did you kill her?"

"What? No, absolutely not."

"Maybe you wanted to hurt your dad for moving on so quickly, for not giving your mother another chance." Trent paused, then elaborated. "It would also free him up to resume things with your mother, since the obstacle—Alicia—would be out of the way."

"Did I hate the woman? Sure, fine," Bethany seethed. "But I didn't kill her. I wouldn't kill her and hurt Dad that way—no matter how mad I am at him."

"Do you know what happened to the missing pentobarbital?" Trent pushed out, obviously having lost all patience.

The Wagners looked at each other, their eyes scanning the other's face like two people who were privy to a secret and wanted to protect it at all costs.

"We need to tell them, Beth," Isaac eventually said.

Amanda feared taking her next breath in case it somehow discouraged either Wagner from speaking.

"I didn't kill Alicia, and I can tell you that Dad wouldn't have either. He loved her. I could see that, as much as I hate to admit it." The woman's face was paling in increments, and her body sagged.

Amanda braced herself for the news that was coming, sensing there would be nothing good about it. "What is it, Bethany?" she gently pressed.

"I can't do it," Bethany blurted out and paced to a corner of the room and started to cry.

Amanda turned her attention to Isaac. "Tell us what we need to know."

Isaac's body became rigid. "It was an insanely busy day, and I was the only certified vet here. I had surgeries lined up, had one cocker spaniel under, in fact, when this labradoodle came in suffering greatly... in organ failure. I was pulled from the operating room, where I left the cocker spaniel under the care of one of our veterinary assistants."

"Where were you?" Trent looked at Bethany.

"I stepped out for a few minutes," she said.

Isaac went on. "Tony came in to pick up Beth for lunch, and I was running around like mad and wanted to end this poor labradoodle's suffering. The owner was having a complete meltdown too, which didn't help things in the waiting room. She was taken into an exam room with her dog. Long story short, I really didn't want to leave the woman. I feared for her well-being, in all honesty. She was acting hysterically, and I didn't want her passing out or having a heart attack or something. I stuck my head out of the room and saw Tony. I asked him to retrieve the pentobarbital from the locker. I gave him the codes, told him where he'd find it, and he went and got it."

It sounded like this woman was quite attached to her dying

pet, and even worse, Amanda didn't like the direction this conversation was headed. It certainly wasn't looking good for Tony. He had access to the drug that killed his wife and Eve Kelley. "So Tony returned with the pentobarbital?" Goosebumps were spreading across her flesh.

"He did."

"Why didn't you leave him with the woman and get the drug yourself?" Amanda longed to poke holes in the man's story.

"I suppose I could have. I just wasn't thinking."

"You weren't thinking because she's your freaking mistress!" Bethany spat. "Might as well tell them everything."

Isaac clenched his jaw and flushed red. He didn't need to add verbal confirmation to his wife's claim. The body language did that.

That might explain why Isaac emphasized the woman's mental and physical state. He probably made it sound much worse than it actually was. "So you sent Tony Bishop to get the pentobarbital," Amanda began, "but how do you know he took out more than what you'd asked for?"

"I know what he handed over, and I recorded that later in the day. There is missing pentobarbital, and the only person who had access to the locker besides myself and Bethany was Tony." When he finished speaking, Isaac looked at Bethany.

"There's no way my dad killed her," Bethany said, wiping her wet cheeks. "None." Bethany met Amanda's gaze. In that moment, Amanda saw the young girl who used to babysit Lindsey, but she couldn't allow herself to get swallowed up by nostalgia—especially not now.

Amanda ran through the possibility that her former friend had killed his wife. He stood to inherit New Belle, among other financial perks—but only if Alicia died before successfully removing him from her will. He had access to her bottles of Sleep Tight. He had changed his career, upheaved his life, for what? And if Tony had killed Eve Kelley too, was it something to do with her lawsuit threatening the welfare of the business? She had it served just days before her death. And his alibi for the morning of Eve's death could be contested. A mistress claiming he was with her wasn't exactly airtight. "Sometimes the people closest to us aren't who they seem," she said, shaking as she spoke.

"Are you going to arrest him?" Bethany's voice was on the edge of a cry and held the desperate note of shock and grief.

"We will need to speak with him," Amanda said firmly.

They left the Wagners and the vet clinic, and returned to the car. Trent was the first to speak.

"No wonder she didn't call you back. She knows her dad did this."

Amanda faced her partner. "No. *You* don't even know that." She was still grasping to believe in Tony's innocence. Why, she didn't know, when the evidence seemed to be pointing a finger at him.

"Come on, Amanda. You have to see how guilty he looks. We can't put off bringing him in anymore."

She hated that she was in this position—that Tony Bishop had put her there. She'd trusted him, and it bit her in the ass. "I know. We'll get the arrest warrant, and bring him in."

THIRTY-FIVE

Amanda banged on the front door after pressing the doorbell twice without luck.

"There might not be anyone home," Trent said, glancing over a shoulder. "Not like we could tell if he's parked in the garage."

He was right, but she hoped he wasn't. She'd just accepted the fact that she was going to be arresting her former friend under suspicion of murder. Now they were in a holding pattern, and she feared she'd lose the nerve to slap cuffs on him.

She was about to knock again when the sound of the garage door opening stopped her cold. She hustled down the pathway to the garage just as Tony Bishop had turned into the drive.

He stopped the car abruptly, the nose of it dipping to the ground then heaving up. He cut the engine and jogged toward Amanda and Trent. His face was ashen, and he was waving a piece of paper in his hand. "I was looking for you. I went to Central, and you weren't there."

"Why not just call me?" she countered.

"Here." He gave her the sheet of paper, which she took with hesitation.

"What is this? And why didn't you answer my question?"

"Please just read it." Tony pointed at it, animated. But it was the tone of his voice and his shaken countenance that really grabbed her attention.

She looked down at the page, holding it for Trent to see as well.

You're next, in Times New Roman font.

She didn't know whether to laugh or take this seriously. Succinct and cheesy, like a line in some horror flick where a group of friends get knocked off one by one. Bethany must have warned Tony they'd be coming for him, and he concocted this ploy. "Is this a joke?"

"Is this a—" Tony raked a hand through his hair. His eyes were wild. "This is a threat against my life!"

"Convenient timing." Trent pushed out his chin, showing no mercy and not making any attempt to be diplomatic.

"We've come to arrest you, Tony." Amanda made a circle with her finger, motioning for him to turn around.

"No. I didn't do anything. You read it." He was panicked and frenzied. "First Alicia, then Eve, and now me."

"You can't expect that we'd believe—" Trent silenced under her gaze.

"Why should we take this seriously, Tony?" Amanda said, stepping in. "You had access to pentobarbital, and you stole some to kill your wife and Eve Kelley."

"I didn't hurt either of them."

"Turn around. Please."

Tony held her gaze, then slowly pivoted, putting his hands on his head. She pulled them behind his back, snapped on the cuffs, and read him his Miranda rights.

"I can't believe you're doing this, Amanda."

"Detective Steele." She pinched her eyes shut just for a second, not believing it either. In less than twenty-four hours, her beloved family friend and sergeant was rushed to the hospital and now she was arresting a former friend.

"Fine, Detective, I'll cooperate," Tony seethed. "But my life was threatened. Doesn't that mean anything?"

"Let us determine that." Trent was being relentless, and it had the back of Amanda's neck tightening. If this was anyone other than Tony, Amanda probably wouldn't even notice.

Tony Bishop was loaded into the back of a cruiser by a uniformed officer who had been there on standby. Amanda told the officer she and Trent would be following them to Central. As Trent drove, she looked at the threatening note she now held in a clear evidence bag.

Trent pointed at it. "So convenient that he presents us with a threat now."

"You keep saying that but—"

"No buts, Amanda. The guy did this. He killed his wife. He killed Eve Kelley."

Silence fell between them, which she ended up breaking.

"Why? Give me a reason." Though she could conjure a couple: money and the freedom to take up with Tina Nash, the nanny. "You know what? Never mind. I can come up with enough on my own."

"I'm sorry, but the simple answer is he's guilty, Amanda."

She met Trent's gaze just before he turned to look out the windshield and pulled into the lot for Central.

He's guilty, Amanda.

Trent had also said that was the simple answer, yet it was anything but.

Amanda entered the interrogation room with a bottle of water. Tony was already seated at the table and facing the door. He didn't look at her when she came in. She put the water in front of him, and still he refused to make eye contact.

She sat across from Tony, and Trent sat beside her. She had a file with her that included Tony's background, a copy of Alicia's will, a printout of the document on Alicia's laptop with her intention to remove Tony as a beneficiary, the flagged threats to the bidders, and also the ones sent to Alicia Gordon and Eve Kelley. She had the threat against him in the evidence bag.

"Why do you have me in here like some criminal?" Tony peered into her eyes, begging for redemption.

"The evidence led us to you. You will be charged with killing your wife unless you can give us something solid to make us believe otherwise."

"It's right there!" He flailed a hand toward the threat directed at him.

"Before we continue, you need to know that our conversation is being recorded." She refused to be swayed by hysterics.

"Fine, I don't care. But whoever killed Alicia and Eve, they must have sent that threat to me."

"Tell us where you got this." Amanda pressed a fingertip to the letter.

Tony lifted his gaze from the table to meet hers. "You know what? Why bother? You're going to believe whatever you want anyway."

The accusation stung. She'd tried to remain objective from the start. "Please." She bit back adding *Tony*.

"I was at work and found it in my desk drawer."

"You returned to work so soon after your wife's death?" Trent asked.

Amanda held up a hand to her partner, and he shook his head.

"Just because she was murdered doesn't mean everything stops—even if it hurts like hell." Grief shadowed his face, and Amanda felt the intensity of his sorrow.

"You were at work, doing what?" she asked, just for the record.

"I was reviewing some marketing campaigns and giving final approvals. Ad deadlines are tomorrow."

"Okay, so you found the letter in your desk drawer... Run us through it," she said.

"Nothing much more to it."

"Why did you open your drawer?"

"I needed my approval stamp."

"That's where you normally keep it? Which drawer?"

"Top, on the left-hand side."

If the threat was legitimate, Amanda would surmise whoever placed the letter there knew Tony would be at work *and* need his stamp. "Who knew you were at work today?"

"Pfft. Everyone I suppose. The front desk people, Scarlett, Harold." Tony lifted his shoulders. "I'm probably forgetting someone. But I was there yesterday too."

"Did you have any visitors? Or is there anyone else who might have known that you would need your stamp today and where you kept it?"

Tony met her gaze. "You're finally taking me seriously."

"It's my job to get to the truth and find justice. Please answer my question."

"No one. Oh, Brad and Leo popped in yesterday when I was finishing up at the office. They stopped by to surprise me. They wanted to go out for dinner, but I'm just not up for that yet."

"Nice that the brothers are close," Amanda said.

"It is."

"They seem to be handling the loss of their mother okay," she said. That would be the second time the two boys would be out this week.

"Like champs, but I think they're putting on a tough front,

just like me. It surprises me they want to go out in public, but I'm not going to discourage it. You can't sit with grief all the time."

Even if it—like misery—likes the company... "We'll investigate this threat, but we have something far more pressing to discuss." The energy in the room shifted in its intensity.

"I didn't kill Alicia or Eve Kelley."

"From my viewpoint, I see evidence of your guilt. For one, this." She produced the printout of Alicia's intended change to her will. She set it on the table, so the wording was facing him. "We got this from Alicia's computer. She was removing you as a beneficiary, Tony."

He held her gaze for a few seconds before turning his focus on the page. A few seconds later, he was pushing the sheet away. "No, why would she?"

"I don't know. Maybe she found out about your affair with Tina?" Amanda stiffened. "You killed Alicia before she could cut you out of an inheritance." Even as she hurled the accusation, she realized it didn't implicate him in Eve Kelley's murder —but something else did.

"I swear I had no idea about this." Tony was heaving for breath.

She was tired of hearing his lies. "And you knew about Eve's lawsuit. It could have seriously threatened New Belle's financial stability."

"No way. It was all hot air. New Belle's lawyers would get the entire thing dismissed. Besides, it would take more than one lawsuit to topple what Alicia built. There was no solid proof that Alicia stole that serum formula from Eve. Not a thing."

Amanda didn't share that confidence. "Alicia had Eve sign an NDA, paid her to keep quiet. I'm sure that wouldn't look good to a judge."

"I don't think it would have taken a good lawyer much effort to make the courts see Eve Kelley had nothing to stand on."

"All right, let's move on," she said. "I asked you if you ever went into the room with the drugs at your daughter's vet clinic. You told me no."

"That's right."

"Except that's a lie." Amanda leaned back in her chair. "I'll give you a chance to reconsider your previous answer."

Minutes ticked off. Finally, she prompted him, "Mr. Bishop."

"You already know the answer." Not a question, but a statement, an accusation, a conclusion.

"Talk," she urged.

"I was at Paws and Claws."

"And when was this?" Trent cut in.

"Two weeks ago. It was a Thursday."

"Just days before your wife died," Trent said drily. "Continue."

She wished her partner was a tad less aggressive.

"Sure. I was there to pick up Bethany for lunch."

"Okay, go on," she encouraged.

"The place was nothing but chaos, and there was this dog. It was really suffering, and"—he swallowed roughly—"Isaac asked for my help. He gave me the code to the drug locker to get him pentobarbital. He didn't want to leave the pet owner, and I couldn't blame him. She was acting rather hysterically."

"So you got the pentobarbital for him?" she asked.

"I did, and I locked everything up behind me."

Amanda found it interesting how Tony added that last tidbit, eliminating any possible defense that someone might have come in after him and taken the pentobarbital.

"Did you help yourself to some extra pentobarbital besides what you got for Mr. Wagner?" Trent asked.

Tony clenched his jaw, leveled his gaze at Trent. "No, I didn't."

While Amanda wanted to believe Tony, there was nothing

and no one to substantiate his claim. There was, however, the letter staring at her from the table. What if it was a legitimate threat and not something that Tony had concocted? What if Tony truly was in danger? What if everything they had against him was circumstantial?

THIRTY-SIX

Amanda and Trent were in the observation room next to Interview One and looking in on Tony Bishop. They were standing mere inches apart.

"He'd have reason to want both Alicia and Eve Kelley dead," Trent said. "You do see that?"

She couldn't look at him, but said, "Of course I do."

He touched her arm, and it had her turning to face him. "And you can see why he'd come up with this *threat?*" He attributed finger quotes to the last word.

"Yes." She swallowed roughly, her answer going down like broken glass.

"Then why are you giving it so much consideration? It's like you're clawing at anything to excuse him."

"It's our job to protect the people in the community. Tony Bishop is one."

He shrugged. "Fine, we'll... what? Give him the benefit of the doubt?"

"We would anyone else."

"I think we've already extended him a lot of rope."

She couldn't even argue that point because she agreed. Her

phone rang. Her heart froze thinking it was an update on Malone, but it was the lab. "Detective Steele."

"It's CSI Donnelly. Blair asked that I call. Sorry this took so long, but I have the results on the tire treads left in the mud at the cabin. As well as the brand of shoe that left the prints next to the window."

Amanda was staring at Trent still, her chest heaving. "And?"

"The tires are factory standard for the Dodge Ram fifteen hundred model."

Dodge Ram... Amanda bounced that around in her mind, knowing she'd seen one in the course of the investigation but couldn't conjure up where. "And the shoes?"

"Cloud Footwear, their Ithan model. We would have been able to confirm immediately had the logo not been damaged. It's positioned right in the middle of the shoe."

"Right where there's a slash," Amanda said.

"That's right. And it's a model they make for men."

"Okay, we figured it was a man's shoe based on size, but this seems to confirm it."

"I'd say so."

"Thanks for this."

"Don't mention it. As I said, I'm just sorry it took so long to get back to you."

Amanda ended the call and shared the results with Trent.

"Alicia Gordon had a visitor who drives a Dodge Ram," he said as if mulling it over.

"Seems so. And I know I've seen one during the course of the investigation. I just can't remember where."

"But it doesn't even need to belong to her killer. Tony Bishop was fooling around with the nanny. What's to say that Alicia wasn't having her own *fun* on the side?"

"We never found anything in her phone records or communications to support her having an affair." She looked back through the one-way mirror at Tony, who was staring into space. Every few seconds, he wiped at his cheeks. She couldn't see tears, but he was visibly distraught. "We need to go back in there and see if we can get any more answers."

"We could, or..."

She turned to Trent. "Or what?"

"We let him cool off for a bit and investigate this threat of his." Trent went to the table in the observation room where she'd set the envelope and returned with it.

"Now you're encouraging that?"

He shrugged. "In the vein of keeping an open mind and protecting the public."

She had a feeling his suggestion was more of a concession for her. "Let me see it again." She held out her hand, and he put the bag in her palm. "The page is creased." How hadn't she noticed that before? Maybe she had but pushed it aside in her effort to remain objective.

"I'm guessing that means something?"

"Harold printed out the threats sent to Alicia Gordon. They have the same crease."

"This threat came from Harold's printer?"

"Maybe. And I remember where I saw a Dodge Ram now."

"Me too. In Harold Armstrong's parking spot at New Belle. Let's go ask Harold some questions, hopefully get some answers."

She glanced in at Tony again. "Okay, but let me explain what we're doing to Tony, er, Mr. Bishop first."

"You don't have to do that, Amanda."

"I know I don't *have* to, but I *want* to."

"All right, I'll wait in the car."

She nodded, and he walked down the hall while she returned to the interview room. She knocked once before entering, extending her former friend another courtesy by doing so.

Just the fact she was going to let him know they were looking into the threat was a courtesy of its own.

He straightened up when she entered. "Tell me you've got the real killer."

"It's not that simple." She leaned against the wall, not wanting to tower over him, but not wanting to take a seat either.

"Of course it is, Amanda. I didn't do it. That means the person who poisoned my Alicia and also Eve Kelley is out there running around free while I'm in here. And my boys are..." He rubbed his jaw. "*My* boys. Guess that's a joke really. Brad's practically a man, and Leo... well, he'll probably end up with Seth, his biological father."

"We never know what the future holds."

"Huh. Isn't that the truth? If you'd told me we'd be here, or that Alicia would be murdered, I never would have believed it."

"Unfortunately, we are in that spot. We're going to investigate that threat you gave us."

His eyes lit, and his expression became brighter. "Does that mean I'm free to go?"

She let out a deep breath and didn't need to say a word as she watched her answer sink into his slumping posture. "I'm sorry, but I can't let you go just yet."

"Even though you know I didn't kill them?"

She hesitated just a second too long.

"You still think I did."

"It's an open investigation. I—"

"Nah. Don't hide behind that lingo, not after all the years we were friends. Be honest with me."

"You want me to be honest? You look guilty as hell. All the times you lied to my face. And Tina Nash? You were sleeping with her? What were you thinking?"

"I didn't mean for it to happen."

"So, what—you just fell into her repeatedly?" Amanda crossed her arms, felt the heat in her cheeks.

"I loved Alicia, but she wasn't always there emotionally. And I need more than just the physical. I want to be with a woman who is actually with me—mind, body, and soul."

Silence fell between them for a few seconds, and she turned to leave.

"Thank you," he said.

She faced him. "I'm not doing this for you. I'm doing this because I'm not about to stick someone in jail without solid evidence against them, and you have received a threat. As an officer of the law, I am duty-bound to investigate the matter."

"Good. Then you'll see I'm innocent. In the meantime, what happens to me?"

"An officer will be here to get you shortly."

"You're putting me in a holding cell? Amanda, please don't do this."

His desperate plea, the sound of her name coming off his lips, tore her apart. The only thing giving her solace was her ability to hide behind the badge. She was just doing her job.

Trent pulled into the parking lot for New Belle, and Amanda pointed to Harold Armstrong's Dodge Ram.

"Right model too," she said. "Maybe we had it right in the first place. He found out about Alicia's plan to sell, and he did what he felt he had to in order to protect his financial future."

"Could be. And with Eve and her lawsuit against New Belle, Armstrong could have been worried that it would hurt the company."

"Except Tony really didn't seem to be."

Trent shrugged. "Two men, two viewpoints."

They both got out of the department car and went over to the truck. She looked closely at the tires.

"Are you looking for mud?" Trent asked. "You really expect to find some after this long?"

"You never know." She moved from the front driver's side to the front passenger's side. A few moments later, she was shaking her head. "Nothing so far, but still have the two back wheels to go." She didn't see any mud until the last tire—driver's side rear. "Look." She pointed, pleased that she'd turned up something for her efforts.

"We'll ask him how he got mud on his tire." He smirked. "Sounds like a line from a country song."

"I'll trust you to know that. As for how the mud is there, I'm quite sure I can tell you already."

Trent got the door for her, and Amanda went straight to the front desk. She observed a large poster displayed on an A-frame. An ad for Abandon, New Belle's latest fragrance. She noted the brand tagline again: *Dare to live the life you deserve.*

"Good morning. Welcome to New Belle. How can I assist you?" This receptionist wasn't the one who'd been there last time they visited.

Amanda went through the brief introductions and asked to speak with Harold Armstrong.

"Mr. Armstrong is currently on a conference call. He should be finished shortly, though."

"Please let him know we're here," Amanda said. "In the meantime, we'd like to speak with Scarlett Dixon." They'd met her before. Scarlett was Alicia and Tony's assistant.

"One minute." The receptionist smiled as she picked up the receiver and placed a call.

Amanda's plan was to talk to anyone who knew where Tony Bishop kept his stamp. They didn't have reason to suspect Scarlett Dixon before, but maybe she had a motive to want Alicia Gordon and Eve Kelley dead that they weren't aware of? Or maybe she was working with someone in this deadly game? Did she stand to lose something if New Belle was sold or fell into receivership? As Alicia's assistant, it was feasible she might be privy to personal information as well—specifically that Alicia took a sleeping aid.

A second or two later, the receptionist said, "Scarlett will be right down for you."

"Thank you."

Amanda and Trent hadn't even had a chance to take a seat in the lobby area before Scarlett was heading their way.

"Ms. Dixon, is there somewhere we could speak privately, perhaps your office area?" Amanda wanted to get closer to Tony's office, and they would get inside before they left.

"Sure. You probably remember it's not much, but I can grab a couple of chairs for you. Follow me." Scarlett took them to her desk. It was positioned between the offices for Alicia Gordon and Tony Bishop, something they knew from their first visit here.

Both offices had their doors shut at the moment. Amanda wondered if they were locked when unattended. She didn't remember Harold or Scarlett unlocking Alicia's office when they'd first looked at it.

"Let me get those chairs." Scarlett went to Tony's office and had the handle twisted and the door cracked before Amanda could stop her.

"We're fine to stand," she told the assistant.

Scarlett turned to face them. "As long you're sure...?"

Amanda glanced at Trent, who nodded. "We're sure," she said.

"All right, then." Scarlett took a seat at her desk. "What can I help you with?"

"We just have a few questions," Amanda began. "Let's start with who has access to Tony's office."

"Who? Let's see. Me—obviously—and well, there's probably quite a few who have been in there. Is there a specific time or day you're interested in?"

There was no way of knowing exactly when the threat had

been left in Tony's drawer, though it could be assumed since Eve's murder. "Let's say this week."

"Huh. Okay..." Scarlett's forehead pinched, forming a straight line between her eyebrows. "Me, Tony, Leo, and Brad came by... One of the models from the marketing campaign. The janitors come in at night."

"When was the model here?" Trent asked.

"Monday morning."

Amanda didn't think the model was in on any of the murders. Did she believe things were platonic between Tony and the model—who knew? He was already sleeping with the nanny. What's to say he drew the line there? "I noticed when you opened his door a minute ago that it wasn't locked. Is that always the case?"

"Uh-huh."

"Then really anyone could get into his office?" Amanda pressed.

"Yes."

That opened the suspect pool, but it could be narrowed down easily enough. "Mr. Bishop told us that he had approvals to make, due by tomorrow, for some ads?"

"Yes, that's right."

"And he normally signs off by hand on those or...?" Amanda was guilty of leading the woman, but she wasn't sure how else to get the answer she was after—namely, did Scarlett Dixon know about the stamp and leave the threat? And for what purpose?

"Heavens, no. He uses a stamp. Saves him a lot of time."

"And where does he keep that?" Trent interjected.

"His top drawer on the left."

"How many people know about his stamp and where he keeps it?" she asked.

"Lots would know about the stamp but not where he keeps it."

"And who would know he'd be in need of it this week?"

"Me. Not sure who else."

"What about Harold Armstrong?" Trent interjected.

"Yeah, he probably did."

Probably wasn't exactly a confidence booster. "Did you know that Alicia Gordon was planning to sell New Belle?" Amanda figured time was running out before they'd be joined by Harold Armstrong, and she wanted to get what she could from Scarlett before that happened.

"You know about that?"

Amanda gave her a pressed-lip smile. "Not much is missed during the course of a murder investigation."

"No, I suppose not, and yes, I knew. *But* I was sworn to confidentiality on the matter, both by Alicia and Mr. Bishop."

Amanda noted the difference in address, which suggested Scarlett had a more relaxed relationship with Alicia and a rather formal one with Tony. "What was your relationship like with Ms. Gordon?"

"She was brilliant." Scarlett's eyes glistened with admiration. "I learned so much from her. Did you know she started New Belle when she was in college? Oh, yeah, I guess you probably do."

Amanda would say that Scarlett's enthusiasm for Alicia was genuine, and she'd admitted to knowing that Alicia was shopping New Belle around. As she had thought before, nothing indicated Scarlett would have motive to kill Alicia Gordon, let alone Eve Kelley. Amanda also didn't sense any ill will about the prospect of the company being sold. Still, Amanda would ask. "What did you think about Ms. Gordon wanting to sell the business?"

"I thought it was a great thing, actually." Scarlett was grinning. "She wanted to spend more time with her son. That's a good thing, right?"

"You weren't worried about your job?" Amanda asked.

"No. I'd find something else, but I'm quite sure that Alicia would have worked it into the deal—that employees of New Belle would stay on board."

"Something like that can't always be guaranteed, even if initially agreed to," Trent pointed out.

Scarlett shook her head. "Alicia would have found some way to make sure that happened. She stood by her word."

Yet Alicia wasn't going to keep her word with regards to the arrangement she'd originally concocted with Eve Kelley. According to Eve, Alicia was going with a higher bidder and cutting Eve out of the deal. "Could we see Tony's office?"

"Sure."

Scarlett saw them inside, and Amanda took in the space. Adequate size, nothing fancy. A nice desk, a nice view, a nice sitting area off to the right.

"Detectives?" A man's voice at the doorway.

Amanda turned around. Harold Armstrong was standing there. And she wasn't quite sure what it was—the mud on his tires, his lie to them about the last time he'd seen Alicia, or just a niggling in her gut—but his presence made the room feel cold.

THIRTY-SEVEN

Just as Amanda came face to face with Harold Armstrong, her phone rang. "One second." She checked the caller ID, and it was her mother. Amanda couldn't risk sending the call the voicemail in case Malone had taken a turn for the worse. "I need to take this." She stepped into the hall. "Mom?"

"The doctors found something on the MRI." Her mother, who was normally full of energy, laid that out like a damp rag.

"What did they...?" Amanda could hardly get herself to form words.

"They haven't said specifically what it is. Just that it could explain why he passed out."

"When will they know?"

"They have more tests and scans to do, but we could know by the end of the day what we're dealing with."

Amanda's body was trembling. "Call me the minute you know more."

"You coming to the hospital later?"

"I will be. Love you, Mom. Tell Dad I love him too."

"Will do. Love you, Mandy Monkey." With that, her

mother hung up, but Amanda stood in the hall, staring into space, holding her phone to her chest.

Trent ducked into the hall, and Scarlett, who was at her desk, looked at her with concern.

"Everything all right?" Trent asked.

Amanda pressed her lips together, could feel warm tears budding in her eyes, and shook her head. "I don't think so." There was no way anything turning up on an MRI could be good news.

"Do you need to leave? I can handle this."

She considered it and, for a few seconds, seriously thought she would take him up on his offer. "No, I'll be fine. Nothing I can do anyway. It's either wait there or wait here and accomplish something."

Trent nodded. "If you change your mind..."

"I know. Thank you." She touched his shoulder, and they returned to Tony's office where Harold was making himself comfortable on a couch in the sitting area. They joined him. Both she and Trent sat in chairs angled toward the couch.

"Detective Stenson said you have questions for me." Harold leaned back, his arms along the top of the cushions.

He was acting rather cavalier considering two homicide detectives wanted a word with him. "When did you last see Alicia Gordon?" she asked.

"I answered that the first time we spoke."

"Sure. Just humor me." Amanda gave him a tight smile.

"The week before she died."

"Before she was *murdered*." Amanda made sure to emphasize the manner of death.

"That's right."

"Where did you get the mud on your truck's tire?" she volleyed back.

Harold met her gaze, and his face became shadows. "I'm not sure. Why?"

"I'm quite sure you know why I'm asking, Mr. Armstrong. Again, if you'd humor me." Her tone was dry, but she couldn't shake that Harold could have good reason to prevent the sale of New Belle—if he'd found out. Unlike Scarlett Dixon with her life and career path ahead of her, he was nearing the end of the road. He wouldn't be the top hire for any company at his age, despite his experience and what he had to offer. Sad but true. And while he had money to invest in New Belle at the beginning, his personal financial situation could have changed. "Were you at the cabin with Alicia?"

His cheeks flooded with color, but he said nothing.

"Answer Detective Steele's question, Mr. Armstrong," Trent prodded.

The older man took a deep, ragged breath. "Very well. Yes, I was there."

"Why were you there, Mr. Armstrong?"

Harold loosened his tie and undid a couple of buttons at his collar.

Suddenly it seemed the man had lost his ability to talk. "Will your prints match the wine bottle and wineglass that Alicia Gordon was drinking from at the cabin?"

He shrugged. "Yeah, I'd guess they would."

"You still haven't told us why you were there. Did you find out about her plan to sell New Belle?" She watched his body language as it stiffened and he crossed his arms, defensive. "Mr. Armstrong," she prompted.

"Yes, all right, I knew."

"You failed to admit this the first time we spoke."

"I know how it might look. I've been here forever, and if I lose this job, well, I'm a dinosaur in the world out there. I won't find anything else."

"And you're not ready for retirement," Amanda said, keeping the narrative going.

"No, I'm not. My wife spends money faster than it comes in. We have a mountain of debt."

His story of not being good with his cash wasn't a new one, but in Harold's case, it gave him motive for murder. "You must have been happy when Alicia died, knowing that the business would stay around longer."

"No. What a horrible thing to say."

"Since you were a close partner of Alicia's, I'm guessing you were aware of her will saying that Tony couldn't sell for a few years?" She was twisting the words of the clause slightly.

"He could sell, but he had to—" He clamped his mouth shut.

"So you were well aware of the stipulations in her will. It must have hurt that you weren't in it." A thought that had just occurred to her.

"Why would I be?"

"I'm sure you saw her as a friend at some point along the way," Trent said.

"She'd be nothing without me."

"Oh." Amanda glanced at Trent.

Harold added, "I don't mean that the way you're taking it."

"It sounds like you're saying her success was because of you, and if you wished, you could bring her down. Did you kill her?" Amanda said.

"Not what I meant."

"Maybe you should start saying what you mean," Amanda said. "And you never told us why you were at the cabin with Ms. Gordon."

"I wanted to talk her out of selling. Is that what you want to hear?"

Amanda shrugged. "We just want to hear the truth."

"Well, that's the truth. And, no, I wasn't thrilled when she told me she was entertaining offers, but at least she had the guts to come to me directly. And she did tell me that she'd make sure

I'd walk away with a generous severance package." When he said that last part, his voice deflated, as if he didn't believe it.

"You didn't think that would happen," Amanda surmised.

"Even if she gave me the numbers she was talking about, I'd be in hock. That doesn't mean I killed her, as you seem intent on implying."

"Run us through the night you were at the cabin with her," Amanda requested.

"We just spoke, drank some wine. She seemed adamant about selling. I wasn't going to change her mind. She then told me about this arrangement she'd made with Eve Kelley. Ludicrous. And I told Alicia as much. At least I was able to twist her thinking on that. Pixie Winks couldn't afford to outbid or even match the highest offer. I told Alicia she had to be smart about the company that she and I had worked hard to build. She couldn't just give it away to Eve Kelley because she felt bad for her."

Amanda realized it was more about Harold being concerned with his own affairs than Eve Kelley's. Also given the timing it sounded as if Alicia was having second thoughts about breaking her deal with Eve. Alicia had told Eve earlier in the day she was going back on her word, yet Harold made it sound like Alicia was struggling with that decision. "Why would Alicia feel bad for Eve?" She was testing just how much Harold knew.

"Eve alleged that Alicia stole the formula for Reborn, but it's all lies."

So he had known that too. "The lawsuit against New Belle, served last Friday, must not have come as a surprise to you, then."

"You bet it was a surprise," he countered, then grimaced. "Alicia's not even cold in the ground, and Eve was circling like a damn vulture. I detest that woman."

"Enough to kill her?" Trent tossed out.

"No, of course not."

"Eve Kelley was murdered on Monday morning," Amanda said. "Not sure if you've heard that news yet or not."

"No, I..." Harold went all pasty-mouthed and pale. "I've been working long hours. I never saw it on the news or read about it."

"She was given an overdose of pentobarbital, like Alicia." A running assumption, as toxicology for Eve still hadn't come back.

"Alicia died of pentobarbital?"

"Surprised we figured that out?" Amanda tried to read his eyes.

"What does it have to do with me? I don't know where to get that drug."

"But you know what it is," she countered.

"Yes."

Amanda had to admit knowledge of the drug alone certainly wasn't damning. It seemed everyone had heard of it. "Did you know that Tony was in this week? That he had deadlines on some marketing ads he needed to approve?" she asked.

"Yes, of course."

"And he'd sign off on these by hand...?"

"He used an approval stamp. It saved time."

"And you know where he kept it?"

"In his desk drawer."

"Which one?"

"Top left. Why are you asking me this?"

"Mr. Bishop received a threat," Amanda said.

"Oh."

"Uh-huh. It was found where his stamp goes, so whoever placed it there presumably knew he'd be needing his stamp soon."

Harold's expression was one of shock, mouth hanging

partially open. "There's only a handful of people who would know that," he said.

Amanda would refrain from pointing out that Harold was one of them. "Where did you print the hate mail that you handed over to us?"

"The printer in my office."

Which Amanda had suspected. "And who has access to it?"

"Just me."

"And you lock your office door or...?"

"No. Alicia had an open-door policy and valued transparency. She understood that privacy was needed at times but didn't believe anyone in a management position should ever lock their door."

"Could we see the printer?" Amanda asked, standing.

"Sure." Harold took them to his office and pointed toward a printer on a credenza. "That's the one I used."

"Could you print something for us?" Amanda nudged her head toward his computer on the desk.

Harold obliged, and the printer whirred to life. It made a little groaning noise as it worked and spit out the page. Creased just like Alicia's hate email and the threat given to Tony Bishop. He'd said other people could enter his office. Conceivably another person could use his printer, but the fact he had a motive to kill couldn't be ignored.

"Mr. Armstrong, we need you to come with us," she said.

"What for?"

"You're under arrest for making a threat against Tony Bishop." They'd also be looking at him more closely for Alicia Gordon's and Eve Kelley's murders. *But one step at a time...* "You can come with us willingly, or we can do the walk through the building. Up to you how you'd like us to handle it." She pulled her cuffs, driving home the mental imagery of his fate if he didn't cooperate.

"I'll go along willingly, but I want a lawyer."

"And that is your right." She proceeded to read him his Miranda rights, and they left New Belle.

THIRTY-EIGHT

Two suspects behind bars—Tony Bishop and Harold Armstrong. Maybe if it wasn't for the dark shadow cast overhead like thunderclouds, Amanda could take some satisfaction in the case getting resolved. But Scott Malone's MRI had revealed "something," and that weighed on her. There were other parts of the arrests that niggled. And which man was the killer—the husband or Harold Armstrong, there for Alicia Gordon since she began New Belle? At this point they could only put pentobarbital in Tony's hands, but they were just getting started with Harold.

He had denied delivering any threat to Tony Bishop, but even if he was guilty, why would he admit it? And despite his pleas of innocence, he made it clear he wouldn't be saying another word until his lawyer arrived. They were securing warrants to confiscate Harold's tablet to see if they could find the emails sent to Alicia, Eve Kelley, and the others who had bid on buying New Belle.

"Detectives."

Amanda and Trent looked up to see Police Chief Jeff

Buchanan standing outside their cubicles. She stood, Trent did too.

"Chief, is there something I can help you with?" she asked him. Buchanan was an unassuming-looking man, in his fifties, with gray hair and a pleasant demeanor. He wore his position of power with grace from outward appearances.

"I was looking for an update on the case, but I've come to find out you have two men in custody for the same murder." His gaze was leveled at her as the senior detective.

She wasn't sure what to make of his words and their delivery. Was he finding it ridiculous she had two suspects being held at the same time? "Both men have given us reason to question their innocence."

"Solid reason, I hope."

"Yes, of course."

Buchanan glanced at Trent. "Which way are things leaning?"

"Still a little early to say, sir," Trent said.

Amanda went on to give the chief the highlights and point out they were in a bit of a holding pattern at the moment. She was interrupted by her phone ringing. She flinched. With Malone in the hospital she wanted to answer, but what sort of impression would that leave on the chief?

"Go ahead, Detective Steele," Buchanan told her. "I'll wait."

Amanda consulted caller ID. "It's my mother. Probably with news about Malone."

Buchanan gestured for her to go ahead and take the call. "Definitely answer."

She didn't wait for further approval. "Mom?" She listened as her mother told her to get to the hospital immediately. The update she had to share wasn't one she was giving over the phone. "I'll be there as soon as I can," Amanda told her. She ended the call, and Buchanan and Trent were watching her. "I guess it's not good news." She swallowed roughly. "My mother wants to tell me in person."

"Go," Buchanan said. "We'll manage here. Besides, as you said, things with the case are at a bit of a standstill while you wait on that lawyer."

"Ah, Chief," Trent said, speaking up. "If it's all right with you, I'd like to go with Amanda."

She had no past history with Buchanan to know how he'd respond to the request.

"Of course, go with her. You're partners." Buchanan gave them a small, yet genuine smile. "Keep me posted, Detective Steele, on Malone's condition."

"I will." She and Trent hustled from the station. That had been her first interaction with Buchanan, and he was all right in her book. Certainly an improvement over his predecessor but that wouldn't be a hard feat.

Trent insisted on driving Amanda to the hospital, and despite her stubborn protests that she'd be fine on her own, he won that particular battle.

Amanda ran through the hospital doors to her mother. Her dad was talking in a huddle with Ida and her sons. Paul's wife was there now, but no sign of his kids. Could she take that as some sort of reassurance? No one needed to say their last good-byes, or was it to shield the Malone grandchildren?

"What is it, Mom?" The words rushed out, but she managed to keep her voice low. They were seated in a grouping of chairs away from everyone else.

"There is a growth in his brain." Her mother paused, letting the dire update sink in.

Tears gathered in Amanda's eyes and fell down her cheeks, which she quickly wiped away, determined to be strong for everyone else. She glanced over at Ida and her sons. What would come of all of them? But maybe she was getting ahead of herself. "What's the prognosis?"

Her mother's eyes filled with tears, and she shook her head. "It's hard to say whether it's cancer or not, but given where it's located, operating will be tricky and require an especially skilled surgeon."

"He's been acting differently. Sometimes moody." Amanda's mind was processing the news in pieces and tried to assign logic—if only as a distraction from acceptance.

"That can be caused by the tumor."

Tumor. Somehow hearing the growth described in that way nailed home the seriousness of the situation. "And how long does he..." Amanda couldn't even bring herself to finish. He was fine just two days ago, up, walking around, talking... Life freaking sucked sometimes!

"Let's not leap to this being the end."

"Mom, it sure sounds like it is!" Her entire body was shaking.

"All I said was that operating on it would be tricky. It's a matter of finding the right doctor, someone who's qualified for this particular surgery."

She blinked away the tears clouding her vision. She could hardly draw a full breath. It felt like her chest was caving in on itself. If she wasn't sitting she'd collapse.

Her mother squeezed Amanda's shoulders. "Just stay strong, okay? Or fake it. Be there for your dad and the Malone family."

Amanda went cold. Then she felt a hand on her shoulder from behind. She expected it would be her father, but it was Trent. She put a hand over his and patted it appreciatively. "I just can't believe that..." She sobbed. Her determination to be strong for everyone else was crumbling like an old stone wall. Her mother hugged her, and Trent stepped back, allowing the two of them space.

A few moments later, Amanda pulled herself together and stood. She had to say something to Ida, Paul, and Sam, but what? There was nothing she could say that would make this better, that would bring Scott Malone's health back, that would bring a qualified doctor to them immediately.

Amanda went to Ida first, grazing her father's arm on the way, and pulled Ida into a tight embrace. Everyone's eyes were full of tears. She offered words of support and sympathy to the family and her father.

Sam, the eldest Malone son, was rigid and cold, trying to remain logical and detached. Amanda recognized the defense mechanism. Deny the bad news, and it didn't exist.

"If the accident never happened," Sam said, "and things didn't play out the way they had, who knows if we'd have learned about this before it was too late to say goodbye."

A blessing amid the darkness but still hard to swallow. Amanda had nothing to say in response but patted his arm.

Amanda turned her gaze to Paul and his wife. She was a pleasant woman Amanda had met a couple of times. She was wearing a hoodie, and when Amanda hugged her, she noticed a gold pin on the sweater with the letters MWHC on it. The same one that Brad Slater's girlfriend, Rachel Sharp, had on her coat.

"Amanda." It was Ida's small voice behind her. "The doctor will be letting us know in a minute or two about visiting Scott."

"I'd love to see him." Her voice traveled back to her ears, sounding like it was coming from a distant place.

"I know." Ida threw her arms around Amanda and wept.

Before Amanda could get around to asking Paul's wife about the pin, the doctor returned. He said that people could visit with Scott Malone but only if they limited it to two people at a time.

"Go," Ida told her.

"Are you sure?"

"I am, and I know you need to get back to work."

"I promise I'll be fast."

"Nonsense. Take your time."

Amanda tried to squeeze the word *time* out of her mind. It wasn't anyone's friend. It only took with no promises or guarantees. "Thank you." She followed the doctor and drew in a deep breath before entering the room. The doctor carried on down the hallway.

She could barely get her legs to move; it felt like they were cemented to the floor. How could she even bring herself to face the man who had mentored her, who helped make her the detective she was today? Yes, she had grown up with her father as a role model, the strong and proud policeman who had climbed the ranks to police chief. But Malone held a special, sacred place in her heart too.

"You going to come in or shadow the doorway?"

She swallowed back her tears and entered. He appeared so pale and small on the bed. She just couldn't get herself to move.

"I know... this isn't the news we wanted to hear, is it?" he said.

"Not at all." She bit down on her bottom lip and shook her head. Warm tears splashed her cheeks. "But we'll find a doctor who will fix you up."

"Come here." He waved for her to approach. "There's nothing to be afraid of. I won't bite."

She smiled and found the strength and resolve to move. When she reached his bedside, she draped herself over him and wrapped him in a hug. She kissed him on the forehead and the cheeks, then put her hand on his face and beard and peered into his eyes. "I'm so sorry." She dropped her head to his chest and cried while Malone swept a hand over her hair. They stayed like that for several minutes; she felt unable to move. It was like the loss she'd experienced of her husband and daughter came rushing back. She'd barely survived that heartbreak, and now here she would likely be facing an enormous loss again—if they couldn't get someone willing to operate. And she wasn't exactly a cup half full type of person.

She pulled back. "I've never told you this, but I love you." This triggered another crying jag, which Malone patiently waited out. She'd gone in there intending to be strong, but that became nothing more than a hopeful wish from the moment she hit the doorway and had seen him.

Malone's eyes were full of tears too. "I love you too, kid."

"You always have my back," she said, repeating what he often told her.

"No matter what side of the grass I'm on."

She hated to hear him talking so lightly of death. "Don't give up on us. We'll find someone."

He took her hand. "There's the chance we won't." His face went sour, then he waved a hand. "All right, we need to cut that out. All the negativity, Ida would have my hide." Malone smiled at her, his lips lifting lazily. "But enough about me. Tell me you've caught that killer you're after."

She palmed her cheeks. Sinking herself into work was the easy part. "We have two suspects in custody."

"Two? You never do anything the easy way."

She nudged his shoulder. "I just follow the evidence."

"One of your suspects the husband?"

She nodded.

"Must have been tough bringing in an old friend."

"Wasn't the easiest, but I assumed the responsibility to uphold the law when I donned the badge."

"That's my girl." Malone smiled at her, but the expression quickly faded.

She probably shouldn't keep him long and give the others a chance to see him. "Just hang in there, okay? You're a tough old goat."

"A tough... *goat*?" He laughed, and it turned into a slight rattle in his chest. He coughed but held up a hand to let her know he was fine.

"It's the truth." Amanda smiled and patted him on the arm and was going to leave, but she was drawn back. She kissed him again on the forehead. "I'll be back to visit soon."

"Do your job, Detective. Close the investigation and get those women justice."

"You got it, Sarge." Amanda left the room with one quick glance back. As much as her legs hadn't wanted to take her to Malone at first, now they didn't want to carry her away from him.

She stepped into the hall. She leaned against the wall to the side of the doorway, burying her face in her hands. Next thing she knew she was being pulled into a warm, strong embrace. Trent. She let it happen. She stayed in his arms and let him hold her as she cried against his shoulder. He was there to support her and comfort her, not judge. He was exactly what she needed in this moment.

THIRTY-NINE

If Amanda caught an hour of sleep last night, it would have been a miracle. There was far too much weighing on her mind. At least she'd had the wherewithal to get ahold of Libby and have Zoe spend the night at her house again. Amanda felt bad for this, but she was in no emotional state to be around Zoe, who was also struggling with her own feelings these days.

She finally pulled herself from bed at eight o'clock. She had filled in Chief Buchanan on Malone's prognosis last night, and he told her that she and Trent could show up later today. And that came as a relief. She was still exhausted and not even particularly motivated. That was, until she heard Malone's voice in her head telling her to get the investigation closed. That was one wish she could make sure happened—even if she was a little late getting started this morning.

Two suspects in custody, but the light of a new day brought on the doubts about both Tony Bishop and Harold Armstrong.

It could be that she was just struggling to accept that her former friend was a killer. Tony Bishop did have access to the drug. He also could have very well gone into Harold's office and printed the threat to himself, then claimed he'd discovered it in his drawer. He benefited financially from Alicia's death.

But Harold also had motive. Even possible opportunity. Though it would be more of a challenge for him to taint Alicia's bottles of Sleep Tight than it would be for Tony to print the threat.

Tony could fit the proportions of the mystery figure in the videos from Pixie Winks and Caffeine Café, but Harold was heavyset. Where did that leave him?

Both men had lied or withheld information from her and Trent, hindering the investigation's progress.

But where would Harold get pentobarbital? In fact, they couldn't even prove that Tony had stolen it from the vet clinic. They only had speculation and extenuating circumstances.

She sank into the couch at her house, put her feet up on the coffee table. She was sipping a coffee, staring blankly into space, and thinking.

Besides Tony or Harold, who had motive to kill Alicia Gordon and Eve Kelley?

It still seemed to her it was someone who didn't want the sale of New Belle to go through. Threats were sent to the bidders to back away, even after Alicia's murder. Thankfully, it would seem the killing stopped with Eve Kelley.

She sipped her coffee.

Harold's office was never locked, which meant anyone could have slipped in there, printed the threat, then placed it in Tony's drawer. If so, that person could have intended to frame Harold. Though that would imply they knew about the distinct crease his printer made in the paper. Then again, maybe his printer was just chosen without that knowledge, though still in the hopes the threat would lead back to his desk. If that happened, the real killer might have seen Harold as a good mark to take the fall. And they might have known about Harold's visit to the cabin.

There were conceivably two visitors to the cabin while Alicia was there—the person who left the tire marks and the one who left the shoeprints. They knew the tires matched to Harold's truck. But what about the shoes?

CSI Donnelly said the sole impressions were a match to Cloud Footwear and their Ithan shoes. They had yet to conduct a search of Harold's home, but when asked, he hadn't even heard of the brand.

Amanda wasn't familiar with them either. She decided now was as good a time as any to google them. She retrieved her laptop and sat at the kitchen counter while she did the search. Now seeing what the shoes looked like, she knew she'd seen them before. She nearly fell off her chair when she realized where.

And then it was as if all the pieces of the case finally clicked together.

Amanda picked up Tony Bishop from holding and was somewhat relieved Trent wasn't in yet. She told Tony her theory, then warned him that if he took one step out of line, she'd have him back behind bars before he could blink. But she wanted him with her when she followed through on her very strong hunch.

"I can't believe this. I'm in shock." Tony kept repeating this the entire way to his house.

They went in the front door, and Brad came down the stairs and stopped short.

"Tony?" He dragged his gaze to Amanda, back to Tony. "What are you doing here?"

"I'm being released."

That's what Amanda had told him to say, and he would be if her theory was right.

"Oh. That's..." Brad's brow pinched. "We don't know who killed Mom, then?"

"You leave that concern to me." Amanda smiled pleasantly at him.

The three of them went to the sitting room.

Just as she took a seat on that dark-gray couch, her phone rang. It was Trent, and she was torn about answering. Maybe she should have messaged him about where she was going and her hunch. That might have been the smart thing to do, and it was the least of what she owed him for his loyalty. But he'd also had the right to sleep in... She rejected the call, sending Trent to voicemail.

Tony sat on the other couch, but she found herself wishing he'd dropped next to her.

Brad came in and sat beside Tony. "So you have no leads at all?" Brad asked her. "What about Mr. Armstrong?"

It was interesting that Brad went right to Harold. It was starting to feel like her hunch was spot on. As she thought at her house, the killer might have used Harold's printer for the threat against Tony in the hopes it would incriminate Harold. If Amanda's theory was right, the killer also knew about Harold being at the cabin. "What about him?" she asked, putting it out there casually. She hoped Tony would pick up on her body language, the unspoken communication to relax.

"I'm quite sure he was jealous of all Mom had going." Brad crossed his legs, getting comfortable. Cocky.

"You don't even know what you're talking about, Brad. You're just a kid," Tony said.

"I'm not a freakin' kid, *Tony*," Brad spat. "If you didn't kill Mom, he probably did."

Yet, this was the first time Brad had come forward with his suspicions about Harold. Amanda was sure she knew why— self-preservation because he could feel time running out. "Well, there *is* circumstantial evidence," she said.

"See?" Brad waved a hand toward Amanda.

"There are also some unanswered questions."

Brad's face hardened. "Like what? He deserves to pay for what he did to my mother—and that other woman."

Eve Kelley always seemed like the postscript in this investigation, and it wasn't right. "It's hard to say, but you let me worry about that." She smiled tightly at Brad, who didn't return the expression. "I wonder why he would have killed Eve, though. Mr. Armstrong didn't have a relationship with her like he did with your mother."

"She was suing New Belle, you know."

Tony turned to him. "How did you know that?"

"I know a lot more about what goes on around here than you think."

Then it wasn't too much a stretch to believe that Brad had uncovered the identities of the bidders, Lopez and Reynolds. "So you think Mr. Armstrong was upset about the lawsuit?" Amanda asked to steer the conversation back around. She hoped that Brad didn't realize she was actually probing his motive.

"She would have destroyed my mother's legacy. Someone needed to protect it." Brad sniffed and glanced away, just briefly, then locked eye contact with Amanda once again.

Amanda bobbed her head slowly as if considering. "I can see that."

"Yep." Brad leaned back into the couch, relaxing just a little, but there was something wild in his eyes.

Amanda needed to detour to less volatile ground. "Your girlfriend seems like a nice person. It was great of her to come for a visit to support you."

"Rachel is great." Brad spoke this as if wary for some reason, and he had reason.

Amanda had done some more googling before she left home. The gold pin that was on Paul's wife's hoodie was the same one Rachel Sharp had. Amanda was aware Paul's wife worked at the MedStar Washington Hospital Center in Washington, DC—MWHC. But that's not where Rachel Sharp worked. The girl was still in college. Amanda had run another search on Rachel's family members. Her mother, Stacy, was a nurse at the hospital. "You two been dating for a while?" Amanda smiled, trying to lighten the air. "That's why you wanted to bring her home to meet your mom?"

"Yeah."

"It's great when we meet *that* someone."

"I don't know if Rachel is *the* one, but she's great." Brad was studying her closely, and though it made Amanda uncomfortable, it also made her more confident in her suspicions. So confident, in fact, she was getting a twisted feeling in her gut. It might be best to get Tony away from Brad, just in case this went sideways.

"Actually, Tony," she began. "I'd like a coffee..."

"Okay." Tony went to get up, but Brad quickly moved down the couch and put a firm grip on Tony's arm.

"What are you do—" The question died on Tony's lips as Brad pulled a syringe from his pocket.

Amanda held up a hand. "You don't want to do this, Brad. This isn't who you are." Bringing Tony may have been a really bad idea, but she wanted Brad to initially be set at ease, so he'd talk. She figured having Tony there would help with that.

"How the hell do you know who I am?" His voice was high and full of panic.

"You're not a killer." She put it out there with as much kindness as she could muster, speaking the lie and doing her best to make it sound truthful.

"You don't know that." He grimaced and swallowed roughly. His eyes were darting about the room. "And he deserves to die. He came in and took over everything. He was just standing by while Mom was determined to sell her company."

"She wanted to spend more time with you," she said.

"No." He snapped his mouth shut. "She cared more about Leo than me. Always had."

Amanda played through the scenario in her mind. Brad Slater had access to the New Belle offices and had recently been there. It wasn't a far reach to see him going into Harold's office, printing the threat against Tony, and then slipping it into Tony's drawer. He could have done it after Scarlett left the office for the day or had vacated her seat for some other reason.

"She loved you, Brad," Tony said. Even facing a threat against his life, he was the picture of calm, even empathy for Brad.

"No. Don't talk to me!" Brad shouted.

"Put the needle down now, Brad. Everything will be okay," Amanda said evenly, hoping to de-escalate the tense situation.

"Mom didn't really care about me or Leo! She wasn't interested in selling to spend more time with us. That's bullshit." Sadness danced across his features and darkened his eyes.

"That's exactly what she wanted," Tony said, drawing away with a wince. The tip of the syringe must have pierced his flesh.

"Shut up, just shut up."

He was a young man, barely older than a child, and he obviously felt so abandoned by his mother. "Where did you get the pentobarbital, Brad? Why kill your own mother?"

Tears fell down his face, and the sudden shift in emotion threw off Amanda's equilibrium.

"Did you take it from Paws and Claws?" Tony asked him.

"No, I didn't take it from Beth's clinic," Brad spat.

"Did Rachel steal it from MedStar for you?" Amanda said.

Brad's eyes snapped to hers, his jaw tight, challenging her. She'd rise to the occasion.

"Stacy Sharp, Rachel's mother, is a nurse at MedStar Washington Hospital Center. Did Rachel steal some pentobarbital for you, so you could kill your mother and Eve Kelley?"

"This is a nightmare," Tony cried out.

"You don't know anything," Brad seethed.

"Did you feel betrayed that your mother was selling the business?" she asked.

"She was never there for me. Never. That damn company of hers always took priority. But now she was going to stop to have time for Leo?" His face shadowed and contorted with grief.

"She ran a multimillion-dollar company and provided for you," Tony said, and Amanda gave him a subtle shake of her head to keep quiet.

"Money isn't the most important thing," Brad said, barely above the level of a whisper.

"What is, then?" Amanda was fishing and had a feeling what the true motivation was the more the boy spoke.

"How is it fair that Leo would have a full-time mom while I didn't?" His eyes narrowed, full of rage. "I'm here on spring break, and what does she do? She takes off to some stupid cabin."

Amanda was piecing it together: this was about a young man who had felt abandoned by his mother. "Did you go to the cabin?"

"You can't prove that."

"You wear Ithan shoes, size eleven, right? I saw them on you the other day when you were heading out with Rachel and Leo."

"So?"

"You left prints in the mud outside the cabin window. You stood out there and watched while your mother died."

Brad released his grip on Tony, and Tony stood.

"You did kill her!" Tony hurled that at Brad, disgust and

rage twisting his face.

Brad began to cry in earnest. "I just wanted her to notice me —to see I even existed."

"She loved you, Brad," Amanda said. "She was looking at your picture when she died."

Brad was sniffling, tears falling in rapid succession. "She was just supposed to fall asleep, but she looked so scared. Still, she deserved it. She didn't care about me! All she cared about was New Belle and Leo, and then you." Brad turned his gaze on Tony and shot up to pursue him.

Amanda stood and pulled her gun from its holster, but she didn't want to fire on Brad. He was messed up, but a kid no less. He needed to get help. "Stop, Brad. I don't want to shoot you. I know you didn't mean to do what you did."

"I meant it." Brad thrust out his chin as he grabbed Tony. Tony bucked against the younger man but wasn't strong enough to free himself.

"I don't think you did. You regret it... terribly. Come on, let Tony go, put down the syringe, and I'll put my gun away."

His eyes snapped to hers, and in that brief second, she grabbed one of the heavier throw pillows and slung it across the room. It hit Brad's hand, and the needle fell to the floor. He fumbled to retrieve it, and Tony quickly moved out of the way at Amanda's prompting. She holstered her gun and closed the distance to Brad while he remained preoccupied with finding the syringe.

She came up next to Brad just as he bolted upright.

"You bitch!" he roared and came at her, the needle in his hand.

Tony shouted, "Watch out!" She juked out of Brad's reach when he jabbed the needle at her. *Close. Too close.* She tried to put some space between them, but he put out a leg. She fell over his foot, spilling onto the wood floor with a whoosh of breath letting out of her lungs. She scrambled onto her back and pulled her gun, just as Brad was lowering over her.

She clocked him on the head with the butt of the Glock's handle. Brad Slater fell unconscious to the floor next to her, the needle falling once again from his hand.

EPILOGUE

TWO DAYS LATER

Happy endings were sometimes bittersweet. Alicia Gordon and Eve Kelley's killer was behind bars, but he was just a child who had wanted his mother's love and attention. Brad had been crying when he was arrested, his heart broken, but there would be no turning back the clock. His mother was gone—at his hands and so was another woman. Malone was still hanging on, fighting like the strong man Amanda knew him to be. They'd found a surgeon out of South Carolina who was praised as one of the best neurosurgeons in North America, and Malone had gone under his knife yesterday. So far, they believed the operation was a success, but until Malone woke up, they wouldn't know for sure.

A new sergeant was coming in from the New York City PD and was due to arrive for a meet-and-greet tomorrow.

"I still don't know what you were thinking going there on your own." Trent was shaking his head as he repeated the sentiment that he'd said a million times since she had given him the scoop.

It was Sunday morning, and she had asked Trent over for brunch, specifically pancakes, which were Zoe's favorite. The child ate about as much as she wore and then retreated to her room with Maria, who she had made up with and insisted had to try Amanda's pancakes.

That left Amanda in the living room with Trent. Becky's advice to get back into the dating world came to mind. But this was Trent. Her partner on the job. Someone with whom there needed to be defined lines.

As good a time as any to discuss the case against Brad Slater... She started the conversation, and they covered it all.

They had been able to confirm that Rachel Sharp had managed to steal pentobarbital from the hospital where her mother worked. As for what happened to the missing inventory at the vet's clinic, that mystery was never solved. Amanda still had a feeling the Wagners were trying to cover something up. Brad Slater's tablet showed the email accounts that were used to send the threats to Alicia, Eve, and Lopez. They also found one addressed to Dale Reynolds, which was likely the one he'd mentioned but couldn't hand over.

Brad was identified by an employee at Caffeine Café, and his stature matched that of the mystery figure in the security videos from both the café and the Pixie Winks warehouse.

While no one at Pixie Winks remembered seeing him there, it was possible he'd disguised himself. Brad refused to confirm or deny. But if he didn't, it was quite likely someone would have recognized him as Alicia Gordon's son and kicked him out of the building.

The wear pattern on Brad's running shoes put him outside the cabin. He told them that he'd slipped out after Tony fell asleep, drove to Gainesville, parked down the road from the cabin, and walked up.

When she and Trent finished speaking, he got off the couch, and she took his empty mug. "Well, I should be going," he said. "Thanks for brunch."

"Not a problem. I just wanted to thank you for being there...

through everything." She didn't need to verbalize it all in detail; Trent would know what she was talking about. How he hadn't left her side once the news had hit about Malone.

"Nowhere else I would have been, Amanda." Soft, husky, emotional. "Keep me posted."

"I will." She walked him to the door, the nagging of her friend's voice in mind. She needed to make her life about more than Zoe and work. "Maybe we could go out for drinks sometime. Just as friends." She was very quick to add the latter part.

He angled his head. "I didn't think you drank."

"Water, iced tea, coffee..." She smiled at him. "Though one sip of wine probably wouldn't be the end of the world."

Trent grinned. "All right. Sounds good."

"All right," she parroted.

He left, and she watched him walk to his Jeep. She was still standing there when he turned around and waved just before he slipped behind the wheel.

A quick wave in return, and she closed the door. She considered pouring another coffee and taking care of something that she'd put off for far too long. Maybe it was time to finally clear the air between her and CSI Blair. A phone call wouldn't work for this conversation. It would need to be done in person, but Amanda couldn't leave the house and Zoe. She made the call anyway, not expecting Blair to answer her work phone, but she did.

"It's Detective— uh, Amanda Steele." She stopped there and swore she heard an audible groan from the other end of the line. She pressed on. "I was wondering if you'd be available to grab a coffee sometime."

There was nothing but silence.

"Emma?" Amanda pulled out the investigator's first name.

"I'm here, but I don't know why you'd want to do that."

"I think you do," Amanda put out there gently.

"Fine. Name the time and place."

They planned to meet tomorrow night at a coffee shop in Manassas. Going there would afford them privacy that they wouldn't get at Hannah's Diner.

She ended the call and dropped off her cup and Trent's to the kitchen, her steps and heart lighter than she'd imagined possible, considering the uncertain state of Malone's health. But as her mother had suggested, Amanda was determined to stay positive. Besides, it hurt far too much to give herself over to the fear that preyed in the background, ready to overcome her.

Her phone rang, and she answered immediately. "Mom. Tell me—"

"He's awake, Amanda." Her mother's smile traveled the line. "The surgery was a success. The doctor expects a full recovery."

Tears rolled down Amanda's cheeks, and the giggles of little girls from down the hall struck her ears. Life was uncertain. It was unfair. It came with zero guarantees, but everyone breathing was blessed by the journey. It was about making the best out of what we were given and being brave enough to claim what we wanted.

Amanda planned to do just that.

A LETTER FROM CAROLYN

Dear reader,

I want to say a huge thank you for choosing to read *Her Frozen Cry*. If you enjoyed it and would like to hear about new releases in the Amanda Steele series, just sign up at the following link. Your email address will never be shared, and you can unsubscribe at any time.

www.bookouture.com/carolyn-arnold

If you loved *Her Frozen Cry*, I would be incredibly grateful if you would write a brief, honest review. Also, if you'd like to continue investigating murder, you'll be happy to know there will be more Detective Amanda Steele books. I also offer several other international bestselling series for you to savor—everything from crime fiction to thrillers and action adventures. One of these series features Detective Madison Knight, another kick-ass female detective, who will risk her life, her badge—whatever it takes—to find justice for murder victims.

Also if you enjoyed being in the Prince William County, Virginia, area, you might want to return in my Brandon Fisher FBI series. Brandon is Becky Tulson's boyfriend and was mentioned in this book, but you'll be able to be there when they meet in *Silent Graves* (book two in my FBI series). These books are perfect for readers who love heart-pounding thrillers and are fascinated with the psychology of serial killers. Each installment is a new case with a fresh bloody trail to follow. Hunt with the FBI's Behavioral Analysis Unit and profile some of the most devious and darkest minds on the planet.

And if you're familiar with the Prince William County, Virginia area, or have done some internet searching, you'll realize some differences between reality and my book. That's me taking creative liberties.

Before signing off, I want to thank Yvonne Van Gaasbeck, a former deputy coroner of Houston County, Georgia, for her help—and patience—in answering my questions about pentobarbital poisoning and its effects on the body.

Last but certainly not least, I love hearing from my readers! You can get in touch on my Facebook page, through Twitter, Goodreads, or my website. This is also a good way to stay notified of my new releases. You can also reach out to me via email at Carolyn@CarolynArnold.net.

Wishing you a thrill a word!

Carolyn Arnold

Connect with CAROLYN ARNOLD online:

carolynarnold.net

facebook.com/AuthorCarolynArnold
twitter.com/Carolyn_Arnold